CW00517708

# The CEO's Companion

## The Caregivers, Volume 4

Rose Fresquez

Published by Rose Fresquez, 2022.

To my editor, Deirdre Lockhart. You're a true blessing from God. Your insights and wisdom have helped shape this story.

To my dearest friend Candace Wright, thank you for being such a Godly example to me, and to those around you. The way you've overcome depression, is an extraordinary testimony that seeking help and turning to Christ is the best weapon to overcome life's struggles. I thought about you as I wrote this story. Thanks for your transparency.

And to all God's children, weighed down by anxiety, depression and all the storms of life; May God use this story to remind you that He's right there, pulling you through your brokenness. Don't hesitate to seek out counseling if you need help and encouragement.

# ACKNOWLEDGEMENTS

I WANT TO THANK THE Lord, my Savior. Without you, Father, there's no point in trying to do anything at all. It's my prayer that I can honor you with my words. I thank you for connecting me with an amazing group of people who helped support me in accomplishing this novel.

To my husband Joel, who works so hard to provide for our family, so that I can stay home and take care of the kids. I'm so blessed that we get to journey through life together.

To my children Isaiah, Caleb, Abigail and Micah, you fill my heart with joy. Thanks for the giggles, laughter and encouragement.

To my insider team, thanks for always suggesting the coolest ideas.

Jerri Hall, Thanks for your support and encouragement always. You're such an inspiration

To Nicole, Deb, Melissa, Marie, Nancy, Linda, Katherine, Elizabeth and Trudy. You ladies are so amazing for the time you invested to brainstorm, beta read and critique my manuscript. Thank you from the bottom of my heart.

# CHAPTER 1

Agony couldn't describe Eric Stone's condition as he lay motionless on the hospital bed, not far from death. He couldn't care less about what the doctor was saying—not when the pain shooting through his back, his knees, and his feet was hard to ignore. Keeping his gaze fixed on the window should get across his disinterest in the doctor's speech so he'd leave Eric alone.

"We're also switching to Tecfidera for your multiple sclerosis. You'll need to take it twice a day." The doctor spoke in his Indian accent. "We need to increase your NSAIDs dose as well. The last thing you need is joint inflammation."

His attention slightly piqued, Eric allowed his gaze to leave the window, even if he didn't shift to meet the doctor's gaze. Adding more treatment to the ten or so he took daily didn't make any sense. He grimaced, shuddering at the thought.

An unpleasant medicinal smell replaced the antiseptic odor. Within the year, he'd been diagnosed with chronic fatigue syndrome, fibromyalgia, multiple sclerosis, and several other diseases he didn't care to remember. He let out a bitter laugh after the doctor pointed out that he possibly had rheumatoid arthritis. A surge of irritability burned through him, and he stiffened his jaw to fight the urge to silence the doctor.

All the treatments these past months hadn't cured his ongoing fevers and fatigue. Not to mention the almost-daily headaches. By now, he should be closer to recovery, not farther from it. What was the point of drowning in ineffective medication? He was done, and so was his patience.

"Eric?"

3

Frowning, he managed a glance at the short man. The doctor had lost him the moment he'd said NSAIDs. *Are you talking to me?*

"The pharmacist will be here to talk you through the side effects of your new treatment...."

The doctor continued his spiel on how critical Eric's condition was, adding different antibiotics to his current treatment and the extra hours he needed to stay in the hospital to see how he would react to the new medicine.

As if any of this should suddenly cure him! He needed to get out of here. Looking back to the window, he focused on the thick snowflakes falling like unwanted rain from the sky. His mood felt as flat and gray as the weather, and he was grateful to be alone when the doctor left, promising to send in a pharmacist and a nurse.

After his days and months blending with no distinction, Eric needed some kind of diversion, but his brain had quit functioning when he'd stopped running his company. How was he supposed to think when he was restless in the confines of the hospital, and if he wasn't here, he was in his parents' guesthouse?

He winced when he tried to shift. The IV and catheter tubes didn't make turning any easier. The bedsores were more unbearable when he was lying on his back, but the side position wasn't practical with all these things inserted in him.

When the nurse and pharmacist walked in, his mom, Regina, came with them.

The chair scraped the tile as she pulled one out from the side and set it closer to the bed. She then touched his forehead, her fingers warm, soothing, and slight tension drifted from his shoulders—until he saw her eyes. Her golden eyes, once so vital, were weary from shedding tears on his behalf, and his teeth ground at the sight.

"Hi, sweetheart."

Hurting her was one of the hardest parts of his illness.

"The doctor told me about your new treatment."

"Yes." Eric swallowed the lump in his throat. His unshed tears were mostly for his parents whenever they stared at him with sorrow-seeped eyes. They were far better off without him.

"Isn't your back hurting?" Her forehead furrowed. "Can we move—?"

"I'm fine." He attempted to shift beneath the covers. Although uncomfortable, the sores were the least of his problems.

"I'm Cox." The dark-haired man bowed, introducing himself as the pharmacist. He then summarized Eric's new medicine and antibiotics.

The nurse did something to Eric's IV bag and checked the catheter. Even if the bathroom was in the same room, Eric could break into a sweat and take twenty minutes to wobble to it and back.

Mom listened more intently to Cox—no surprise there since she was in charge of making sure Eric didn't skip a dose of medicine.

Being nurtured by his mom as a grown man was humiliating, but he hadn't made it easy on the caregivers she had hired for him. As of now, he only had a physical therapist and a psychiatrist.

After the pharmacist ended his lecture and received Mom's promise to pick up medicine before Eric's dismissal, the man left, and the nurse told Eric she was bringing him water and antibiotics to see how his body reacted.

Mom cleared her throat and clasped her hands on her pencil skirt. "There's this woman who volunteers at the hospital. I asked her to come and visit with you."

What did a hospital volunteer have to do with him? Mom worked at the hospital, unless the volunteer was another one of her friends, but he already had a mom who over nurtured him. He didn't need two women sympathizing with him.

"Mom," he croaked, but when he met her shiny eyes, the resistance died in his mouth. His parents had rearranged their routine to accommodate his demands, yet he acted like a rebellious teen when he refused to let caregivers tend to him.

She was eyeing him with hope-filled eyes.

Just great. He let out a heavy sigh. "What kind of visitation?"

Even as he asked, he wanted to remind Mom he wasn't interested in interacting with anybody.

"She usually visits patients—mostly elderly but also babies who need someone to hold them. Their moms are usually ill and can't tend to them."

Eric was forty-four, but he looked and moved like an old man. As for babies, he was treated like one lately, and that was confirmed when the heavyset nurse with kind eyes returned. When she held out her palm with two blue capsules, he grimaced.

Mom stood and slid a hand behind Eric's neck, easing it up as he pulled to sit up. When he swallowed the pills and washed them down with water, his stomach churned. It wasn't unusual to feel nauseated whenever he took medicine lately, even when he didn't need to throw up.

"Isn't your lunchtime over by now?" he asked his mom. He could only handle ten minutes of her sad scrutiny.

She looked at the wall clock displaying eleven forty. "I still have some time. I want to stay until Joy shows up."

Joy? Oh. The volunteer she was talking about.

Eric lay back and struggled to turn to his side, to the arm not strapped with the IV. He yawned, his eyelids heavy. Now would be a good time to sleep, but he'd not taken his hallucination pills. He shivered at the thought of the hooded figures that haunted him when he fell asleep. Scratch sleep.

With resting off the agenda, he had no choice but to stare at the gloomy day through the window. Mom talked about the pastor she'd asked to come pray for Eric whenever he got home that night.

*Prayer.* He'd done it several times before and after losing his family. He hadn't blamed God, still clung to Him while he had work to keep him distracted. But, when the illness stripped him of any escape and left him helpless, he'd developed major doubts about faith and everything he'd ever believed in. All he wanted was his old life back, but that was impossible since his family couldn't be resurrected.

The only good thing going for him lately was the hope that God was going to end his time on earth—soon.

# CHAPTER 2

Joy Musana nestled the sleepy infant into the crib and stood aside to admire his chubby cheeks. He was so adorable sucking as his eyes closed. The tight way he was swaddled in the striped blanket reminded her of the tamales she'd made in a cooking class last month.

Her heart melted when she looked around the room lit by fluorescent light. The six other babies' chests rose and fell. They were so precious and innocent, yet a tightness squeezed in her chest for the four whose moms weren't available. Three of the mothers had undergone post-labor surgeries and were still in recovery, while one baby's mom had passed away last night. She'd had complications during childbirth.

The volunteer name tag scratched Joy's hand when she rested her fingers on her chest and let out a shuddered breath. As her eyes itched with unshed tears, she made a mental note to say extra prayers for that little one.

When she left the nursery, she retrieved her green backpack handbag from the lounge. In an hour or so, hospital staff would be filling the room for their lunch.

Before she could forget, she grabbed a pen from her bag and scribbled in her palm—"Pray for orphaned baby." If she glanced at it throughout the day, she could keep the prayers flowing.

While shouldering her backpack, she eyed the microwave. Eleven fifty and almost time to visit her next patient.

In the hallway, an old man stooped behind a wheelchair with his hands holding his lower back as he eyed the elevator down the hall. He must be taking a break from pushing the gray-haired woman in the chair.

8

"Do you need any help pushing the chair?" Joy asked as they both craned their necks in her direction.

"That will be wonderful, honey," the woman said in a hoarse voice. "My husband might break his back before I make it to the doctor."

"Thank you." The man straightened his stance, stepping away from the back of the chair, his expression lightening. "We're headed to the third floor."

"That's where I'm going." Joy adjusted her shoulder pack. It wasn't big, but it fit her wallet and the small gifts and artwork she brought to hand out to patients.

As they entered the elevator, she asked about the couple's hospital visit.

"I have a follow-up for my hip surgery." The woman clasped her hands on her floral pants.

Good thing it was a follow-up, rather than being admitted. "I hope it goes well," Joy said as the elevator deposited them on the third floor. "Do you know where you're supposed to go?"

"They want us to start at the lab." The man waved toward a sign.

Although Joy wasn't a staff member, Pleasant View Hospital wasn't too big. She'd spent enough time visiting patients to know where each department was located.

After dropping them off at the lab and wishing them a good day, she walked back in search of the examination room she'd specifically come for today. As she passed the welcome desk, she greeted a couple of nurses, and they waved back, one of them greeting her by name.

Her stay in Pleasant View was supposed to be six months when her friend, Ruby, invited her for a visit. But the moment Joy started volunteering, God opened up opportunities for her to extend her stay.

If she was going to make it through the rest of the American states and a few countries, she was running out of time. She'd wanted to conclude her travels within six years before she turned forty—that was if she lived to be forty. She needed a plan. Both financial and chronological.

She glanced up to the wall to read the number on one of the rooms—301. One more to her destination.

She normally went to rooms where patients had filled in a hospital form requesting company during their stay. Today's assignment was different. The children's psychiatrist had asked her to visit her son who had follow-up tests for several disorders.

She put her hands under the automatic dispenser on the wall. The cool liquid gel dropped in her palm, and she rubbed her hands together before knocking on the half-open door.

"Come in." A feminine voice sounded. It had to be the psychiatrist.

When Joy opened the door, the familiar scent of antiseptic and medicine engulfed her. Even if the hospital smell brought back unsettling memories, she felt a sense of fulfillment whenever she volunteered at the hospital. Strong and fearless was her new way of life, as long as she wasn't the patient. Volunteering comforted her, reminded her she was well and others could depend on her instead of the other way around.

When she caught Regina's gaze, a sad smile lifted the woman's cheeks. "Hi there, Joy."

"Hi." Joy shrugged off her backpack and set it on the counter by the sink.

With Regina's strawberry-blonde hair clipped in a short bob, she looked younger than sixty-five. Joy had done the math when she read Regina's bio on the wall where they hung hospital staff photos.

As she approached Regina, Joy stared at the man on the hospital bed. Fluid-filled blisters blotched his face, and dull eyes fixated on the ceiling as if he wanted to be left alone. Regina stood and tucked the hem of her black blouse into her cream pencil skirt. She then reached for the empty chair from the corner, scraping it against the tile when she scooted it next to the one she'd sat in.

"Eric, this is Joy." She touched a strand of the man's unkempt brown hair. It would make a perfect wig for a hairless patient.

Eric's head shifted. Hazel eyes rimmed in shadows fixed on her, and briefly, she saw something deeper than physical pain. A shard of sorrow pierced her chest.

He turned back to stare at the ceiling, wincing, and touched his stomach beneath the light blanket. He was probably in pain and uncomfortable with the IV tube in his arm.

"Hi, Eric." She finally remembered her manners.

"Hi." He swallowed, his voice raspy.

His jaw could be square, but it was hard to tell with the scraggly beard poking through his pale skin. Just above the neckline of his hospital gown, thin skin stretched over extremely pointy collarbones. Her heart sinking, she lowered her gaze to his fisted left hand, clenched tight as if against pain or a circumstance he could only fight in his mind. She could imagine this man, likely tall and robust, full of life and determination before this frailty struck him down.

The unpleasant sharpness expanded in her chest... as if she'd swallowed something whole.

That Eric wasn't attempting to look at his mom or Joy could indicate he'd received unnerving news from the doctor before she showed up.

*Oh Lord, please make him well.* For his mom's sake and the rest of his family members. He probably had a wife.

Someone cleared their throat, and Joy blinked out of her stupor.

It was Regina. Joy heated. If Eric assumed she was staring at him, he didn't notice or decided not to say anything, making her grateful for his silence.

She flopped on the chair next to Regina.

"He started new medicine today." Regina squeezed the frail tissue in her hand. No doubt she'd used it to wipe her tears several times.

Had they found out what he was suffering from? Was it another prescription to treat new symptoms? More endless medication in hopes he would recover? But Joy held back on those questions and asked instead, "How long is he staying here?"

"I assume you're asking me and not my mother?" Eric asked in a clipped tone as his jaw twitched.

Regina sent Joy an apologetic look. But it was understandable, and Joy, of all people, should know not to ask about the patient right in front of them.

"You, I mean—"

"I'm leaving today," Eric snapped, then winced and let out a sharp breath.

"Are you okay?" Joy and Regina asked simultaneously.

"What an odd question to ask a pati—" He gagged at his last words, and Joy leaped up, instinctively unzipping and yanking off her sweatshirt.

Just as she laid it on his chest, Eric's mouth forced out and deposited a stench of yellow liquid over the butterfly hoodie.

Regina pressed the nurse call button from his bed, and a couple of nurses burst through the door.

"Everything okay?" one asked.

"I think it's the new medicine he took." Regina hovered over him, her voice panicked.

"I shouldn't have come here in the first place!" Eric growled, his forehead glistening. "I need to go home now!"

Joy stepped forward, eager to lend a hand, but the nurses were hushing him as one lifted his head while another one tossed the soiled hoodie into a trash bag. So she stepped back, not wanting to be in the way.

"We will go home soon, sweetheart." Regina took a deep breath where she stood on the other side of the IV.

While the nurses cared for Eric, Joy walked to Regina and put a comforting hand on her shoulder. "Can I get you some water?"

Reina shook her head, but then shifted and took Joy's hand. "Let's let the nurses do their job for now."

Regina needed a break, and if Joy could only get acquainted with Eric, she'd give the woman the break she deserved.

"Can I talk to you for a moment?" Regina asked once they stepped out of the room.

Joy stared at her hands, the ink from the prayer request she'd jotted down earlier was now smudged in her palm. When she washed her hands again, she'd have to add Eric to the people she needed to pray for throughout the day.

"I have a sink in my office," Regina offered in an attempt to guess Joy's thoughts.

Nodding, Joy fell in step with Regina's strides. Her heels clicked against the tile among the announcements ringing through the hospital PA system.

In Regina's fourth-floor office, Joy washed her hands and then settled on the comfy chair with padded armrests where Regina ushered her. Colorful pictures of Winnie-the-Pooh characters seemed to come alive on the walls, while interactive toys likely used in counseling sessions awaited their usefulness on the shelves.

"Would you like some lunch?" Regina handed over a water bottle and took the bright-orange couch across from her.

"I'm fine, thanks." Joy wasn't hungry, not with Eric's discomfort fresh in her mind.

"How are the triplets doing?" Regina asked, which wasn't a surprise since she'd been the kids' counselor after their grandpa died three months ago.

"They ask about their grandpa often, but their grandma is doing a good job."

A seriousness crossed Regina's face as she moved the fresh wild-flower bouquet aside on the table. "You were so good with that man on his deathbed, no wonder his wife hired you to nanny their grand-kids."

Joy's cheeks burned. Embarrassed by the praise, she had to redirect her sight to the computer. Framed pictures of a bunch of kids and adults that she couldn't see clearly from here surrounded it.

"How often do you watch the triplets again?"

Joy met Regina's gaze.

"Half days, four times a week." To give their grandma a break.

"Speaking of work." Regina brushed a strand of her short hair from her forehead. "I wanted to know if you'd like to work for me the other half of your days?"

Joy blinked. Surely, she didn't mean Joy working as a counselor. "You have a business outside the hospital?"

Regina tapped the knee she'd crossed over the other. "My son."

Joy's lips pressed together, holding back a question. Regina must be too old to have a toddler, unless she'd adopted one.

"Eric," Regina clarified.

"I'm not a nurse." If she was looking for a caregiver... "I don't think I'm qualified to—"

"I've had excellent recommendations about you from several staff members. You're perfect for this job." Regina's lips pressed into a thin line. "Eric has made it clear he doesn't want any more care-givers."

Regina talked about the length of time Eric had been sick, the various treatments he'd undergone, and the three caregivers she'd hired only to have to let them go. "He's so irritable and doesn't want anyone around him."

Joy nodded. She'd likely be acting like him if she were in his place.

"He used to not be like that." Regina sniffled, her amber eyes glassy, and Joy pulled out a tissue from the box on the table and handed it to her. "He's been through so much. But again, if I tell you everything about him, you'll not have much to talk about when you visit with him."

Regina seemed hopeful Joy would work for her, but that may not be an option.

"If he doesn't want anyone around, why would he want me there?"

"Because I'm not hiring you as medical staff."

Joy shifted in her seat, focusing on a springy image of Tigger. The triplets loved Tigger. What had they thought of seeing his image as Regina tried to explain they wouldn't be seeing their grandfather again?

Joy shook her head, refocusing. She already had a nanny job and wanted some afternoons open for spontaneity, but people like Eric were probably the reason God kept her in Colorado. If only God could give her some more time, she would be grateful even if she made it to two other countries. More importantly, she wanted to cheer up those who were hurting. Like Eric. She leaned forward. "What do you want me to do?"

"Same thing you do when you come to the hospital. Visit with Eric, keep him company." Regina drew out a breath. "He doesn't know this, but he could use a friend."

As the compassion and pain in Regina's eyes tugged at Joy's heart, she thought of her mom and the extent she'd gone to make Joy comfortable when she was ill. Joy didn't want long-term commitments, but as long as she still had Wednesdays open, she could keep her hospital engagements and help Regina. "How often do you want me to come?"

Regina's face lit up. "As many days and hours as you'd like."

Even if Joy hadn't been up for company, she'd still enjoyed temporary visits from other people besides having Mom sobbing endlessly at her bedside.

"I'll help on one condition."

"You name it."

"I'll not accept payment."

Regina's brows squeezed together. "Why?"

Joy did it for free at the hospital, and her reward was seeing smiles from patients who appreciated her presence. Among the many blessings she'd had from her illness was a stranger paying her hospital bill.

"I just want to. He might not even want me there."

"He will, but he doesn't know that yet." The wrinkles uncreased from Regina's brows, and she stood from the couch with her arms spread out for a hug.

Joy stood and hugged her back.

"Thank you so much." Regina cupped Joy's cheek. "You're God sent."

"I hope so."

Eric's sullen face flashed in her mind once again as she reached for her backpack. She had no idea why her dad's condition pressed on her.

"Please don't tell me you've had second thoughts already." Regina's voice interrupted her thoughts.

Joy may not have the best memory, and she might have missed something from Regina's mention of her son's past diagnosis. "Did you say Eric was tested for Lyme disease?"

Regina rubbed her forehead. "He was negative, though."

That had been the case with Joy's dad. She gripped the straps of her bag, uncomfortable prying, but it couldn't hurt to stick her nose into things where someone's health was concerned. "When was the last time they tested him for it?"

"Four months ago."

Joy ticked off her fingers to make her calculations from the time Eric started being sick up until four months ago. The Lyme didn't show in Dad's blood when they'd done the original diagnosis, but they saw a Lyme disease specialist much later. By then, it was too late for him.

"I hate to say this when I'm not a doctor, but it might not hurt to have Eric checked out for Lyme disease again."

Regina leaned against her desk and crossed her hands. "The doctor will think I'm crazy, and that's if I get Eric to accept another blood test today." She narrowed her brows. "Why would you think he needs another Lyme disease test?"

"My dad had Lyme disease." Joy swallowed and told Regina about her dad. Yes, God was in control, but it was hard not to wonder if the other fierce symptoms wouldn't have developed if they'd done another test on her dad right away.

"Oh, honey." Regina closed the gap between them and squeezed Joy's shoulder. "I'm so sorry."

Joy fought the tears clogging her throat.

"I'm gonna have to get Eric tested again before we go home today."

Eric could have something very different from Lyme disease, but his symptoms were similar to her dad's. She needed to refocus on something rather than mourning. "Will Monday be too far for me to start?"

"Serious?" Regina grinned. "That will be wonderful." Then her brows drew together. "I know the hospital ran a background check on you already, but the Stone security team might do the same so we can get you access to the house."

Who wouldn't run background checks these days? "I expected that to be the case."

"I'd normally have people sign a nondisclosure agreement, but I'm trusting you to keep and respect Eric's privacy if he opens up to you."

"O–kay." What kind of privacy? Joy wasn't one to go talking about people's lives. The only people she talked to often were Ruby, her grandpa, and her mom. "If you'd like, I can sign it."

Regina brushed her off with a wave. "Not necessary. I just want-ed you to know my son is very private."

Which would be a good reason for him not to want her there.

Regina jotted down the address on her business card and handed it over. "I'll call you to meet with security soon."

With a promise to pray for Eric and to see Regina in five days, Joy left.

As hospital announcements paged doctors over the PA system, she walked toward the end of the hallway to the window to voice a silent prayer. For those on their deathbeds and for the doctors to be successful as they worked with high-risk procedures. She prayed for the orphaned baby to find a home if he didn't have a dad or a family member to claim him. Then her prayers switched to Eric.

*Whatever disease he has, please, God, heal him. Give the doctors wisdom so they can pinpoint the source of his illness soon.*

Was this a disease that would end his life?

Suddenly overpowered by melancholy, she pressed her head against the glass and peered at the crisp white snow. It didn't feel as refreshing as it had earlier this morning. She'd entertained the idea of painting the falling snow on the buildings below the hospital, but maybe another day.

Monday, Tuesday, Thursday, and Friday. Four half days for four months. She'd wait until Ruby's wedding to figure out her next state to visit. Would it be enough time to connect with Eric? And that was if he needed her presence.

# CHAPTER 3

January seemed to drag on as if the cold temperature froze even the passage of time.... Could winter get any more exasperating?

Eric ground his teeth and glared at the snow beyond the floor-to-ceiling windows of his parents' guesthouse. The wind flung swirling snow in a glittering spiral across the yard.

As frigid as it was outside, the sting of coldness wouldn't numb him any more than he already felt physically and emotionally.

"Mr. Stone." Tessa's voice demanded attention.

She stood in front of him, her skin the same color as the mahogany padded ottoman he was resting his foot on. Where did Mom hire all these young people from? "I'm going to try to move your fingers next."

Eric tightened his fingers over the sweatpants on his legs.

"My fingers are fine." If anything, they were his only normal working parts. He used them to scratch the itchy rash on his body. "You may go now."

"I just..." Tessa pressed her lips together, obviously thinking better of her words before continuing. "Can we get our five-minute walk?"

"I can get myself to the bathroom." Not exactly, but he wanted to prove he was capable of taking care of himself. "That counts as a walk."

Five minutes was how long it took him to hobble to the bathroom with a walker.

At forty-four, he'd expected to be skiing, snowshoeing, bungee jumping, or undergoing something adventurous this time of the year.

Instead, he was stuck in the confines of his childhood home dealing with a mysterious disease.

He shifted in the leather swivel recliner, wincing at the pain radiating from his bottom.

"Um, can I help you back to bed?" Tessa peered at the adjustable hospital bed in the sunroom, perhaps noticing his discomfort.

"I'll get it!" His tone came out sharper than he would rather react, but couldn't she see he wanted to be left alone? Besides, it didn't matter if he lay down or sat up. He was in pain either way.

Tessa seemed to get the message. Without a word, she bent down and gathered the exercise balls she'd brought for him to use, but he wasn't in the mood for more than foot-muscle exercises.

"I'll see you tomorrow then?" She hovered a few feet from him, her eyes wide, her posture timid.

He couldn't blame the woman for doubting her job security. She'd only worked with him a little over two weeks, and he'd fired her last week—not that he hired her in the first place. Instead, his parents had hope in his recovery and insisted he needed a physical therapist.

They were the only reason he'd put up with this repetitive assault. All the people they hired to take care of him, he insisted his mom send their information to his accountant to be paid. The least he could do was to pay for his medical bills.

He didn't meet Tessa's gaze when she reminded him of his morning medicine, but his stomach lurched. The mention of tablets brought a distasteful smell, and he swallowed, fighting the urge to gag. He lifted a hand.

"I'll take it later." Skip it entirely.

"I'll leave it on your bedside table."

He grunted a response, keeping his gaze on the window and the snowcapped mountains beyond the property.

Heels clicked on the hallway tile that connected to the main house. He didn't have to swivel his chair to know his mom was dressed and ready for work.

"Are you leaving already?" Mom's voice sounded as she spoke to Tessa.

"Mr. Stone isn't up for a walk today."

"Did he take his medicine?" Mom asked.

"He'll take it later."

Eric cringed, feeling like a helpless toddler while they talked about him as if he wasn't even around. But again, he *was* like a child if he couldn't get himself to the bathroom without the aid of walkers and canes.

His face itched, and he scratched his bearded jaw, grimacing when he scratched too hard. He avoided looking in the mirror lately, scared he'd be terrified by what he saw.

The heels clicked again, accompanied by Mom's voice. "Good morning, my darling."

Eric huffed.

Then her gentle hand touched his cheek as she bent to look at him. Those amber eyes with a golden hue met his, and his heart ached more for his mother.

"I would like you to take the new antibiotics." Concern carried in her voice. "I know you can't stand medicine anymore, but with the chronic Lyme disease you've now been diagnosed with..." She shook her head, her words faltering.

*Lyme disease.* He'd tested positive for all the other diseases he was being treated for. Lyme disease shouldn't be a surprise. Was there anything he wouldn't test positive for? His body seemed a source of mystery bacteria, viruses, and illnesses.

When he stared at her teary eyes, his throat tightened. So much for coming home to recover from whatever this was. He nodded, rather than objected, only because he couldn't handle Mom sobbing anymore.

She let out a sigh of relief and left for the kitchen, then returned with three amber canisters of jingling pills and a glass tumbler with a lid and a straw.

The first two pills slid down fine. But, as he swallowed the blue pill, it stuck in his throat, and he held his chest with one hand while using the other to hold the cup and sip water through the straw. Man, that stubborn pill wouldn't budge, and it was scratching his throat.

His stomach let out an involuntary reflex, and saliva flooded his mouth. As it swirled with all the water he'd forced down, warm moisture stirred in his mouth, and he bent in search of the tiny bucket that was usually next to his chair. Where was it?

He pressed his hand harder to his chest as he gagged. Even if he walked to the bathroom, he wouldn't make it at his snail's pace.

"Oh no, sweetheart." Mom hurried away and returned with a bucket just in time for him to retch up a gush of vomit. The whole capsule landed in the bucket with the protein shake he'd taken that morning.

Her gentle hand brushed back his hair from his face. He was past due for a haircut, but he couldn't deal with that while he had no reason to. Shaky, he rinsed his mouth and ran a hand over his face. Clammy skin met his touch, and his whole body trembled. He pulled the lever on the side of the chair and leaned his head back to calm his tense muscles.

Mom called for Tessa to take the messy bucket. Thankfully, Mom's sweet jasmine scent diluted the smell.

"I know you'll feel better," Mom repeated the words. "Now that we know what needs to be treated."

"I don't know." Breathless, he closed his eyes. Even moving his arm was an effort as he massaged his temples. "I don't."

"People recover from Lyme disease every day."

He didn't have to know her well to hear the forced cheer in her tones. Even if he had Lyme disease, this was an extreme case, just like all his other diseases.

"Your dad will be working from home until noon."

He hoped it wasn't because of him. "I don't need to be babysat." He kept his eyes closed, needing to rest them. But the headless shadow figure appeared, and he instantly opened them.

"By the way"—Mom cleared her throat—"Joy will be here to keep you company during the day—someone you can talk to, besides your health care attendants."

Hadn't he made it clear he didn't want any more attendants? They'd gone through this conversation countless times these last six months. "I have plenty of friends to talk to."

"Yet you don't want them to come and visit. You refuse to take their calls."

He wanted to be alone... alone without an audience. He drew out a breath, needing to be gentle as he declined her offer.

"I don't need a nanny or caregivers." Whatever they called them.

"She's not a nanny." The golden flecks in Mom's eyes shone, her sorrow deep. "She doesn't want me to pay her. She wants to visit as a friend. I thought you could use one."

*Great.* He'd driven his mom to such desperation she was enlisting strangers to visit him. There was no sense in arguing, and he didn't have the strength anyway. Joy would get the message and leave.

"You didn't get a chance to visit with her in the hospital."

Oh. It was her. The woman he'd almost puked on—he'd ruined her sweater or something, hadn't he? Double great. Seeing her again would be humiliating.

His mom sputtered details of what time his caretaker would show up. "You've spent so much time alone, and it's not good for you."

Little surprise she'd say that. The therapist had told him that too. He'd recommended Eric interact with people besides his dad and mom, but Eric had told his friends he wasn't up for talking. Whenever they called, Mom had to answer and relay their message. He'd also had to limit calls from his siblings to once a month.

"Your dad will stay until Joy arrives," Mom continued and wanted to know if he needed to move to his bed.

His bottom hurt. The soft leather should be comfortable, but it wasn't. He needed to switch positions, but he'd rather have a stranger help than have his mom do any more.

"I'm fine."

With a promise that the chef would bring his midmorning smoothie, Mom disregarded the bumps on his forehead, as usual, and planted a soft kiss before leaving. He almost rolled his eyes, but the sentiment reminded him of when he was a terrified four-year-old mourning his mom. Regina's kind eyes and embrace had soothed his panicked heart. "It's okay, sweetheart. I'll take care of you," she'd said and kissed him on the cheek. She and Kyle had done just that, ever since they brought him into their home.

Well, he was a child, and as long as he was helpless in his childhood home, he'd better expect to be spoon-fed.

After she left, he glanced toward the kitchen next to the hallway where she'd vanished. From the main room where he sat, he could see the entire guesthouse, minus the five bedrooms down another hallway. Tessa wasn't in the kitchen, and when he looked back to the sunroom where his daybed was, she wasn't there either.

He breathed out low and deep. Alone at last.

He gripped the chair's armrest and pushed up. After what seemed like five minutes or however long, he stood. Keeping his hand on the chair for support, he bent and reached for his cane.

His brain was spinning and woozy. By the time he shuffled into the sunroom, he felt like he'd been hit by a truck.

Fully spent, he didn't have the strength to make it to the rug by the chair. His feet were too weak to climb the bed or chair, which was only inches away. He lowered himself on the floor and laid down on his stomach. The cool tile soothed the painful sores. He'd stay on the floor until Sabastian showed up with his smoothie.

Who would've guessed he was a man who once ran a successful billion-dollar company and had several investments around the world? All the money and genius doctors couldn't pinpoint what was wrong with him. Hmm, he was now lying hopelessly on the floor.

He once had a wife and ten kids. The moment they died, he'd never felt at home in the house where he'd raised his kids. The Peak, his childhood home, was as comfortable as he'd ever be.

Tears pricked his eyes. He'd cried and mourned for years over his family—pretended to move on by distracting himself with work—but the illness had awoken a beast of darkness that continued to overshadow him daily.

SEVERAL MINUTES LATER, Eric shifted to his side. He pushed down the pillow, feeling more propped than he wanted to. Sabastian had helped him move to the couch when he'd brought the smoothie.

Eric blinked at the sudden shuffling of feet and voices from the guesthouse kitchen.

All he needed to do was lift his head to see the people in the adjoining kitchen and main room, but he wasn't up to the task, not while his head throbbed like it was about to fall off his neck.

He recognized his dad, Kyle's voice when he spoke again.

"This cabinet has all the medicine Eric needs." Dad relayed medical tasks to someone who may not last longer than an hour. "Regina left instructions in a spreadsheet on the iPad, including the type of medicine and the time to administer it."

"O–kay." The feminine voice sounded hesitant—a good sign. If him puking on her sweater hadn't scared her off, a better look at his frightful face would send her packing. Surely, she hadn't had time to study his beastly appearance in the hospital.

Dad pointed out the hallway to the bathroom and the five bedrooms. "In case the weather is bad and you can't get home, you're always welcome to stay the night."

"I hate driving in the snow." Her peppy voice grated Eric's nerves as it disturbed their somber house. "I'll no doubt take you up on the offer. Thank you."

"Let's meet Eric," Dad said, and footsteps sounded louder as they approached—Dad's familiar Hush Puppies making squishy sounds while her steps were whisper soft.

Eric could sit, but he had no idea how long he would survive staying still. Laying down was a safer option.

"Eric?"

He turned to look up at his dad, dressed in a black coat and a blue shirt that reflected his eyes. When Kyle smiled, Eric forced his cheeks to lift into some semblance of one as well.

"I believe you've already met Joy?"

The woman next to Dad offered a warm smile.

"Hi again." As she waved with enthusiasm, her bobbed spiral curls bounced around her jaw.

The genuineness in her smile brought a welcome contrast to the sorrowful smiles he got the moment people looked at his scraggly face. "I'm sure you don't remember me, but—"

He cleared his throat. "I do."

How could he forget her when he'd left a memory on their first encounter?

At roughly five five, she was taller than he remembered. The blue butterfly pattern on her white sweater, with more butterflies on her sock-clad feet—no wonder her steps were so quiet—intrigued him.

As if aware of his perusal, she fumbled with her backpack straps before sliding it off. "I got something for you."

He doubted anything she had would lift his spirits, and he was right when she set a colorful cube on the table. "I'd brought it for you in the hospital, but I didn't get the chance to…"

As she trailed off with a shrug, Dad thanked her for being thoughtful. "Eric used to have a collection of Rubik's cubes."

Ages ago. He could barely remember what age he'd obsessed about it. Lately, he had no interest or desire to do anything other than lay down.

His gaze wandered back to his dad when he clamped Eric on the shoulder. His touch was lighter than anything he'd given him as a frightened child. Maybe he knew Eric was even more afraid now. "Let Joy know if you need help getting anything from the house."

Eric switched his focus to her then, her spotless brown skin making him cautious of his scaly rash, and he touched his face. "I'll be fine." He hadn't intended to be sharp, but that was his tone lately. Everyone should be miserable like him, and if they weren't, then it was his job to make it happen.

Dad told him about the health care company he was analyzing that afternoon. "I might be late getting home." He adjusted his navy tie. "How does my tie look?"

"Like you're ready to take over the world."

After giving him a wistful smile, Dad wished him a good day, then wished Joy the best of luck before he left.

She sat in the navy armchair across from Eric. Now, if she could lose that sunny smile, his day might be normal with the proper dosage of misery he prescribed.

Joy's eyes met his gaze and held it. They were the most extraordinary brown eyes he'd ever seen, and for one awful moment, he thought she could see right through the dark recesses of his heart.

Exposed, he cringed, then dismissed the unnerving thought with a scowl.

"Are you going to stare at me the entire time?"

With her hands resting on her sky blue tights, she crisscrossed her outstretched feet, making herself at home as if she'd been here before. "I was considering how to approach our first conversation."

With her face so vibrant, she looked more ready to take on anything the world threw at her than Dad did. Too bad the world had thrown Eric at her. If she was counting on conversation, she had the wrong man. "I hope I haven't given you the impression I'm good company."

Her mouth curved up. "You're better company than last time we met."

With vomit. What a way to make a first impression. He winced, and as if reading his mind, she touched her sweater. "Don't worry. I have more than enough sweaters to last me this winter."

Butterflies. His ten-year-old daughter loved butterflies. For a second, he pictured Joy as one of those adults who might have the heart of a child. Getting excited about every living thing they came across. Believing all things could work out for good. Trusting everyone she met.

Man, was she the wrong person to enter his space. He needed to send her off in peace before he destroyed something in her or vice versa. "Listen, Joy..."

Her smile widened, and she scooted, moving the chair forward. Her name suited her, and she perked up as if awaiting the best news of her life. Being the opposite of anything related to Joy, his tone—his whole being, really—went cold. "Your talents might be best used at the hospital."

As her smile vanished, she tucked a springy strand of her hair behind her ear. Her discomfort should make him feel good about himself, but it didn't. Ugh. But he *needed* to get his point across. It was for her own good as well as his. So he closed his eyes, afraid to look at her as he fired her before her first day. "I prefer to be alone."

In his misery.

# CHAPTER 4

O f all the states Joy Musana had visited so far, Colorado hadn't left her lacking inspiration. She'd only been in Pleasant View for the summer, fall, and now winter, but from the seasons she'd experienced here, she was already anticipating spring to be as breathtaking as the others.

Speaking of scenery, this house had one of the best mountain views. Good thing she brought her sketchbook. She'd expected Eric not to want her around, and given the circumstances, he'd been polite.

So she was giving him the space he needed—if standing in the kitchen where she could still peek at him now and then counted as space.

The rooms, while classy, were so bland, void of color with their white walls, cabinets, and couches, like a blank canvas still waiting for someone to bring them to life. But the snowcapped mountains were a perfect distraction, and as she moved the pencil on the white paper to draw an arch, peace with her decision to be here soothed her.

Black and white wouldn't do the picture justice. Why didn't she bring her paint kit, too? Carrying her art tub might have been too much on the first day, but her fingers were itching to do more than a pencil sketch.

She would have to study the view so she could paint it when she got home.

As she moved into the living room and sat on the white couch, she eyed the black leather recliner by the window. Eric must rest there whenever he needed a break from lying on the couch or the hospital bed in the sunroom.

When she'd looked him in the eye the way she'd done at the hospital, her heart ached at the anguish there. She sensed a certain pain, affliction beyond his physical wounds.

*"He's been through so much...."* Regina's words kept repeating in Joy's mind.

What had he been through?

"Ow." Eric groaned, and Joy peered into the sunroom. One of his hands braced on the floor. He didn't seem like he was falling off the couch, and although she didn't want to be running to him, she let her pencil clatter on the floor and rushed to him, in case he needed help.

Since she'd been here for over an hour, he must need to use the bathroom by now. "Can I help you stand?"

"Do I look like I need help?"

Her shoulders tensed, and she clasped her hands together. Too bad there wasn't a handbook of what she was supposed to do besides talk and offer company. He was in no mood for her visit. Considering the cold weather, perhaps a warm drink would help his stomach or indigestion if he had any.

"Can I get you some herbal tea?"

With his one hand pressed on the white sheepskin rug, he glared at her beneath drawn-together brows. "Do I look like I need tea?"

The tea she drank whenever she was angry might be the perfect antidote. Feeling small under his scrutiny, she shifted her feet, her socks slipping on the white tile. Um, okay. Visiting with hospital patients who'd requested company was different from being unwanted in someone's home. She hugged her arms around herself, switching her weight to her other leg. The quiet room made it so uncomfortably silent.

"Can I, um, play some music?"

He rolled his eyes, panting as if he'd run a marathon. "Yeah, music should be the perfect solution to all my problems."

Music, really? Of all things, she had to blurt out to an indignant man! He probably thought she was dumb.

Now she needed to come up with a way to revive herself with a better response. Silence passed between them as she looked everywhere in the room except at him, her gaze pausing on the flat-screen TV above the fireplace. A movie might be a good distraction, but he had the TV off for a reason.

Maybe she could read him one of those books on the shelf nestled in the corner? Hmm, but she would have to first find out what he wanted to read about.

There was a walker between the couch and hospital bed. Had he been trying to reach his walker? She could drag it in front of him in case he wanted to go to the bathroom or around the house.

Sensing his critical gaze, she shifted her feet again and tightened her grip around herself. On the wall behind the couch, two abstract paintings displayed intriguing details about the heart. She'd need more time to look at those later.

She then looked through the window, the need to say something, anything, clogging her throat.

"Nice view." It was true.

He snorted, and that was Joy's cue to make herself scarce.

Although she'd packed playing cards in her utility bag, he didn't seem to be in a state to do anything today or ever. "Let me know if you need anything."

She ambled back to the living room, and the coolness of the tile seeped through her socks. Ignoring the fluffy white couches and Eric's brooding black recliner, she picked up her pencil and headed to the kitchen.

"If you think you're here to help me, you're wrong."

Perhaps that spreadsheet had a step-by-step plan to help with the man's surly mood. She grabbed the iPad as a lifeline, but the spreadsheet offered nothing related to her job. Though, apparently, she needed to give him medicine at two.

*Great!* If he couldn't talk to her, how was he going to accept the medicine?

She pulled open the cabinet and eyed the amber tablet canisters. Each was labeled with a different color sticker displaying the time it was to be consumed.

A loud thump and groan had her dashing back to him.

He was on the rug, wincing as he rubbed his forehead. Ouch, he must have hit his head.

"Are you going to get me the walker or what?"

She reached for the walker and wheeled it to his side. He gripped the edge of the table and stood.

*You're welcome,* she wanted to say when he got to the walker, but that would be cynical. A terrible attitude to care for a patient.

"Let me get you an ice pack." She tipped her head, trying to get a good look at the bruise.

"If you think that'll heal all my diseases, then be my guest."

How rude! Her body quivered. She still went to find an ice pack while he made his way to the bathroom at a tortoise pace.

Being upset and giving Eric a piece of her mind was the right thing to do, but she had no right to be mad or complain. She was alive and healthy, having been given a second chance, while he was sick. She could certainly give him a second chance as well.

It was almost one when a dark-haired man with tan skin appeared in the kitchen carrying a tray of two steaming bowls of soup. Joy met him earlier when she arrived at the main house. He looked to be four or five years younger than she was, but the grim line on his face made him appear older. Maybe gloominess was a requirement for anyone who worked with Eric.

"Sabastian, right?" She knew it was his name, but she was trying for friendliness, desperate for a warm face besides Eric's parents who weren't going to be around when she was.

As Sabastian nodded, she took the tray and carried it to the dining table, set for three.

He pushed back one of the yellow barstools further down the counter. "Are you sure you don't need anything besides soup?"

She detected an accent.

Even though Regina told her she'd be offered meals by their chef, Joy had packed a lunch with no expectations to be catered for. So, when he'd asked what she wanted for lunch, she'd said whatever Eric had whenever he ate.

"I'll be fine. Thank you."

Sabastian peered at where Eric was now slouched in the living room recliner. "Do you know if Mr. Stone needs my help to get to the bathroom?"

Thank goodness the chef helped Eric sometimes. Otherwise, he would be hurt if his bathroom breaks were anything like the one she'd witnessed earlier.

"He went earlier, but I'll let you ask him."

When Sabastian went to talk to Eric, he had a different tone, calmer than the one he'd used with her.

"He wants to eat in the living room." Sabastian returned to her side. "If you need anything in the main kitchen, help yourself anytime."

She'd be fine food-wise, but she might need to squeeze conversation out of him before she starved for it. "Will do. Thank you."

When she took the tray to the coffee table and sat across from Eric, she didn't know if he believed in God like his mom, but she'd already felt awkward enough around him. Having her eyes closed would be more awkward, so she asked, "Is it okay to pray?"

"Whatever you want." He stared at his steaming bowl as if lost in thought.

After praying aloud, she noticed the coffee table was almost the same height as the couch and it was trickier with Eric's taller frame to hunch while reaching for the spoon.

His hands were shaking as he lifted the spoon from the bowl to his mouth. Half the carrots and celery from the soup spilled on his gray sweatpants and his navy sweatshirt, but he didn't seem to mind. So she didn't comment, except for passing him a napkin.

The clinking of spoons against porcelain bowls was the only noise.

"I'm done." He shoved the half-empty bowl to the side as she polished off her vegetable soup. She might need her peanut butter and jelly sandwich after all. But, for now, she needed to get him his medicine.

If she succeeded, she'd consider her day a victory.

When she returned from the kitchen with his medicine, Eric acted like a child and crossed his hands over his chest.

She stood there in a staring contest with the saucer of pills and a glass of water.

"Make me." He lifted an eyebrow.

"I'm not going to make you do anything, but I was told to—"

"Guess what?" He tilted his head to one side.

At least he was talking. Her curiosity piqued, she played along. "What's that?"

"Thanks to you, Mom had me poked and probed with more tests, and now I'm taking more medicine."

"So you, um, tested positive for—"

"Lyme disease, like all the other things I tested positive for."

Her heart sank, and her shoulders fell. It was terrible that he had Lyme disease, but at least he was being treated for the infection.

"I'm sorry." Not for being responsible for him getting treatment, but for him having another disease among the many others.

He dragged a hand through his rumpled hair, and his voice was softer when he spoke this time. "Join the line for the ten thousand others who feel sorry for me."

His anguish demanded her attention, and she wanted to ask how bad his Lyme disease had gotten. But she doubted he was in the mood to discuss his health. As much as she wanted to force him, to talk to him, and to push him to take medicine, she had no idea how to. He was an adult, and she wasn't equipped to demand a patient take treatment against their will.

She left him alone and kept herself busy. With a pen, she drew flowers and butterflies in her palm.

Problem was Eric was the center of her thoughts and she found herself thinking of drawing him.

Giving in, she put her art pens in the container and grabbed her sketchbook. She started by sketching his face and shaggy hair and beard from what her mind remembered.

When Regina returned that evening, Joy hung around for less than three minutes to let her know she was looking forward to seeing Eric tomorrow. What she didn't tell his loving mother was the medicine he refused to take or how she'd rather be hanging out with someone who enjoyed her company.

IF YOU LOVE THOSE WHO *love you, what credit is that to you?* The words replayed in the back of Joy's head before she punched the four digits to enter a code in her phone app. The wide black gate rose for her to drive beneath it, and she passed the words *The Peak at Stone Estate* engraved on a curved and chiseled-smooth rock.

Regina had wasted no time in having Joy meet with their security team on Saturday before she started work. They'd programmed her fingerprints and synced her phone into the Stones' security.

Whether it was going to be a good day or not, Joy embraced the words she'd read in the Bible last night. She drove the long paved road on a private drive lined with evergreens and leafless trees. Although the snow still covered the hillside, the road had been plowed and salted.

Almost five miles later, she drove up the hill to a three-story limestone house where the wide cobblestone driveway presented several parking possibilities. At the bend by the fountain, she turned to the right to park closer to the guesthouse entrance.

Although she could let herself in through the guesthouse entrance, doing so felt awkward after just one day on the so-called job.

With one more look in the rearview mirror, she rustled her hair to keep the curls in place. Since her last chemo treatment four years ago, her hair growth seemed slower, but she was grateful to have her familiar vibrant locks.

When she stepped out of her green Sentra, she spread out her hands and breathed in the crisp air. It wasn't snowing today. Whew! And lazy clouds offered hope the sun would shine one day soon.

The modern house looked like a mini-hotel. On the far side, another detached building connected to the house via a closed-in breezeway. She pointed to each black garage door as she counted five wide enough to fit two cars each. It was almost, if not more than, 20,000 international vacations worth.

Joy had been tempted to look up its value on Zillow, but after Regina had pointed out something about nondisclosure and Eric's privacy, Joy wouldn't feel any peace about snooping.

Hoisting her backpack purse, she grabbed her picnic basket and utility tote from the back of the car.

She'd originally intended to work four hours at The Peak, but although Eric made it clear he didn't want anyone around, he needed someone to keep an eye on him so he didn't fall while navigating his way through the house. She intended to stay until Regina or Kyle got home. Despite Sabastian's existence in the home, his presence in the guesthouse seemed minimal.

She rang the doorbell, but no one answered.

She'd never had to scan her fingers to unlock a building, but again, it shouldn't be a surprise. The country she'd grown up in was still behind on technology, let alone the advanced type.

"Good morning, Sabastian," she called as she peered around for the chef who wasn't in sight.

The house smelled of decadent pastries, mixed with the scent of the fresh flowers on the black granite kitchen island. She walked toward the lit long hallway leading to the guesthouse kitchen.

When she peeked toward the sunroom, Sabastian was bending by the bed as if propping pillows behind Eric's head. After putting the half-gallon of Simply Lemonade and her fruits and vegetables in the fridge, she washed her hands before heading to the sunroom.

Making his exit, Sabastian greeted her, then added, "Let me know if you need something else for lunch besides soup."

She told him soup would be perfect, then ambled toward Eric and greeted him. He didn't look at her when he grunted out a hello and pulled the plush fleece blanket to his waist.

He was wearing a white T-shirt instead of the navy sweatshirt he'd worn yesterday. Although standing a few feet from him, she could smell the faint scent of his conditioner.

"Did you sleep well?" she prodded, hoping for better luck at conversation today.

He clasped his hands behind his head, and his Adam's apple dipped. "What do you think?"

What did she think? It was going to be another long day. Had she been that curt to her mom and the two friends who visited during her recovery?

She returned to the kitchen and read her notes on the iPad.

Nothing was different from yesterday's notes—oh. Something was highlighted in blue. Joy strained her eyes to read the detail. Amitriptyline to take with a snack at four. More notes were added in italics: *Decided to split his medicine throughout the day, so he doesn't take all of it at once.*

Maybe she'd have better luck handling medicine today. Joy returned to her drawing and dragged the pencil to create more sketches of Eric. It wasn't as easy as she'd hoped. She ripped out and crumpled the pages, tossing them on the floor only to start over again.

She couldn't get his jaw and ears right. If she could only map out his brain on paper, she would get a better understanding of his anger.

When Sabastian showed up with lunch, this time he brought her a sandwich with her soup.

"I hope you didn't go out of your way to fix this."

He shrugged, handing her the tray. "Hope you eat meat. It's a steak sandwich."

The savory aroma made her mouth water. "I can't wait." She thanked him. "Would you like to join us?" After all, there was no reason for him to eat alone.

Sabastian stifled a chuckle. "Mr. Stone likes to be left alone."

"I've noticed."

Sabastian didn't linger to add to her comment.

Eric didn't seem thrilled having her sit with him yesterday, but he also didn't send her away. So she went through the same regimen when she took their lunch into the sunroom and prayed over it. They didn't talk to each other, but again, he didn't send her away.

The real test would be after lunch when she got his medicine.

Hmm. She pushed up from her seat and strode into the kitchen, then poured lemonade into a mug and microwaved it. Perhaps drinking something besides water would make his medicine less unappealing.

Eric was slumped on the couch, leaning his head back, but he sat up when she neared.

"What's that?" He eyed the mug as she put out the saucer of medicine.

"It's something warm for your medicine."

His brow lifted, and he scratched his shaggy beard. "Do you even know what medicine you're giving me?"

"Antibiotics."

"For?"

"Lyme disease and, uh, swollen joints." Inflammation but she hadn't thought of it in time to respond.

"I'll pass." He rubbed his hands over his thighs beneath navy sweats.

Uh, not good. "It will help you feel better."

"And you're a doctor now, huh?"

Despite his unreadable expression, he didn't appear as intimidating as yesterday, but still, this job was harder than she'd expected. Joy set the cup on the table, lowered herself, and peered directly into his sunken hazel eyes. This should make it hard for him to defy her to her face.

He stared back defiantly at first, and she sucked in a breath.

Then his eyes seemed to soften and revealed a hint of green. The sorrow there wrenched her heart and compelled her to speak.

"Don't you want to feel better?" Her voice emerged as a whisper.

He held her gaze, then snapped, "No! I've had enough medicine already." He scrubbed his forehead, his fingers rasping over his scabs. "Sometimes the medicine makes me feel worse...." He expressed his concerns about the side effects and what he hated most was feeling foggy. "I have to do this for the rest of my life. I don't think skipping from time to time will make a difference."

What could she say? She wouldn't want to deal with brain fog or develop ulcers or any of those many side effects.

"What's in the cup anyway?"

Hmm? She looked up, surprised he'd said something in a somewhat normal voice. "Some kind of tea... not exactly."

"I'll try it." He took the mug and lifted it to his mouth, then asked, "What kind of tea is this again?"

"Um... citrusy kind."

His lips twitched. Maybe it was her imagination, but she thought she saw a ghost of a smile.

Clearly, he'd had a change of heart about the medicine. If he recovered from Lyme disease, perhaps all the other diseases would eventually vanish from his blood. "You're sure you don't want to take your tablets?"

"I'm sure."

Oh boy. He was going to get worse under her care. She stood and walked back to the kitchen. How was she supposed to force a grown man to take his medicine? She would have to text Regina and let her know why she didn't succeed playing doctor or nurse.

"Don't entertain the idea of telling my mom."

His words sounded over her shoulder, and she spun to meet his knowing gaze. How did he know she was going to tattle?

She squared her shoulders, giving him her best professional look. "You've left me no choice."

"I..." He clenched his hands, and his voice dipped. "I. Don't. Need. A babysitter."

Perhaps she was acting like a babysitter if she was threatening to tell on him. What was she going to do? At the counter, she glanced at her phone. Tempted to reach for it and fire a text to Regina.

*God, what can I do?*

It wasn't enough prayer to get an answer, so for the next hour or so, Joy sat in the living room and focused on drawing. Even if she had her paint today, the white sofas and spotless kitchen with its white cupboards offered no place for her to make a mess.

The Peak at Stone Estate.

Did they call it The Peak because their house was up on a hill? It stood out among the few spread apart in the surrounding area.

She imagined what The Peak looked like in the summertime. The beautiful flower garden had to attract butterflies.

She sketched butterflies and flowers as she pictured the types of flowers in their garden. Definitely wild roses—they were hardy enough for the mountain climate. Tulips—they did well in the snow. She'd read about that when she was encouraging Ruby to talk to the landlord so they could plant tulips for the spring in the complex garden.

At some point during her drawing, Eric hobbled on the walker to the recliner in the main room. He was panting, no doubt exhausted, by the time he sat.

Torn between running to give him a hand and letting him do it himself, she forced herself not to move.

He was closer to her now. Although the main room was spacious enough to keep them from being in each other's space, she sensed his nearness. Whenever she thought she could hear his breathing, the room shrank and closed in on her.

Eric was staring out the window, his mouth in a grim line.

The silence seemed to stretch with him in the room. Perhaps, just as uncomfortable, he felt the need to complain. "You can tell my mom I'm not your type of patient."

Is that what he wanted—her to quit? Obviously, he didn't want anyone to get close to him. That's how she'd felt, how a teeny part of her still felt, but the friends who ignored her request to be left alone had made a difference in her life.

"Why don't you tell her?"

Staying silent, he dragged out a frustrated breath.

With his gaze at the window, she felt emboldened to give a firm response. "I made a commitment to be here."

"I free you from that obligation."

She'd have to try a lot longer than two days. "Thanks." Eric could very well be her new assignment from God—the reason she may have to spend the entire summer in Colorado.

Forgetting her current project, she flipped to a fresh page of her sketchbook and started drawing him. The seated position would make a great portrait. With his minimal mobility, she might get the drawing done before she left for the evening.

She retrieved her phone from the kitchen and scrolled through her apps, then tapped her classical music playlist. The soothing instrumental chords relaxed her as she drew his chin. She doubted he'd notice that she was drawing him.

She waited for him to protest about the music, but he didn't say anything or move.

Good.

Uneasy whenever he winced and scratched the rash on his arms and his face, she fought the urge to run and offer help. Unless he asked, she'd better keep drawing.

The more she drew his face and studied the shape of his defined jaw, then his nose, the more she saw how different he'd be without the beard. She couldn't stop imagining what he looked like before the skin rash, the unruly hair, and the wild beard.

Through the corner of her eyes, she saw him push the lever and lean back in the chair. He yawned, exhausted perhaps, and by the time she added the beard to the chin, his chest was rising and falling in an even rhythm.

She didn't add the rash on his face. It was temporary, and he was going to be okay eventually.

With the natural light radiating through the floor-to-ceiling windows, she studied him. He looked so vulnerable laying there, so hurt with affliction.

Her chest constricted with a pain so intense, she could scarcely breathe.

She wanted to share his pain, ached to sacrifice everything for him, do anything or go through anything God threw at her, so she could help Eric get better.

*Oh Lord, I don't know what Eric has been through, but please, heal him, comfort him, and make him well.*

A lump clogged her throat. At that moment, she didn't care if she never traveled to another state or place as long as she stayed until he was better.

She didn't want to stay in one place for too long or get attached to more people, but maybe he was the reason she'd come to Pleasant View.

# CHAPTER 5

With the brisk midmorning air, Joy strolled with Ruby along the quaint shops on Pleasant View's main street. The town felt so magical with the twinkling strings of lights and the towering snowcapped mountains surrounding them.

"Aren't you glad we ate lunch at your office café?" Joy tucked her gloved hands in her jacket pockets as she studied an overly priced menu on the big wooden sign before one of the cafés they passed.

"This town is not for the poor and faint." Ruby pulled Joy's hand to the side when a tall woman emerged from one of the designer boutiques. "Speaking of wealth…" Her jaw dropped as her gaze followed the woman dressed in tight jeans and orange pumps and carrying two full bags with the store logo.

"Did you see her handbag?" Ruby touched both hands on her cheeks reddened from the cold as she ogled the woman's bag.

Joy hadn't noticed, but knowing Ruby's purse addiction, Joy urged her forward and away from the boutique just in case it had whatever handbag her friend was swooning over.

"Chanel…" Ruby sighed dramatically. "Chanel. Do you know how expensive those handbags are?"

Joy could guess what some paintings cost, but handbags were overrated. "The woman is probably a model, and even if you can afford that kind of handbag, you have enough purses to last you a lifetime."

"Just like your art supplies?" Ruby, only a year younger than Joy, huffed and adjusted her cozy gray-knit hat over her long brown hair.

They'd met in San Francisco when Ruby had rented the Airbnb home next door to Joy's grandpa's house. Joy was still new in America, and her dad had just died. When Ruby returned to Colorado, they'd stayed in touch. Then, once Joy was diagnosed with cancer, Ruby had flown back to visit her twice during Joy's chemotherapy. Ruby was one of the two friends Joy still had, and she preferred the long distances between her friends. With her cancer-risk factor, she couldn't let anyone depend on her.

"Should we check the prices at that hair salon?" Grasping Joy's sleeve, Ruby drew Joy forward.

"That's the flyer we looked at last week." Joy reminded her. They'd been price matching for a hairstylist for Ruby's wedding.

Ruby waved her free hand. "Those ones can't even come to the ranch."

Joy agreed and still reminded Ruby of the stylist she'd talked to who was willing to commute to the ranch venue on the morning of the wedding. Lights winked at her as if encouraging her choice, a single icicle dripped from the nearest sign, and chilly air filled her lungs.

Joy freed her arm, making room for passersby while people walked in and out of banks, unique designer boutiques, and random houses painted in vibrant colors.

"How long is your lunchtime?" she asked her friend as the hobby shop sign—Alpine Hobby and Craft Shop—came into view, its red letters on white background Christmassy even without the crafty candy canes they'd removed from the sign after the holiday season.

Still in her scrubs, Ruby snuggled her coat closed. "I got someone to work my afternoon shift."

Which was always hard with their dental practice being one of the two in the area and busy all year long.

Joy swung open the door, and the bell jingled. "I just need a few supplies."

"For your patient," Ruby added the quotation with her fingers. "I can't believe you're planning to go back when he doesn't want you there."

Pressing her lips tight, Joy entered the warm shop and breathed in the sweet scents of paint and homemade candles. Oh, she could just hug the whole place! Willow wreaths hung from the walls while spools of yarn and ribbon spilled from handwoven baskets dangling from the rafters and each pine shelf beckoned her to investigate the unique treasure it held. But she shouldn't have told Ruby anything about her first day at the Stone residence. She'd been too drained to make dinner that night, a task she'd taken on since moving in with her friend. Telling her why they had to order takeout seemed necessary. She scooted past a shelf of hand-blown glass vases and stained-glass window decorations positioned too near the entryway. "I think he needs me."

"I thought the triplets and the hospital patients needed you." Ruby walked into the store and waited for Joy to close the door.

She paused before a display of cutesy craft projects nestled on potpourri. Making a personal connection with the hospital patients was always hard. She never got to see most of them once they were transferred or discharged, but it was for the best to keep her from getting attached, only to have them die.

"I don't know who needs me, but I need to be patient with Eric." He was different, too prickly for her to get attached to.

"Hello." An elderly woman smiled from behind the counter where she was organizing beaded bracelets on the rack. "Let me know if you need help finding anything."

"I should get a job here and enjoy all the discounts." Joy picked up a stray handmade card from the hardwood floor. She then stacked it behind the other cards in the basket on the table.

"That would be nice. I have a hard time attracting full-time employees."

"That's the downside to having a shop in a tourist town." Ruby was already trying on one of the crocheted scarves and wrapping it around her neck.

"Weekdays are not very busy. This is my time for a break."

Joy asked about the teenagers who helped her a few times when she shopped.

The woman fluffed gray hair away from her face. "I only have them here on Fridays to Sundays."

"Joy!" Ruby, now perusing a table not too far from the counter, lifted round yellow earrings and flicked them to catch the light. "For you."

Joy gave her a thumbs-up, but earrings were not in her budget that day. She had no money to squander on luxury. "I'm here for the art supplies."

"By the way," the woman said from the counter, "I will have the caterpillars by mid-April."

Joy grinned, already picturing the butterflies. "Really?"

The woman beamed. "You'll also be happy to know that most of the art supplies are forty percent off this week."

Soaring, Joy practically floated to the art section along the wall. She breathed in deeply, loving the store's happy-place smell of hand-made lotions, citrusy soaps, and aromatic scents.

She picked up a twelve-pack of paintbrushes. Even though she had some at home, the tips were getting frail. Forty percent off was a good deal. Most times, she shopped for the big supplies in a town outside Pleasant View.

"I figured you would need this." Ruby pushed over a small shopping cart.

"Thanks." Joy tossed in the brushes and then reached for the pack of acrylic paint. "Twelve." She scanned the colors as her mind worked on the perfect ones for Eric's painting.

White was always good when she had to mix colors. She'd get the twenty-four pack since it had a bottle of white paint.

"What are you going to paint for your special patient?" A couple of tables behind Joy, Ruby sniffed and squeezed the sample lotion into her hand.

Joy tapped her chin, eyeing the bright colors in the cart. Whatever picture she painted had to have the right tone to match that fancy house. Something with a subtle green or a color representing life. "I'm not so sure yet."

She turned back to the wall and selected a box of acrylic art pens. When she scanned the row of canvas boards, she cringed a bit since the firm painting canvas was still expensive even with the discount.

But if she was taking it into Kyle and Regina's house, it needed to fit the rest of the decor. She'd better use whatever was left of her paycheck after her share of the rent.

When she joined Ruby at the lotion booth, her friend had a stash of jewelry on the table and two lotions. Joy breathed in the lotion's soft scent, its aroma soothing her.

"These are homemade." Ruby was reading a tan label on one of the lotions. "Lavender essential oil, peppermint..."

Joy picked up the sample tube and squeezed it in her hands. "This is so soft."

"Smells good too." Ruby put her palm to her nose, inhaling as she closed her eyes.

Joy had to agree after imitating her friend to sniff the lotion. But she'd already overspent on art supplies. "I'll have to buy some next month."

"Skin rash cream." Ruby read the next jar, and Joy snatched it from her hand.

Eczema, dermatitis, infections, unusual skin rashes, and all kinds of hard rashes. Eric.

The iPad spreadsheet showed he took medicine for his skin rash. But *did* he take it, or was it one of those he told his mom he wouldn't consume? Could he use a cream, and would he be offended if she got it for him?

Hmm.

"You don't have a rash?" Ruby's brows drew together.

"Eric does."

"Oh." Ruby tilted her head to the side as if in warning. "And how are you going to persuade him to use it?"

Joy had no idea. Just like she had no idea how to get him to take his medicine. "I have my ways."

Sure she did. She almost rolled her eyes. But even if she didn't have ways, God did, and she'd count on that any day.

At the cash register, Ruby talked about her dinner plans with her fiancé that night. "You should join us."

"I'm not coming as the third wheel." Joy put the items on the wooden counter.

"Nate's going to be there."

"Who?" She spun to look at her friend.

Uh-oh. Ruby was biting her fingernail the way she did whenever she was up to something.

"Hudson's brother. The best man?"

Not again. This time Joy did roll her eyes. "I have to paint."

When the woman told her the total, Joy said she'd pay for Ruby's items too. She hated using a credit card. After all, Ruby only had two items, and she'd been so good to her.

"I'll pay for my own stuff." Ruby tried to reach for her items, but Joy swatted her hand away and urged the older woman to continue with the order.

"We have plenty of time before dinner." Ruby resumed her conversation while Joy paid. "You can paint before then."

"Do I have to meet the best man tonight?" The wedding was over three months away.

"Sort of." Ruby bundled her coat tighter as they walked out of the store. A burst of cold air swirled around them, tickling Joy's curls across her neck.

"I'll come if our meeting has anything to do with your wedding."

"Yes!" Ruby clapped and linked their arms.

"And if this is another one of your matchmaking endeavors"—Joy stopped walking to stare her friend in the eye—"I'll not be your maid of honor." She was joking; well, mostly. She *was* serious when she reminded her of the last two dates she'd set her up with.

"Okay, I have to agree Hudson's friends weren't my best setup attempts." Then Ruby raised her hand in honor like a scout. "I promise we will be talking about the wedding tonight."

When they met for dinner that evening, Ruby's promise to talk about the wedding only lasted until the waiter served them their drinks.

She and her fiancé were lost in each other, and he curled his arm around her waist, whispering into her ear while Ruby giggled.

Observing them from across the table felt uncomfortable. It wasn't inappropriate, but being seated next to a stranger made it hard to know where to look rather than her half-empty water glass.

Nate cleared his throat over the gentle music playing in the background, but the couple didn't even hear him.

"So, Joy"—his brown eyes shone beneath the restaurant's soft lights—"Ruby said you like to travel."

"She did?"

Just like she'd expected, Ruby *had* set her up with her future brother-in-law, even after Joy made her clarify the reason behind the invitation. She managed a glance at her friend so she could give her a cold glare to freeze her blood. But again, why would she keep her away from her fiancé for a moment?

"What else did she say?" Joy managed a fake smile.

He squared his shoulders and gaped at her dreamily, then added a shrug as an impish grin kicked up the corners of his lips. "That you're beautiful... and single?"

Nate looked like a nice guy, and he was attractive. But Joy wasn't interested in dating. Even if she were, she wouldn't want anything to interfere with Ruby's wedding. If she and Nate went out and things didn't work out between now and the twenty-fifth of May...

It could make for an awkward wedding weekend.

She was grateful to have driven separately. Maybe she hadn't trusted her friend to keep her word.

"I'm sorry." She winced apologetically to Nate. "I'm going to have to leave. I have an engagement in a few...." She hadn't outlined the butterflies on the canvas she'd painted earlier.

"We haven't even ordered." He peered into the other part of the restaurant where each table was occupied, and then back to her. "I thought we're going to—"

"Talk about the wedding, and since we're done..." She pushed back the chair to stand as their server returned to take their orders.

"Where are you going?"

Ruby, her hand clasped in the crook of Hudson's arm, finally noticed.

"I need to touch base with the painting and deliver it soon." Joy hated being rude, but Ruby had broken a promise. And Joy'd already tortured herself through two dates Ruby set up. Life was too short to sit through another dinner with a guy who assumed he was on a blind date. She'd wasted too many opportunities and didn't have time to lose.

"Let's eat quickly before you go." Hudson pointed to the waiter, who had his pad and pen ready to jot their orders down.

While Nate pleaded she stay, Ruby insisted she was being ridiculous.

Ruby might be right, but for this once, Joy was okay being ridiculous. She was at peace with her decision, or so she'd thought until she entered the apartment and stood alone in the kitchen. As she stared through the window at the dotted lights shining from other buildings, a sense of unease roiled her tummy.

Had she done the right thing running away from her friend's dinner? Yes. No.

She surrendered the dinner debacle when her gaze rested on the easel propping her painting.

The peaceful teal and gray drew her in, becoming even more relaxing when she studied the round seed head on the canvas. Although its petals were floating away, it was still vibrant and strong enough to attract the butterflies.

She tilted her head to the side, and exhilaration ran through her. Whether Eric liked the picture or not, he'd inspired her to create it.

# CHAPTER 6

Eric stared at the overhanging lights by the bookshelf, a focal point he needed to relax. It had been two a.m. when he last looked at his bedside clock. He let his body relax and closed his eyes, craving a peaceful rest but being embraced by darkness.

He was jogging in the mountains, a familiar trail, where he breathed in the fresh mountain air. It was the perfect pace for him to take in the view, the colorful bright yellow and orange trees nestled in between the pines.

When he ran further down the mountain, the trail wound into a... tunnel?

"Eric!"

He shuddered at the creepy voice echoing from the tunnel, and when he turned to go back, a blanket of darkness draped in front of him, turning the world pitch black.

He gasped and spun around in search of any light. Instead, he saw a shadow moving... his shadow he assumed when he took a step forward and it imitated him.

No... there were more shadows?

He kicked up his speed, panting and running as fast as he could into the dark endless tunnel, but the shadows were moving faster.

A dim light glowed far ahead. An opening. He breathed out slowly, relieved to be headed back in the light.

A scream tossed him in a frenzy, and one of the shadows flung barbed wire over Eric's head. As he fought to leap, he yelped when it scratched his arm.

A shadow with glowing red eyes stood in front of him, laughing at him.

Eric struggled to free himself from billions of smooth shiny wires, but they trapped him completely.

"Help!" he shouted, but his throat was tight as if he were choking. He couldn't breathe, his mind felt fuzzy, and then he heard a loud thump.

It was him. He looked back at the light in the room. Then he sighed, grateful to be anywhere but that tunnel. The cool tile was refreshing against his damp shirt and face.

*That tunnel again.* What was up with that creepy place haunting his sleep most nights?

He touched his throbbing arm, then his leg. Ouch. His head seemed like someone had pounded a hammer to it. His rapid breathing provided the only noise in the guesthouse.

*No more sleeping for me. Please, God.*

If only He could hear Eric's prayers. What was the point in praying if God was closed off to him?

*I can put up with lying down all day, but the nightmares!*

His teeth chattered as cold permeated him from the tile and his sweat. He crawled toward his bed and reached for the trash can where he'd tossed the evening pills Mom had given him. Three tablets remained wrapped in tissue. Which was for hallucination and night terrors? The tablets bounced in his shaky hand as he contemplated taking all three. But taking hallucination medicine had an aftermath. He would end up making trips to the bathroom for the rest of the night. It was hard to win either way.

He closed his fist around the tablets and pushed up, gripping the edge of the bed to stand. Using the walker, he made his way through the guesthouse, turning on every light as he walked to his bedroom and the master bathroom. He needed a shower.

He didn't need to use the walker in the bathroom with all the handlebars his parents installed.

Water cascaded over him, and he let the shower spray his face. He relaxed on the chair as warmth pummeled his skin while the soothing sound of water whispered over his head. Then he applied the shampoo in his hair, lathering himself and aiming his head toward the jet. He needed a haircut, but he wasn't up for such a daunting task.

When he got out of the shower, he sat on the leather bench while towel drying his hair. As he reached for his T-shirt from the shelf beneath the bench, he gave in and let his gaze rest on his reflection in front of him.

The scratches and bumps on his face... The hard twist to his lips and the scraggly hair on his neck... The eyes were disproportionately bigger than the rest of his body and looked as if they were about to pop out... The dark shadows under those eyes, shadows that would terrify kids and adults... He was no different from the malnourished kids he'd started organizations to help.

No doubt, his appearance scared Joy away. She didn't show up yesterday, and he hadn't asked Mom why.

Who cared if she quit? A slight twinge pinched his heart. She was gone, and that's what he wanted, right?

Even though he wanted to be alone, Joy *had* crossed his mind once or twice. Okay, maybe more than twice. He'd already aligned and misaligned the Rubik's cube three times. Tinkering with something rather than staring at the mountains all day had been relaxing.

Warmth teased his heart when he thought of the odd drink she considered tea. It had him almost laughing during his seclusion.

And what was with her staring him in the eye? She hadn't been gaping at his frog-like skin, but instead, she held his gaze and spoke with tenderness. One look into those warm eyes diffused his defiance. He'd almost taken her medicine. It was for the best that she wasn't coming back.

"All I can say, God, is You've attacked me." Eric whispered more to himself this time than to God since He wasn't listening. The God he knew to be compassionate, kind, and loving, but not to Eric—not anymore.

All the days he'd woken up with a purpose hadn't prepared him for this season in his life—a season of having no idea if he was going to be alive tomorrow, or if he went to bed, if he would be killed by shadows and headless figures.

"GOOD MORNING, MR. STONE."

Eric tipped his head as Sabastian, their chef in his late twenties, showed up with Eric's protein shake. After nine years of Sabastian working for them, Eric had given up reminding him to drop the formalities. Eric had also stopped encouraging him to open a restaurant rather than work for his family, who were barely home.

Sabastian would rather stay and manage the maintenance team at The Peak, among the random jobs he did to occupy his time.

"How's your morning, Sabastian?" Eric asked, pleased to see someone, anyone after last night's nightmares.

Sabastian frowned, probably surprised Eric had initiated a conversation. Those days of him being polite were way past gone, unlike today, of course.

"Not too bad," Sabastian finally responded, and a faint smile tipped his mouth. "You showered early today."

"It's that kind of day."

Not that Sabastian needed to know about his dreams. Eric's counselor was the only one who knew his night terrors. Mom and Dad knew he needed medicine to lull his hallucinations, but he'd never shared the gory details.

Besides the aches from the fall, he was feeling slightly stronger today and preferred to sit in the living room than the sunroom.

When Tessa arrived at eight, he didn't complain about his sore arm or leg from falling off the bed. He instead let the therapist flex his feet and even agreed to walk—well, hobble was more like it—from the main house and back to the guesthouse. A much longer walk than the bathroom.

Mom spent most of the time that morning on the guestroom couch busy clicking the keyboard as she typed away.

Joy probably told her of his defiance with medicine, which would explain why Mom worked from home to see that he took his medicine. It didn't help that the doctor added another at eleven thirty for his indigestion.

"Medicine and water," Mom announced when she walked over and held out her palm. Two round tablets and a blue capsule. *Eww.* A shudder coursed through him.

As if aware he'd chucked his medicine in the trash yesterday, she waited.

"You don't have to guard me as I take my medicine."

Mom brushed him off with a wave. "In case you throw up, I'd better stick around."

She was on to his plan. Left with no choice, he gulped down the first tablet, then the second, and swallowed. He winced as he stared at the blue capsule, the one he dreaded most. He'd chucked it in the trash yesterday, wrapping it with tissues. It wasn't like it was going to make a difference to his recovery. So he stared through the window, buying time and hoping she'd leave.

"I know how hard that particular tablet is on you," Mom said, but Eric kept his gaze on the snowflakes dancing in the air.

He gritted his teeth. He was done with snow. Even if he didn't go outside much, the cloudy sky made him feel desolate—as if he would never recover. However, after the eerie nightmare, he should be thankful for any kind of daylight.

When the front door jerked open, Mom turned, and Eric used that moment to toss the capsule in the trash can which was meant to be his throw-up bucket.

"Joy. Welcome, darling." Mom's eyes glowed like she was talking to one of her kids.

Eric turned as the woman set her bag down at the entrance and then hung her jacket on the hook. He'd barely taken the time to study her appearance these last two times.

Her smile, genuine and vibrant and warm, contrasted the hazy day. He almost chortled at the smiley face on her yellow sweater. The dusting of snow flakes on her hair made snow seem fun to look at.

"Thank you, Regina." Joy eased out of her backpack.

What was with the toddler-sized backpack? *Interesting.*

"You look well, Eric."

He blinked. He'd been staring at her far too long, hadn't he? Heat crept up the back of his neck. To Joy, he was Eric, not Mr. Stone. He was grateful that someone besides his parents and friends called him Eric. "You came back?"

"I didn't say I was leaving, did I?" She shrugged, her smile a ray of life and possibilities. "I brought you something."

Without giving him time to respond, she strode with easy grace toward the entrance and grabbed the utility bag.

Mom's cheeks lifted as she looked at him, no doubt pleased he didn't have a smart remark.

Something about Joy made him think she was capable of diffusing his irritation, and that irritated him even more. As much as he should warm up to her smile, he could feel his brows draw together when she presented him with something wrapped in white tissue paper.

"Open it," she urged with enthusiasm, more excited about the gift than he was.

When he stared at the butterfly design on the paper like it was about to bite him, Mom took it from Joy. People like her shouldn't be here with him.

"Aren't you such a sweetheart?" Mom said, paper crunching as she ripped open a canvas and tossed the paper on the floor.

"Butterflies." Mom beamed, then grinned at Joy's neon-green butterfly-print socks. "You definitely like butterflies. Did you paint this?"

"Yes." Joy's response was a whisper of uncertainty.

"Oh my!" Mom's jaw opened, and her eyes widened, leaving him suddenly curious to see the picture. But he had to stay put, feigning disinterest.

When Mom handed him the canvas, he had to admit the abstract painting was refreshing. Peaceful.

White, gray, and teal. As he reached to touch the wilted dandelion, it reminded him of his life. His shaky finger moved to one of the three butterflies. Somehow, they looked like they were breathing life into the dead plant.

There was more to the picture. He needed to figure it out. A hidden message...

He found himself peeking at Joy, amazed she had such talent. Her face was the shape of a heart, and her eyes somehow its focal point, deep and rich and caring. It seemed every feature was perfectly set to draw one's attention to them—soft lashes curled over them while strong dark brows highlighted them, a delicate nose separated them, and tender lips balanced them. Stunned, he almost couldn't breathe as he absorbed her vitality, her zest for life he'd lost.

She swallowed when her gaze met his, tinkered with the hem of her blouse, obviously uncomfortable.

So was he if his body heating up was any indication. Not wanting to say much about the picture, he thanked her, then set it on the table. He'd study it later when he had no audience.

He hoped he didn't appear uninterested in her gift, but if she thought so, she didn't show it since she was already talking to Mom. "Are there things you need me to do when I'm here?"

"You're so sweet, but you don't have to do anything."

"I would rather be useful whenever I'm not chatting with Eric."

*Chatting?* If she considered his snapping at her the last two times "chats," then she was more interesting than he assumed her to be.

She glanced at him. "But then he might need to rest, and I'll be left doing nothing."

Deep down, he was pleased to see her again. Her presence was refreshing. He didn't remember the last time he fell asleep peacefully. When she'd played that lullaby-style classical music, it lulled him to sleep, and he'd not been startled awake from a terror.

"I have to eat anyway." Joy continued. "You said your chef does other house chores. Maybe I can help him fix snacks, dishes, you name it."

"Of course, you can do anything you want." Mom touched Joy's cheek. "I'll let Sabastian know you would love to help."

"Sounds like a plan." Joy scooped up the gift wrap off the floor and took the trash with her to the kitchen.

Mom wished Eric a great day and followed Joy. "Eric just took his midmorning medicine. If you can see to it that he gets a snack before his lunch..."

His meal times changed whenever they added a new prescription to his daily intake. Most meds required him not to have an empty stomach, but with his mouth sores still lurking and his lack of appetite, he only managed to force down smoothies and soups.

Again, he wasn't too sure what to think of Joy when she brought him an almond and banana smoothie half an hour later. Instead of leaving him alone as Sabastian did, she returned with one of the swivel lounge chairs from the living room. She set it across from him and sat. They stared at each other for one awkward moment before she rubbed her hands together.

"Are you waiting to pray for your food or something?" She squared her shoulders.

Joy... Joy. She was something else. "Do I have a sign that shouts 'prayer' on my face?" He didn't mean to be rude. It was more a question to himself, wondering what prayer meant these days.

"I'm sorry, I just—"

"Are you planning to stay the whole time I'm downing a smoothie?"

He liked her being around the house, but not this close.

She touched her chin as if thinking about her response. "If you want me to stay."

"I'm fine!" Alone.

Her face crumpled, but she bounced back with a tight smile. "I get it. You don't want me here, but your mom thought you could use a friend. If you'd rather I don't come, that's okay too." Those brown eyes seeped into his as if she could see his inner thoughts and how he wanted her around. "Regina will not give up on bringing more friends to you. That's what parents do."

How did she know what parents did? Unless she was a parent, but as he looked at her dark leggings where her fingers rested, he didn't see a ring. Maybe she was a single mom. Wait, why would she be volunteering if she had a kid?

"Can you at least give me two weeks?" Her words interfered with his thoughts. "Just so your mom knows we both tried and just didn't get along."

He didn't want her to quit. He nodded instead.

"Since you don't want to talk, the silence drives me crazy. Can I play music?"

"Sure." His gruff voice grated his throat, and his neck burned again.

"I'll let you be. Let me know if you need anything."

Deflated, he tightened his grip on the smoothie. Why did being responsible for her saddened face hurt so much? Like stepping on a butterfly.

As the hour dragged on, he forced down the smoothie in small sips and listened to her soothing music, instrumental gospel songs, most of which were familiar. Now and then, he stole glances at her. Mainly because he wanted to apologize for his behavior and hoped she would look his way.

But she was on the couch, intent on whatever she was writing just like last time she played music.

The lyrical instruments were soothing. After setting the glass on the ottoman, he pushed back the lever, and his body settled in. Soothed by the music, he let his body become heavy and his eyes close.

He had no idea how long he slept, but he woke with a start, rubbing at his groggy eyes when he saw Joy sitting in the chair across from him. Her head was tucked down in the book on her lap as her pencil skimmed the page.

When her eyes lifted to his, she jumped, and her book fell on the floor. The pencil clattered. "You're awake."

Despite his mood, she'd stayed close while he slept. She was probably scared of his grumpiness. No wonder she startled when she saw him awake. He nodded, swiping his dry lips.

"You were supposed to take your medicine an hour ago, but I didn't want to wake you."

He appreciated her consideration. Did she know how much he needed that rest?

"Thanks." His coarse voice rasped his throat again, and his head still hurt. She wanted to be useful, right? "Can I have some ibuprofen?"

Her mouth opened in surprise. She nodded, then stood. "Okay. Sabastian brought your soup, and I have it in the fridge. I'll get it with your medicine."

He had to eat before his usual medicine, and he was feeling good today. "I don't want to take my regular medicine." It kinda felt good to talk to her in a normal way as if she would understand.

"I know." The corners of her mouth folded into a smile. "I saw tablets in your trash can."

Laughter burbled in his chest. "Do you always say exactly what's on your mind?"

"Sometimes." That smile turned impish, pushing her cheeks up beneath her eyes—eyes aglow.

She left and returned holding a tray with a glass straw cup and two bowls. "Would you like to switch seats?" She pointed to the kitchen, to the dining table set for three. "In case you're tired of that chair."

She was right, and he didn't feel a need to argue. He appreciated her carrying their soup to the table and letting him struggle to find his cane. After going to the bathroom, he joined her at the table.

She closed her eyes to pray silently for her food, but he closed his eyes too. It could be the uninterrupted sleep he'd had, but he felt stronger as he sat without leaning back in his chair.

"I hate medicine," he repeated after he swallowed the brown pills for his headache.

Joy passed him a napkin. "You were loud and clear the first day I gave it to you, and—"

"The trash can," he finished her sentence.

"This medicine is new, for something different. What if you try it, just like with me, give it two weeks and see?"

"I've done that for the last year, giving medicine chances and hoping they'll be effective." With his spoon, he gestured toward himself. He hoped she could see as easily as he could feel that they hadn't helped.

He moved his spoon in the green soup. He ignored the bland taste, but he couldn't have onions, garlic, or other high-flavored spices due to his sensitive stomach.

"Two weeks?" she repeated, her dark eyes piercing almost through him.

He wanted to say yes for her sake. Did his mom train her to plead? Groaning, he lifted the spoonful to his mouth. Lukewarm, almost tasteless.

"If you have any reason to fight for your life," she whispered, "just keep trying."

Spoons clinked as they ate, Joy biting into what seemed to be a peanut butter and jelly sandwich.

Problem was, he didn't want to torture himself with night terrors, pain, and bedsores or bother his parents with worry about his discomfort anymore. He'd become a burden, and he hated it.

Was it too early to plead with God to end his life so he could join his wife and kids?

It wasn't like he had a purpose. His best friend, Brady, had stepped in to oversee the charities Eric started in different countries. As long as the money rolled in for those poor children, he was at peace.

As for Stone Enterprise? Well, he assumed his company's president had things under control and people's jobs were secure. He hadn't bothered to check his phone or any media in fear of his name or company being talked about. The last thing he needed was reminders of what he'd lost. Stocks, investments, and the current value of his company were useless if he was stuck.

That was just a slice, but the terrifying reality was that anyone who got close to him died.

As soon as Joy cleared the table, she talked him into playing Sudoku, a number placement game that challenged his short-term memory.

When his parents returned home and she said goodbye, he felt emptier and more downhearted after she left. How strange was that!

# CHAPTER 7

On a Thursday afternoon when Joy arrived during her second week with Eric, her painting was hanging in the sunroom. He complained about its location on the wall and wanted it moved. Pleased he liked her painting, she offered to help and asked Sabastian for a ladder and hook.

As soon as she moved the canvas to where Eric wanted it, she peered at him sitting in the recliner.

"Is that angled enough?" Joy stepped down the ladder and stood to the side awaiting his approval.

"Hmm." He leaned back in the recliner and set the Rubik's cube on the table. Seconds passed as he rubbed at his scraggly beard. He gazed at his hospital bed and the couch, then back to the picture. "It looks slightly crooked." He was far too particular. "I want to see it from every angle in any chair I sit on in this room."

Joy stepped back on the stool and adjusted the picture.

"Perfect. Right there is good," Eric said.

"Whew!" Stepping down, she dramatically wiped at her brow, and he half-smiled. He had a sweet smile. "You should smile often."

His smile vanished, and he glanced at the window.

She followed his gaze to the window and the large snowflakes swirling down. It was the beginning of February, and Joy was starting to shove Colorado down her list of favorite places. Even if they'd had some snowless days, the snow hadn't vanished from the ground since late October.

Since last week when she'd given Eric the painting and they'd played Sudoku, he'd softened toward her. He didn't say much about his life, rarely seemed interested in chatting, but he'd asked her to play the classic music on her playlist a couple of times. One day, he even said he found her picture relaxing and peaceful, claiming the colors were refreshing.

She'd stopped asking him to join her for prayers since she had no idea where he stood with his faith, so, more comfortable with him now, she just closed her eyes and prayed silently for her meals.

As for medicine, he took it some days and refused other days, depending on what mood he was in. By moods, he had a few swings. He could be chill one hour, and the next two hours, he'd be lying down in discomfort.

She folded the stool as Eric picked up the nicely aligned cube. He sure liked it. She might have to get him another one—maybe one of those ones where the colors appeared to change from different angles.

"I'm going to take the stool back, and I'll—"

"You shouldn't drive in this weather." His voice rose with some emotion. Fear? Maybe even panic. "Stay the night."

He cared. She wasn't confident driving on snowy roads with her Sentra, but if his parents showed up early enough, she could still make it home. She stared at the clock by his bed next to the couch. It was almost five. Regina normally got home at six, and Kyle returned around seven, depending on how far away his work projects were.

"I'll call Regina and see if she's on her way.... Or if I can go now—"

"No!"

Joy blinked, jolting back a bit at his sharp tone.

His brows drew together, and furrows crinkled the space between them. A pensive cast dulled his eyes. "It's not safe."

"O–kay." She still needed to talk to Regina. Did Eric lose a loved one in a snowstorm accident?

Her phone chimed from the kitchen, and she carried the stool back with her. After taking the stool to the utility closet, she went to check her phone and brought up a message from her roommate.

Ruby: If you haven't left, I would recommend you stay the night at work.

Ruby knew Joy wasn't familiar with driving in the snow, and Joy appreciated her thoughtfulness.

Joy: Are the roads that bad?

Ruby: There's a bad accident on Elk and 82. Stuck in traffic, and cars are sliding off the road.

They both took 82 to get home.

Joy: Eric's parents are not home yet.

Ruby: check if they can host you for the night.

Kyle had extended the invitation on her first day at work.

Joy: They will.

Ruby: good.

Joy: Will pray for your safety.

Ruby: stay safe too.

Eric's parents' traffic should be the opposite route, but if Regina drove from the hospital, she still had to take 82. Hopefully, the opposite direction wasn't bad.

After texts with Ruby, her phone rang, and she answered a call from Regina.

"Joy, I'll be home late." Regina spoke over car horns and sirens. "Tonight might be a good night for you to stay the night for your safety. It's bad out here already and will be getting worse as it gets later. Kyle won't be home until later. He's in traffic but two miles ahead of me." Regina continued uttering directions for Joy to read the spreadsheet for Eric's medicine at seven, in case Regina wasn't home by then.

When she hung up, Joy returned to the sunroom.

Eric eyed her. "Please tell me you're not driving in this."

"I'll stay."

When he blew out a long breath as if he'd been holding it, Joy ambled toward the bookshelf and closer to the window. Snow slid off the tan covering over the deck furniture. It was hard to see the entire deck, but she glimpsed a structure or more on the other side of the yard.

"What buildings are back there?"

As she spun to look at Eric, his brow lifted. "Curious, huh?"

She nodded.

"If you can find someone to play tennis or basketball with you, there's courts there."

What else did this property have? "Do you have a pool too?"

"And a hot tub." He said it matter-of-factly as he closed his eyes.

"A hot tub?" No way could she keep the thrill out of her voice. It would be perfect on such a chilly day.

"You're welcome to use anything on this property, of course. The pool is heated."

It must be one of those pools in a glass house or something.

She would have to be extra comfortable to go swimming or use their hot tub. Who were these people and what other jobs did they have besides Regina being a counselor and Kyle being an analyst, whatever that meant?

Now that she didn't have to drive in the snow, there was one thing she could do during her stay. She could play in the snow, possibly tomorrow since it was starting to get dark.

JUST BEFORE SEVEN THIRTY, Eric's parents returned home and joined them in the guesthouse, and the tension in Eric's shoulders seemed to loosen, leaving Joy curious over his stress. Sabastian served them beef stew, and Regina insisted he stay and eat.

With only three chairs around the dining table, Joy moved the swivel chair closer to the circle and sat in it. Sabastian and Eric's parents occupied the three chairs while Eric lounged in his recliner close by.

Regina prayed for their dinner and thanked God for the blessings and good health. Joy shifted in the chair, warmed when Regina thanked God for her presence.

They said amen collectively, except for Eric. His mouth was pressed into a thin line.

He'd already eaten his soup when he'd taken his medicine at seven. Joy hadn't been hungry enough to eat with him then.

When his mother asked about his day, he just shook his head. "Still in a chair."

She gazed at Joy, the curved modern light illuminating curious eyes that seemed eager for more details.

"We listened to music." Joy stirred the steamy bowl of soup. "We played a board game too."

"Ma—what?" Eric closed his eyes, perhaps attempting to remember.

"Mankala."

Kyle leaned forward. "You'll have to teach us that game sometime."

Eric's lips twitched, and he opened his eyes. "It's a ridiculous game with stones. With Joy's vague explanation, you'll never win."

When Regina said she'd never heard of the game, Joy explained it was popular in Africa. Then Regina asked Sabastian about his day.

"Good." He then stuck his chin to his bowl. In other words, he was done talking.

So Joy asked them about the drive home.

"It was a disaster out there." Regina touched her husband's shoulder. "Unless you have a different view of the road?"

With his tie slightly loosened, Kyle set the spoon back in the bowl, and his eyes looked tired. "Good thing we can work from home tomorrow."

"What exactly do you do, Kyle?" The vague explanation he'd given her when they met left Joy curious.

He wiped the napkin on his mouth. "In meetings and conference calls, research analysts interpret data, demonstrate what they learn, and explain its value from a business perspective." He moved the spoon in his steaming bowl. "We also solve problems in business, logistics, healthcare, and other fields."

His work must be intriguing because he traveled around the country sometimes. She took another sip of the mouthwatering soup and dabbed a napkin on her mouth. "You're a good cook, Sabastian."

"He's spoiled us," Regina added. "I have a hard time appreciating restaurant food."

Sabastian gripped the back of his neck, appearing embarrassed.

After dinner, Joy helped Sabastian to clear the dishes, and Kyle prayed, then watched Eric stagger to the sunroom. "I'll see you in the morning, son."

"'Night, Dad." Eric climbed onto his bed and slid under the blanket.

Joy bid Kyle and Eric good night while Regina offered to show Joy to her room.

"Glad you chose to stay the night." Regina's house shoes padded the tile as she linked arms with Joy in the hallway.

Breathing in the soft flowery scent, Joy smiled. "I appreciate you letting me stay."

"We should've given you a tour of the house on the first day." Regina shook her head, strands of strawberry-blonde hair tickling Joy's neck with them so close. "You can always watch the virtual tour from the TV."

She might take a virtual tour because she wanted to know what the rest of the house looked like. She'd eventually get around to it. "I don't need to tour the entire house."

Regina pointed to the half-open door on the left. "That's Eric's room." She hesitated as if about to say something she shouldn't, then apparently decided against it. "He prefers sleeping in the sunroom."

Joy's mouth parted to ask why he slept on the hospital bed and in the sunroom, but Regina was already swinging open another door down the hall to the right.

"You can wear anything in the closet." Leaning against the door-jamb, Regina ushered Joy to enter.

Her socks slipped a little on the ashy hardwood floor as Joy spun around the spacious room to get a better look. The polished floors flowed toward a wall of sweeping white drapes, the snowy view beyond them likely stunning in daylight. Across from them, the king bed with a white covering made her self-conscious to sleep in it. Even if she intended to shower, she'd better make sure she didn't have any brush pens in her backpack.... Oh, it was still in the main room.

"There's a bathroom in here, and..."

While Regina pointed out the perks, the luxury faux fur blanket fascinated Joy. Her fingers itched to touch the fabric, and she did.

Soft fabric slid past her fingertips as she sat to test the bed out. "This is so nice." Beyond nice. She glanced up to the spiny recessed lighting and the landscape photography on the wall, then to Regina and thanked her for her hospitality.

"You're volunteering to take care of my son."

When Regina left, Joy investigated the rest of the room. The walk-in closet had three chests of drawers and then racks of clothing. Men's dress shirts and polos lined one of the racks. The tags were still on some of them. Another rack against the wall carried women's dresses, and one rack contained dress shoes, tennis shoes, boots, and different shoes in various sizes.

She almost laughed, feeling as if she was shopping.

Even if she wasn't going anywhere, she tried on different shoes—stilettos, pumps, and knee-high boots, and then she tried on some dresses while she looked in the closet's full-length mirror. If the guesthouse's closet was bigger than the living room she shared with Ruby, then she wanted to take a virtual tour and see the closets in the main house.

In the drawer labeled women's pajamas, Joy picked out a small size pair of bottoms and a matching shirt. The long-sleeved shirt would keep her cozy. They probably switched clothes out for each season since all the pajamas were long sleeves.

Refreshed after the shower, she stretched out on the bed.

It was like a five-star hotel room—actually, better since she didn't have to pay for lodging.

She slid from the bed and knelt on the cozy rug. She could sleep on the rug just fine, but she wouldn't pass up on that sumptuous bed.

She thanked God for a great day and Eric's bearable attitude lately. She also prayed for those in the hospital, the orphaned babies, in particular, and those whose moms were ill. *God, take care of all Your children.*

She then prayed for Eric. *Regardless of the chronic incurable diseases, Lord, You have the power to heal Eric. You're the potter; he's the clay. Please mold him, make him new.*

When she slid into the satin sheets, she was tempted to text Ruby about the luxurious bedroom, but her phone was in the kitchen. Ruby had texted earlier to let Joy know she made it home safely, so there was no urgency in getting out of the comfy covers.

With the multiswitch remote on the nightstand, Joy turned off the main lights and kept on the square desk lamp.

She then took the pen from the nightstand and jotted reminders in her palm.

Texting Tao, the triplet's grandmother, first thing in the morning to let her know Joy wouldn't be making it to her house.

It was either being in a new bed or being overly energized, but Joy wasn't sleepy. So she spent a few minutes drawing an intricate design around the notes on her palm. It was relaxing, and by the time she finished, her eyelids were feeling heavy. So she called it a night.

# CHAPTER 8

Surrounded by six clowns, Eric spun around in the tunnel as he fought to shove his way out of the tight circle. He shivered at their maniacal laughter while they pushed him back into the center of the circle.

Eric swung his hand at one of the creepy clowns, trying not to look at the blood dripping from its eyes and gumming up around its black teeth. "Get out of my way!"

"You think you can escape?" The tall clown's mouth wobbled the words past red lips before he gripped Eric's shoulders.

*Ouch!* Eric yelped when claws squeezed his collarbone so tight it crackled.

The white-faced clown joined the creepy clown to hoist Eric and toss him in the air.

"Put me down!" Eric yelled as he floated.

While the glowering clowns laughed, Eric struggled down, flinging his hands as if he were swimming, but he couldn't move.

Suddenly the tunnel went twice as dark. Maybe the clowns turned into skeletons because Eric was now floating above bright white skeletons as they held framed pictures of his kids and drew creepy faces over them.

His wife walked in, deflated.

"Josie?"

Fire engulfed the tunnel. "Josie, run!" Eric struggled down, but she was standing, shaking her head, and tears slid down her cheek.

Why wasn't she running? With the smoke billowing thick around him, she stood caught in the flames. He had to save her!

Eric fought harder as the skeletons tossed the pictures into the fire where his wife stood. With all his might, he kicked his feet and hands to get down, but once he did, Josie was consumed. Feeling like his chest was ripped in two, he shrieked.

"No!"

He dropped to his knees, struggling to breathe, suffocating beneath the smoke. Josie. "No! *Noooo!*"

With his throat parched as if he'd hiked through a desert, he gulped for breath.

"It's okay." A refreshing and tender voice echoed in his head, and soft hands touched his forehead, his chin, his shoulder. "Are you all right?"

That melodic voice... It was familiar, the kind that soothed his terrors.

"It's okay.... It's okay." Tenderness whispered in the voice—an angel's voice. "I'm here."

When he opened his eyes, the familiar face beneath the bright light was the comfort he craved.

"Joy." He breathed her name as if she were the air he needed.

"Yes?" Kneeling by his bed, she squeezed his hand. "Are you okay?"

He nodded and squeezed her hand back. Soft and assuring, it held onto him, a lifeline drawing him out of the darkness, and he clung to it, not wanting to let go. His loud breathing offered the only background noise.

"Let me get you some water."

"No." He tightened his grip on her hand. Water was the last thing on his mind. What if the clowns or skeletons returned while she was gone?

"The water is right here." She gestured to the coffee table where he had his glass tumbler from last night. So he let go of her hand while she retrieved the glass, then returned. As he struggled to sit, she slid her warm hand behind his neck to help him. After she took the water back to the table, she dragged the armchair closer to his bed.

"Did you have a bad dream?" She tilted her neck to the side, her brows creased.

"All the time." Day and night, he had nightmares.

"Is that why you sleep out here?"

He rubbed a shaky hand over his forehead, then nodded. "The doctor comes here sometimes." Especially when he'd just returned home and was very ill. "It's easier to be examined in a spacious room."

"That's not good."

"I've not been nice to you." Compelled to apologize, he focused on her face, on those eyes that seemed to carry the love of Jesus in them. Joy had put up with his nasty attitude for almost two weeks. "I'm sorry."

She frowned as if she had no idea what he was talking about. "Given the circumstances, I think you've been good enough."

Maybe this week he'd tried, but he could do better. Nice of her to downplay his tantrums. "You don't have to let me off the hook so easily."

"I want to."

A silence passed between them as if she were letting him wake up from his dream. He stared at the floral design on her flannels—the green brought out the lightness in her brown skin, and the pajamas fit her as if specifically tailored for her.

His gaze darted to the dandelion painting on the wall. Thankfully, he could see the soothing picture from his bed and from the two other chairs he normally sat on. He'd looked at it several times since she gave it to him, and the flapping butterflies drawn to the dead dandelion warmed his heart. It almost seemed like the picture was talking to him.

"You're the patient whisperer, huh?"

She chuckled. She had a good laugh. "I wish. Otherwise, my music and tactics would've worked on you by now."

If only she had any idea. He closed his eyes. With the butterflies and the dandelion engraved in his memory, he wanted to relay what her presence meant to him so far. "When you played that classical music, it was the first time I slept in a long time."

"Oh. You wanted to be quiet that day, but—"

"It seems you have a hard time listening." He opened his eyes when she unclasped her hand from his and rubbed her thumb through her inked palm.

"I'm afraid you're getting to know me a little." Shyness edged her smile as it wobbled.

"I don't know your last name."

Her brown eyes danced in the light. "Musana."

"Sounds tribal. Ethnic."

"It's Ugandan, from my dad's side." The smile vanished, and the glow died in her eyes.

Pain gripped Eric's heart. Mom recently told him about Joy's dad dying of Lyme disease. In honor of her dad and her request he get tested, looking back, Eric was glad to have agreed to that extra set of blood tests.

"I'm sorry about your dad."

"Thanks."

He shifted slightly to his back. Even though he'd been taking antibiotics for his bedsores, the pressure still stung his skin. "When did your dad die?"

"Ten years ago."

He had so many questions. It had been so long since he'd had a conversation with anyone. He didn't lack anyone to talk to, but he refused to do so.

"Did your dad die in Uganda?" He wanted to know how she came to be in America if she was a Ugandan citizen.

"San Francisco."

Eric closed his eyes as he soaked in her response. Of all the states and cities, she'd been in the same one where he used to live.

"I should let you sleep."

"No. Tell me more." He wasn't about to go back in that haunted tunnel. Not tonight anyway. "I like to keep my eyes closed when I'm listening sometimes." Or even talking. He was wired oddly.

She let out a breath. "My mom met Dad on her mission trip in Uganda. She never left the country. My two brothers and I were born there."

"Where are your brothers now?"

"They are missionaries—one in Tanzania and one in Zimbabwe." She cleared her throat, her voice soothing. "When my dad got ill, we moved back to San Francisco, to my grandfather's house. We thought America would have better doctors for him...." She talked about her dad's complications from the ill-fated disease she assumed resulted from the untreated Lyme disease. "He didn't even know he got bit by a tick. All the medicine and treatments prescribed treated symptoms, rather than the disease itself. Getting pneumonia was the last straw."

His heart slammed in his chest for her loss. He wished he could tell her the pain of her loss would go away sometime soon, but that wasn't the case. Unless she had a metal heart. Instead, all he could say was "I'm sorry for your loss."

He now understood why she volunteered in the hospital and why she was concerned for him and told his mom.

"Thank you for talking me into getting tested." Not that he would recover from the chronic state, but he could be taking the right medicine for once.

"You're welcome." She palmed vibrant curls away from her face, but they danced right back into place. "Do you remember being bitten by a tick?"

Vaguely. No wonder the virus built in his system for so long. "I went hunting with some friends, and the little bug was on my hair briefly." At least, he'd thought it was brief. "My buddy yanked it from my hair, and I thought that was the end of it."

Plus, they'd tested him two months into his illness. "I'm sure my mom has told you I have more things going on than Lyme disease."

"Besides the mystery diseases, she said you've been through a lot. She hoped someday, if I'm here long enough, you'd tell me your story."

If Mom hadn't told her about his family, then that was a topic best left alone. And tonight, after the nightmare of his family, he'd rather listen to her.

He opened his eyes again, shifting his head to look at her flawless face. "Do you have family here in Pleasant View?"

"Just my friend." She clasped her hands in her lap. "When I came here, I didn't plan to stay longer than three months...."

He learned she was interested in traveling to twenty more states she hadn't visited yet. She also wanted to travel to other countries while she volunteered. The same work she was doing in Pleasant View.

A twinge of unease pinged him. She wasn't planning to stay in Pleasant View long. He'd never been a long-term resident after he went away to college and then started his business.

"What countries do you want to visit?"

"New Zealand, Australia, anywhere in South America"—she ticked her fingers as she continued her list—"Malaysia." Her eyes sparkled under the light. "There's this little island there. I hear it has the best butterfly sanctuary." She spoke of butterflies with such fondness as she glided her hands to imitate flapping wings.

Eric knew the island—an exchange student who lived in Padang had spent two years with Eric's family. With a connection in the country, he felt the urge to make her dream come true, like tomorrow. If he weren't confined by his health, he'd want to be there with her, just to see her bright eyes and awed reaction when she strode through a kaleidoscope of butterflies.

She had quite a plan. Nothing involved work or making money.

"I assume you already have a passport?"

"I do."

Unless she had a lot of money saved up for her trips, she may never leave Pleasant View.

"Besides volunteering, what else do you do?"

She rested her hand on the bed, and a tender motherliness tipped her lips and lit her eyes. "I take care of the cutest four-year-olds...." She described the triplets and their grandma. Her shoulders slumped when she mentioned their grandpa's death. It had been the way she'd started working for the family before she began taking care of him.

That wasn't enough money to pay for a vacation, not if she paid rent. Even the cheapest apartment in Pleasant View cost a fortune. But it wasn't his place to squash her dream.

With his neck hurting, he wanted to shift. Apparently noticing his discomfort, she stood and moved her chair to the other side of the bed. "You can turn your head now if you want to."

The bed dipped beneath his weight when he turned. He could raise the bed by pushing a button, but he didn't want anything interfering with this moment.

When he looked at the nightstand clock, it was three fifteen. Almost morning.

He was being inconsiderate to interfere with her sleep. "I should let you go back to sleep."

She must have sensed his dread because she just smiled. "It's your turn to tell me about you."

"I'm inside all day. Not much to tell."

"Any other family, besides your parents?"

He closed his eyes, the agony so deep he could scarcely breathe. He doubted he'd ever be able to talk about his family. One breath. Then another. The tightness in his chest remained, but he could breathe again. "I have seven brothers... and three sisters." Talking about them was better than talking about his loss. "We're a blended family."

"By blended, you mean...?"

"Diverse. Adopted." He didn't define his siblings that way at all since Kyle and Regina loved them unconditionally. But speaking about his siblings was better than bringing up the dead while he felt like one. "I have siblings from different parts of the country, and some foreign exchange students have become part of our family."

"That's so wonderful." A genuine smile curved her lips and crinkled the edges of her eyes.

"What did you do before you, um..."

"Business. Financial stuff." How nice that Joy had no clue who he was. No wonder she was easy to connect with. But her prying might force him to say things he didn't want to talk about. So he switched the conversation back to her.

"Before you became an artist, nanny, and volunteer"—or whatever else she did—"what did you do?"

"I was the development manager of my dad's orphanage. But we couldn't afford to hire many people, so I did all the administrative jobs." She talked about the online business degree she'd acquired through one of the international colleges in America. "I always wanted to pursue art, but my parents didn't think it was a practical career."

"You're an extraordinary artist." Her art would sell for a fortune at auctions. "If you can paint like that without a degree, I don't even think you need one." He'd been to several art shows and auctions, but he'd never felt as drawn to an image as he did to hers.

"You're so kind to think my art is—"

"It's true." It had nothing to do with courteousness—and she ought to know him well enough by now to realize that.

She was fumbling with the hem of his blanket as if she was uncomfortable with his honesty. Feeling awkward, he had to close his eyes once more.

The night went on as he asked about her family and learned her mom was engaged and lived in San Francisco with her grandpa.

Her voice was so soothing. As she spoke about her faith in God and her doubts after her dad died, he could feel his muscles relax, and he yawned.

"You should get some sleep," she whispered, and he was suddenly filled with an emptiness he hadn't felt until recently. The same emptiness he felt whenever she left at the end of the day.

He spent his days alone in the guesthouse, his nightmares haunted him, and he didn't mind it. But now he didn't want to be alone.

"Talk to me some more." His words came out as a plea.

"Maybe I can read you the Bible while you fall asleep." She didn't seem too sure of her offer, perhaps assuming he had something against the Bible. "It might help keep those bad dreams away."

"Sure."

It *had* been a while since he'd been open to reading his Bible, but as long as Joy was around, it didn't hurt to listen, even if God's word wasn't going to do anything for him.

Her melodic voice washed over him as she read the familiar words from a psalm.

"'You have searched me, Lord, and you know me.... If I say, Surely the darkness will hide me and the light will become night around me, even the darkness will not be dark to you; the night will shine like the day, for darkness is as light to you.'"

Seeing some of God's light whenever he was trapped in that nightmare tunnel sure would help. He seemed to see the light in the distance, but he could never escape the tunnel to reach that hopeful destination.

"'I praise you because I am fearfully and wonderfully made....'" She kept reading. "'All the days ordained for me were written in your book before one of them came to be...'"

Regardless of what he did, how long he waited before his last breath on earth, God had a plan and a day designated for his last breath. He'd read Psalm 139 many times, but he'd never registered that line until now.

His ten kids and wife... God had already decided they'd die before Eric.

Some comfort came from knowing Eric couldn't have saved them, no matter what.

It didn't erase the sting, didn't wash away the confusion, which was now his companion, but he let out a slow breath. His chest rose heavily, and her voice grew more distant as he drifted off to sleep.

He woke up with a start when a hand tapped his shoulder. His eyes were groggy as he winced in the rays of morning light shining through the window.

"Good morning, sweetheart."

He blinked when he registered his mom smiling as if amused about something—probably him since he was always awake and in his recliner when she came to check on him in the mornings.

"Sabastian didn't want to wake you." Mom peered at the bed, and Eric followed her gaze to Joy.

Something twisted inside him at the sight of her closed eyes, her head resting at the edge of the bed. *What an angel!* Her breathing was steady, and short tendrils of her rumpled curls almost touched the open Bible she'd braced over the blanket on his feet. He longed to reach out and read whatever notes she had scribbled in her palm.

Mom put a hand to her chest and mouthed, "So sweet."

Eric's heart warmed. She'd stayed by his side the rest of the night. But if he didn't want to give his mom any ideas, he'd better explain.

"I had a bad dream."

"I'm glad she was here." Mom handed him two of his three morning pills. "Sabastian will be in with your breakfast soon. You can take your other tablet then."

He didn't let his mind think about the medicine as he swallowed both pills at once without gagging. Maybe he wanted to feel better so he could take Joy to her dream butterfly sanctuary? As a friend, of course. Were they friends yet?

One week she was the villain of his story, and the next week, he was entertaining the idea of her as a friend? When did that happen?

# CHAPTER 9

Heat burned the back of Joy's neck when she opened her eyes to see Eric lying down and Regina standing there.

"Oh, hi." She jumped to stand, flinched, and rubbed at her groggy eyes. Why was it so bright? She stared through the window at the crisp white snow with little diamonds glistening in brilliant, if frigid, sunlight.

"Good morning, Joy." Regina's smile was gentle. She was dressed in casual flowy pants and a button-down blouse. Different from her usual suits at the hospital. "When you're ready for breakfast, text Sabastian, and he'll bring it down here."

Joy fingered her curls, brushing them away from her cheeks and trying not to wonder what they looked like after sleeping so askew. "I can just have a protein shake like Eric."

Still lying on his back, he locked his gaze with hers, and her heart skipped as amusement teased the corners of his lips. "I'll not feel left out if you eat bacon and whatever else without me."

"Okay." Struggling to maintain a straight face, she just shrugged. She liked bacon, but she didn't trust herself to respond with an argument since surely her tongue would be tied.

"Remember to bring Eric his other tablet during his breakfast." Regina then reminded her to read the updated notes on the iPad spreadsheet and urged her to reach out in case she had any questions or needed anything. "I'm working from home today."

As Joy surveyed the snowdrifts with over twelve inches piled high in the open areas, her heart went out for the plow drivers. They'd be working all day to clear the roads.

When she closed the Bible to put it away, something slid out and fell. She scooped up a picture of eight to ten kids between ages four and sixteen. All toothy grins and huddled by the lit Christmas tree. Black, white, Hispanic, and Asian kids.

"What's that?" Regina asked, so Joy turned it her way.

Eric leaped to snatch it from her, and his face fell when he gave it a cursory glance before tucking it under his pillow.

Regina's mouth folded, and with unspoken words, she gave Joy a curt nod. Then she took a step backward, glanced at Eric.

Since he'd turned to the side, his back to them, it was Joy's cue to vacate. "I'm going to go wash off and change."

As Joy walked back to her room, melancholy washed over her.

Were those his kids?

No? *A blended family.* He'd said that about his siblings. What happened to his siblings? He didn't seem troubled when he spoke about them last night. Regina didn't mention losing a child either.

Before she showered, Joy went to the kitchen and fired a quick text to Ruby to see how she was doing. Without waiting for a response, she typed another text to Tao to let her know she couldn't make it to her house.

The response was immediate.

Tao: I didn't expect you to drive in snow.

Today's snow was ideal to take the kids sledding on the hill in their backyard and perfect to build a snowman.

Joy: Give hugs to the boys for me. I'll miss them.

Tao: They'll miss you too. See you Monday.

With that, she went to shower and changed into a V-neck teal sweater from the new clothes in the closet. The stretchy insulated tights were comfortable and fit her perfectly.

By the time she returned to the main room and peered into the sunroom, Eric wasn't on his bed. The blanket was nicely tucked in. Sabastian had to have done that. Whenever Joy arrived, the house always looked clean and smelled of lemon disinfectant. Eric's bed was nicely tucked in if he wasn't resting in it. Joy had yet to meet the house cleaner, unless the chef did all the work around the house.

The smell of bacon carried her feet to the tray on the kitchen counter. Her mouth watered when she peeked through the glass lid covering the omelet and bacon.

She hadn't seen Eric eat solid food, so the eggs and bacon must be hers. The brownish smoothie in a glass with a straw had to be his breakfast.

*A brown smoothie...* Hmm. Eric could take his medicine without even knowing.

An idea struck her, and she paced to the iPad for instructions on Eric's medicine.

As she'd assumed, it was the blue capsule he hated. The cabinet was louder than she wanted when she slid it open and pulled out the canister, then retrieved the capsule.

She looked down the hallway connecting to the main house. Nobody was there. Her heart was racing as she peered over the hallway to the guest bedrooms, then to the sunroom.

How did thieves succeed at robbing any house? She could barely breathe just sneaking medicine in Eric's smoothie.

She split open the capsule. *This is wrong.*

But it felt right. Eric could never recover if he kept skipping medicine.

Last night he'd been so normal—vulnerable, almost—and somewhat carefree. Anxiety and fear flitted through his panicked eyes, then subsided as they spoke. She'd wanted to stay awake and watch him sleep the entire time, but she'd ended up drifting to sleep.

Her hands were shaking when she poured the ground powder into the glass. Oh no! Some of it spilled at the rim of the glass and on the tray.

She winced, her heart beating even faster as she opened the drawers in search of a tall spoon. She wanted something to reach the bottom of the glass and stir through the smoothie. A paper towel—did they even have anything like that in here? She looked on the counter and let out a breath upon seeing the roll.

The barstool scraped the tile when she tripped over it while reaching for the paper towel.

By the time she finished wiping the tray and glass of any residue, her heart was thrumming so loud it rivaled any bass backbeat on her playlist today.

Eric's cane clicked on the title, and she straightened her sweater, then leaned against the counter and folded her arms.

*Stay cool.*

"Hi." She waved, her voice squeaking too loud.

His hair was damp, and stray long locks clung to his forehead. His navy sweatshirt had a globe, and white puff print framed the words *Mission Tour.*

Her heart jolted a beat. It was a strange feeling. Maybe because he held her hand last night and clung to her, not wanting her to leave. Could be that they shared a bond of sickness, a connection of some sort. Either way, something had happened last night, something she would rather not entertain.

"You okay?" His brows drew together when he approached.

"Um... breakfast? Um, yes, no?" She squared her shoulders and moved away from the white tile counter. "Ready to eat?"

"Should I be concerned about you?"

Very much so. First, she put medicine in his drink against his knowledge, and now, she was gawking at him. She carried the tray over to the table where he joined her.

"No praying today?"

At his reminder, she paused midchew, having taken a bite or two of her bacon without even realizing it.

"Oh." She put the bacon over the omelet on her plate. With her heart heavy with conviction, she couldn't even pray or look Eric in the eye.

She should think better before acting next time.

She put her head in her hands. "I'm sorry! I put medicine in your smoothie."

Whew! Her chest felt lighter, but as she opened her eyes and met his saddened ones, she regretted her actions.

He rubbed at his brown beard where a few gray strands glistened, closed his eyes, and took a breath.

Joy bounced her knee under the table, waiting for him to say something. Her heart sank. If only she knew what he was thinking!

"I want you to feel better." Her voice faltered. "But you kept refusing medicine, and I..." There was no excuse for her behavior. "I thought it was a good idea at the time.... I'm so sorry."

After a long moment, Eric opened his eyes and reached for the glass. She nearly gasped when he sipped through the straw, then set the glass back on the table.

"Why didn't you just ask me to take the medicine?"

Good thing he had a sense of humor after all. She managed a mirthless laugh. "Turns out I didn't record your responses all those times...." His determination and intent on not taking medicine.

"How many times have you snuck medicine in my smoothie?"

"Today was my first. Clearly, I'm not good at sneaking things."

He shook his head. "You're very terrible at it."

His tone, light with amusement, soothed her, and she told him how she'd spilled half the medicine.

He cackled. "I'll be okay with half a dose today. It's not my worst day after all."

Whew, the tension left her shoulders, and she asked what she'd wanted to know for the last few days. "Why do you just drink smoothies and soups?"

He dabbed a napkin on his mouth.

"Sores. I rarely have an appetite." He tapped his finger on the glass. "As long as I take the protein shakes, it seems to fill me up well."

He told her how many times he ate out of necessity rather than hunger. "If it weren't for medicine, I'd be skipping the smoothies as well."

"My mom used to make me Cream of Wheat whenever I was sick." She closed her eyes for a moment, craving the smooth hot cereal. "It has that creamy taste, so yummy."

"I'll have Sabastian make it sometime." He then pointed at her plate. "Eat before your food gets cold."

Joy forked up some eggs.

*Hmm.* They were scrumptious. She could taste the mushrooms, spinach, peppers, and maybe onions. Best omelet she'd ever had. Her fork clinked on the white porcelain when she speared another bite. "This is so good."

"Sabastian is right there. You can tell him yourself."

Before Joy could turn, Sabastian appeared with a bowl of fresh fruit. "I forgot this."

She'd assumed he was talking to Eric until he set the bowl in front of her.

"The eggs are so delicious." It was hard to see his dark hair with the chef hat covering his head. "Thank you for breakfast."

"Have you decided what you want to drink?" he asked, ignoring her compliment.

Being served felt odd. "I have my tea. I'll just microwave some water later."

"I'll get you water and—"

"I will be fine, but thank you," she interrupted.

When Sabastian left, she stared at the full bowl. "Unless Sabastian is joining us, I can't eat all this."

"Good luck getting him to join us at the table."

"Your mom did last night."

"Only she can make him."

"He's quiet," Joy said, not wanting to gossip, but perhaps Eric knew the man well enough. "Is he new?"

"He's always been that way." Eric took a sip of his smoothie through the straw. "He's been here for nine years."

Joy almost choked on her grape. She coughed to clear the lump of juice from the fruit.

"He's family." Eric handed her a napkin. "At least, that's how we see it. He went to culinary school and insisted on staying here as our chef instead of starting his own kitchen."

"Maybe you make him feel at home." That's how Joy felt in Regina and Kyle's presence.

Beyond the window, it had stopped snowing. Her fingers itched to touch the snow. The triplets came to mind. The last snow they'd played in had been hardening in lumps of ice.

"Thinking of new ways to poison my smoothie?"

She couldn't help but chuckle when she dragged her gaze to him. He was handsome, even with the unshaved beard and skin rash. She hadn't felt there was a good time to give him the cream she'd bought at the hobby shop, but would now be a good time? Would he be offended? Only one way to find out.

"I... bought you some medicine for, um, your skin."

His eyebrow lifted. "You did?"

She nodded. "I went to buy some art supplies and saw the locally made creams. I thought about you."

His nodding was rather appreciative. "As long as it doesn't have that overbearing smell." He winced as if engulfed by a bitter memory.

"I smelled one of the samples." Not the exact cream. "It had a subtle minty scent."

"I'll try it and see.... Couldn't do any worse to my face than it already looks."

His face was fine, but the rash had to be annoying.

Now that the awkward conversation was out of the way, she didn't want to stretch it out and motioned her head toward the window. "Would you like to walk in the snow?"

Eric leaned back and ran a hand over his face. "My physical therapist would be proud of you trying to get me walking outside."

She'd never seen him walk from the guesthouse, but again, it was a struggle for him to get to the bathroom. If he let her help him, they could walk to the front, so he could get some fresh air.

"Would you like to come?"

"Have fun." He waved a hand. "There's probably coats and winter gear in your closet."

If it were warmer outside, she'd insist on him joining her.

"Can I get you anything before I go?"

When he shook his head, she stood to clear the table. Not wanting to add more work for Sabastian, she hand-washed their dishes in the guesthouse kitchen sink.

# CHAPTER 10

J ust like Eric had pointed out, Joy found a winter section in the walk-in closet. She rummaged through several boots for her size. The knitted winter hat was so soft and warm on her head, she had to speed up on getting the gloves so she could get out and cool off in the snow.

Intending to build a snowman, Joy took the red top she'd worn yesterday to tie around the snowman's neck. On her way out, she stopped by the refrigerator for three blueberries and a baby carrot. Then she waved at Eric, who was still slouched on the dining chair. He waved back.

A while later, she'd rolled snow and stacked the three mounds together for a snowman. She bit into a clump of snow stuck to her gloves, and it melted on her tongue. *So good!* She then poked in the carrot for the nose, two berries for the eyes, and one for a mouth. Tying the red blouse around the snowman's wide neck proved tricky, but she pulled at the shirt's arms and the stretchy fabric cooperated enough for her to tie a knot.

Standing to the side, she tilted her head to admire her creation. "Hmm!" The mouth was too small, but at least she could tell it was a mouth.

She had to take a picture for the triplets. As she reached for her phone from the sheepskin coat, Joy sensed someone watching her. She spun toward the tall window.

Eric was in his recliner, hand on his chin, expression grim, and eyes intent on her or the snowman.

He had to miss being outside. She would be, if she were in his place. But with his face so pensive, perhaps he was in a trance and not looking at her after all.

She smiled and waved so hard her whole body moved.

He lifted his hand and waved back. He wasn't in a trance after all. What she wouldn't give to earn a smile out of him! She didn't expect him to be cheerful with everything he had going on, but she desperately wanted him to smile. He did have a great smile that should be seen often.

She ran back to the snowman, its face directed to the window where Eric could see it. Joy stood next to it and motioned her hands to the snow as if presenting it to Eric. She then adjusted her fluffy scarf and leaned closer to the snowman and made a silly face before snapping one, two, and three selfies with the snowman.

Finally, Eric's cheeks lifted, and Joy's stomach somersaulted. She turned around with her back to Eric, to take another picture with him in the background.

Snap.

The brisk air blew at her hand when she slid off the glove to look at the picture.

Steam flew from her mouth as she strained her eyes and zoomed in on Eric, his subtle smile giving her a priceless sense of accomplishment. If she could get a smile out of him once a day, that could assure her she was in the right place.

When she lifted the phone and waved it at him, he all but rolled his eyes, amusement twitching at the corners of his cheeks.

Okay. That wasn't so bad.

How long since he'd breathed in fresh air? From the house, he went to the hospital. Did he ever go anywhere else lately?

If he touched snow, he would get a taste of winter.

She scooped a handful of snow and packed it tight in her palm before returning to the warm house.

After taking off her boots and setting them on the mud tray by the door, she tugged off her hat and put it on the boots. With her teeth, she yanked off the one glove, needing the other to hold the snow so the cold didn't sting her palm.

"Got you something," she said when she walked toward Eric.

His brows furrowed while he stared at her gloved hand. "What do you want me to do with that?"

"You couldn't come outside, so I thought I could bring some outside to you! You might want to touch and feel the snow."

He grunted. "You're out of your mind."

But then he reached for the snow, and his fingers brushed against her gloved palm as he took the ball. He winced at the coolness when the snow melted against his fingers. He switched it to his other hand, liquid dripping beneath his fingers.

"Sorry it's cold."

"It's fine." He handed it back to her.

"Don't you want to taste it?"

"Definitely not." He wiped his damp hands on his sweats. "Thanks."

Joy took the snow to the sink to put it in a Ziploc bag and freeze it, just in case Eric needed it again. She then unrolled a handful of paper towels and brought them to him to dry his hands.

"Aren't you a little late for that?" He eyed the damp watermark on his sweats.

In case the damp spot seeped into his skin, she bent and wiped over his leg.

"I'm fine." His warm breath hit her neck, and a rush of heat coursed through her as she stood.

Eric's face was unreadable, and as for her—what was with her stomach flop?

It had been a long time since she'd dated, and of course, Eric being comfortable with her finally had to be the reason she was feeling a bit cozy and jumbled up.

She needed to wash her clothes and clean up the boots. A few moments to regroup. "Can I get you anything?"

"You forgot to turn on the music."

She took a couple of steps backward and tripped over the ottoman, blocking the tumble with her palm on the tile. "I'm okay." Well, mostly. She *was* suddenly breathless. Right, he was staring with an arched brow. "Music. Got it."

"Classical," he spoke over her shoulder.

Whew, what was that all about? She wasn't supposed to get attached to Eric, let alone develop feelings for him.

After she turned on the music, it was past eleven, and she went to get the winter hat and the rest of the clothes she'd worn last night. She needed to leave everything clean before she left that evening. That was if the roads were better by then.

In the guest laundry room, she swung open the white cabinets in search of detergent but didn't find any. She peered up to the decorative LED light, taking a minute to indulge her new habit to study each room in this house. Everything was modern and fancy.

On her way to the main house to look for laundry soap, she peeked at Eric. His head was leaning back in the chair, probably sleeping. She retrieved a throw from the ottoman and covered him from his feet to his shoulders.

He didn't even move a bit. He must be exhausted after last night's nightmares.

INSTRUMENTAL GOSPEL music drifted through the main house when Joy walked into the kitchen. Sabastian wasn't there, so she ambled toward the living room.

It smelled of flowers and sweet fragrances. Was it from the diffuser against the wall? With black-and-white photos of big cities on the walls, she stood to study the one above the white sofa—

"Hey there, Joy?"

She jumped, holding her racing heart at the sound of Regina's voice.

Regina stood on the side adjoining the main room, and Joy hadn't looked that far yet. It was high time she took that virtual tour. "Come over here."

Joy walked around the long sectional couch and past the winding staircase. The soft rug cushioned her stockinged feet.

She sat at the edge of the sofa where Regina motioned for her to sit across from her, then glanced up to the abstract linear chandelier. "You have a beautiful house."

"Eric had it redesigned when the neighbors sold us their land." Regina slid the laptop to the side of the glass coffee table. "He wanted enough room for all his siblings to stay whenever the family gathered for the annual reunion."

Having this much money, of course, they'd have a reunion. The fireplace mantel displayed three frames of pictures. With Eric's comment about a blended family, not to mention the picture he'd yanked out of her hand, Joy motioned to it. "Are those your kids?"

Regina smiled, stood, and walked to the mantel shelf. She reached for one of the frames. "They are quite a handful."

Joy joined her.

"There's Eric."

Joy leaned into Regina for a good look. Handsome with short brown hair, he was the tallest in the bunch—she counted twelve boys, two girls, and a baby with a pink hat and swaddled in a pink blanket.

With dark skin, light skin, olive skin, and you name it, they gathered in front of a gazebo. Eric was holding the baby up, and all the other boys grinned mischievously and reached their hands out as if they were fighting to get the baby from him.

"Such a beautiful family."

"Four of them were exchange students, but they all call me Mom." Regina drew out a breath, opened her mouth as if ready to say something, but closed her lips, then put back the frame and reached for another.

It was Eric floating above the rapids. The lush forest to the side reminded Joy of Uganda. "Where's this place?"

"Two years ago." Regina tilted the photo to the light and studied it. "Eric went to visit his friend in Uganda, and they did some adventures." Her eyes glistened, and Joy's heart ached.

"I'm sorry." She touched Regina's shoulder. Seeing her son happy once and knowing he was now dealing with chronic illness or even depression had to be hard. But there seemed to be more to her sadness.

The picture from Eric's Bible came to mind. Did it have anything to do with the kids while they were young? "Are all your kids okay? Did any of them die?"

Regina reached for the other frame with a bunch of kids. Was it the same kids from the earlier picture?

"Eric and his siblings." Regina touched their faces. "It was taken after our daughter was born."

That explained why there was an infant with all the teenagers. "We didn't think we'd ever have biological children." She chuckled. "And then I hit forty and got pregnant."

"Are these some of the same kids from the picture earlier?"

Regina shook her head. "That's a story for Eric to tell. He's very private, and I have to respect his wishes."

"Did he—"

"Excuse me, ma'am." They both turned toward Sabastian, standing further in the main living room. "What time would you like your lunch?"

Regina tilted her head to one side. "Sabastian... Sabastian, aren't you a dear? That omelet you made this morning will hold me for another two hours." She glanced at Joy. "But Joy might want something."

"Detergent." That's what she'd come for.

"I'll do the laundry," he said.

"I got it." No way would she let him wash her underwear.

"You don't need to do laundry." Regina set the photo back on the mantel. "The housekeeper will be here tomorrow morning. Plus, you can keep any of the clothes you wear while you're here."

That explained why most of the clothes in the closet had tags on them. But she needed to keep herself busier than just drawing pictures, which would mostly be of Eric. "I still want the detergent though."

As she followed Sabastian to the kitchen, she wanted to ask him about Eric. Had he lost his family? Did something tragic happen to the kids in the picture? Did he blame himself for someone's death?

But she'd barely had a five-minute conversation with Sabastian, certainly not enough for him to open up.

"Can I help you make lunch?" she asked when they arrived at the kitchen and she rested her hand on the granite island.

His thick brows drew together. "Aren't you supposed to be keeping Mr. Stone company?"

This would be the first question he asked that didn't involve food. Intrigued, she touched one of the fluffy looking petals in the vase.

"He's sleeping right now, and there's no urgency in me doing laundry."

Sabastian stared at her as if trying to figure her out, but then she clasped her fingers, studying the smudged ink beneath the pendant lights. "What's for lunch?"

"Tell me what you want to eat, and I'll fix it."

"I'll eat whatever Eric eats." Although his food was plain, she didn't want Eric to feel left out every time she ate something delicious.

Sabastian swung open the stainless fridge and pulled out three glass containers with chopped vegetables. "Mr. Stone doesn't eat anything with spices in it." He then pointed to the sink, against the wall. "Feel free to wash your hands."

Eric had warned her of Sabastian's quietness, so Joy would use this opportunity to strike some conversation. "How do you know Eric?"

"You should ask him." Sabastian handed her a kitchen towel for her dripping hands.

"He doesn't talk much." Opening up specifically.

He reached for one of the nonstick pots hanging above the sink. "This is the most I've heard his voice since he got sick." A ghost of a smile curved Sabastian's mouth. "He told me about your citrus tea."

He'd talked about her tea in a way that made Sabastian almost smile? Her chest bubbled. "What exactly did he say?"

"Like you said, he doesn't say much. Especially lately."

She'd assumed she was the only one he didn't talk to. "I hope he feels better."

"He's a good man." Sabastian then asked her to get the chicken broth from one of the bottom cabinets.

They made soup while she pried and poked Sabastian with personal questions. She learned he'd been homeless when Eric found him and paid for his culinary school. "He gave me my life back. I owe him."

Eric hadn't pointed out that he'd sponsored Sabastian or met him on the streets. In fact, he considered Sabastian a family member. "I don't think he expects you to pay him back."

Just that simple conversation revealed something unique about Eric—he was compassionate. Joy didn't take the revelation lightly.

When she sat down with Eric two hours later, he looked refreshed from his nap and asked for his medicine this time. He swallowed it before they had their soup. "I'll get it done with."

"Why are you eating the bland food when we have a chef?" he asked, dabbing his mouth with a white cloth napkin.

"You're eating it."

"You don't have to eat it because of me."

"People run the race for the cure when they don't have cancer."

He frowned, seeming confused by her response, but she was already ladling another spoon into the bowl.

The spoons clanked against porcelain bowls as instrumental classical music played in the background.

With Eric's parents at home, Joy didn't need to stay until five or later. "I'm going to get some laundry done after lunch, and then—"

"I hope you're staying another night."

"It's not snowing anymore."

"You grew up in Uganda where it doesn't snow." He set his bowl to the side and narrowed his gaze at her. His eyes didn't look hollow. Perhaps the nap helped. "Then you moved to San Francisco. Trust me when I say the roads are worse today than they were yesterday."

That was if her car could get her across town. Speaking of which... "My car is parked outside." Probably buried in snow.

"That solves that." Eric leaned back as if pleased with himself.

She ran her fingers over the rim of her lemonade glass as she thought of a comeback. "My two-week trial is over. I'm not sure if you still want me to tell your mom things won't work out."

He rubbed his chin, lost in thought. "I need more time—six months or even a year—so I can make a better decision."

He wanted her here. Her heart swelled with happiness or something beyond it. She didn't have plans for tomorrow, besides painting and Saturday chores. As long as she made it to church on Sunday, by then the snow should at least be cleared from the road.

As it turned out, she wasn't ready to let go of him yet either.

"More time then, huh?" She held his hopeful gaze, and he scrunched his face. Something dark lay buried deep in his heart, and she hoped he'd open up to her or at least try.

# CHAPTER 11

The following days, Eric still felt restless, but Joy was the highlight of his days. In the two weeks since she'd stayed the night, he'd enjoyed listening to her talk about the kids she took care of, the patients she visited, and the interesting people she encountered. She had positive stories about her mailman, the triplets' grandma, the craft store's owner.... The list went on. As a perennially cheerful person, she could wear down one's melancholy with her positive view of life.

Whenever she asked about him, he claimed not to have much going for him and switched the conversation back to her.

One day, on a forty-degree midafternoon without snow, she convinced him to go out on the porch. Five minutes of breathing in fresh air had felt good.

Wednesdays and weekends seemed longer when Joy didn't come to The Peak.

Even on those days, he found himself staring at her painting as her vibrant smile flashed through his mind. From the first day, he'd known her smile was contagious—dangerous even if it cheered him up—and he'd already caught too many disorders.

For the first time in a long time, he felt compelled to push himself and take any kind of medicine. The cream she'd given seemed to have lessened the rash on his face. He'd have Sabastian call the number labeled on the jar, so he could order more.

On Wednesday when his PT showed, Eric didn't mind going through the routine stretches and walking exercises. An hour later, his psychiatrist showed up for their twice-a-month meeting, and Eric didn't dread answering when Ian asked about Eric's recent dreams. He told him all the details he remembered from the dark tunnel.

"And you still haven't escaped the tunnel?" Ian ran a hand over his shaven jaw as he spoke meditatively.

"No."

Eric always wished he could get to the light on the other end.

"The hallucination medicine hasn't given you any more side effects, I presume?" Ian's brown eyes were intent on Eric as if he knew something about his medicine intake. "I didn't get your refill call."

Eric had eliminated several prescriptions from his system. "I stopped taking them."

Ian brushed something off his V-neck sweater. Much younger than Eric, he remained tactical enough to convince Eric to share with him.

"Is there a reason you stopped taking it?"

Even though he'd ditched the medicine before Joy showed up, she had a say in him accomplishing his plan. "My new caretaker plays music."

Ian crossed one leg over the other. "You have a new caretaker?"

Eric nodded, realizing it was the first time he'd mentioned Joy to his counselor. "She likes music." Either that or she knew what he needed and played it for him. "I find it relaxing and don't get hallucinations as much."

Joy had synced her music to the kitchen iPad, and he listened to some of the songs at night. "I've been sleeping a lot better lately."

Ian nodded and smiled, pointing his chin at Eric. "Your eyes look better."

No kidding. "You never told me they looked terrible."

The man rubbed his hands over his slacks. "Have you talked to anyone about your wife and kids?"

Eric's body stiffened. That conversation wasn't up for discussion. He talked to God a few times, yelling and crying during the past four agonizing years.

"It's about time you tell someone how you feel."

"My family knows."

"Besides your family."

His few close friends knew he didn't want their company now. He'd even pleaded with Mom to cancel their annual summer reunion until further notice. "If you haven't noticed, I don't get out much to meet people to talk to."

Ian gave him a knowing look. "I think this caretaker might be the perfect friend to talk to."

Joy had more important and exciting things to think about than Eric's dampening memories.

Ian chose not to prescribe any medicine for him that day. "Take a break from Celexa. You don't look at all depressed."

Eric cringed hearing Ian say it out loud. Anxiety and depression. Why didn't they call it something else?

In his defense, with all the medicine he'd taken for the last seven months, someone was most likely to get anxiety attacks.

WHEN JOY SHOWED UP the next day, Eric was waiting in the living room recliner.

"Happy Valentine's Day," she said with a smile that lit up the room. Even his heart rose in his chest when she set two bags down in the kitchen and walked to him with a small red bag.

"You're late." After all, he'd checked the time several times before sitting down.

"I texted Sabastian to let you know, but maybe he hasn't checked his phone yet." She rambled on about the stop she made at the hospital to deliver valentine cards to the patients, then another stop at the store.

"I'm teasing." Eric peered at her radiant face. Then his gaze dragged down to her tan sweater. The color added a glow to her skin while a big heart encased with sparkly pink flowers centered on her blouse. "I didn't realize it's Valentine's Day."

He should've bought her something, a thank you for her time. He needed to get in touch with his accountant to start paying her.

"I got you something." She handed him the red bag, her sweet scent emanating in the room. She shrugged as he unwrapped a jar of the cream. "It's not the best valentine gift, but—"

"I'm going to pay you for it this time." He set it on the ottoman and reached for another gift, unwrapping a jar just like it.

"It's a gift." She rubbed her forearms, bunching up the sweater sleeves by her elbows.

"You must have noticed that it's working. That's why I will pay."

"I'll not accept your money." Her dainty chin jutted up while he retrieved something else from the bag. It was light. His fingers slid over another canvas, and when he looked at the picture, he nearly swallowed his tongue.

"Are you okay, Eric?" Joy edged closer and knelt to peer at him as he studied the abstract tunnel painting. Unlike the recurring tunnel in his dream, this one didn't have clowns, ghosts, or skeletons. It was dark, and a boy in a yellow shirt had outstretched hands, his back to the opening of the tunnel. It was like he'd escaped it and was reveling in the bright light.

How did she know about this tunnel?

His hands shaking, he clenched his teeth to keep them from chattering as he felt more exposed than he wanted to.

"Eric?" Joy whispered, kneeling beside him. She reached to touch his hand, but he pulled his fingers away.

He had to get it together. It wasn't her fault he had demons.

She took the picture and set it down. "Did I do something to up-set you?"

He shook his head, touching his head as if he could erase the haunted images flashing from his dreams. "Just give me a moment."

She left. The microwave whirred on. Then several beeps came, and she returned with a cup of her citrus tea.

Despite himself, he took the mug. He didn't want her to feel bad about her gifts or the tea. Honestly, he liked her painting a lot better. It had life as opposed to the traps in the dream.

"Thank you," he finally said, staring at her on the floor where she knelt, ready to catch him should he fall.

He took a sip of the tea and winced. "This is disgusting."

She bit her lower lip. "I thought you didn't mind tasteless things."

Maybe he was reacquiring his taste buds. "Have you ever drank this before?"

"When I'm upset."

"In other words, it was that bad, and you couldn't care less about the taste."

She reached for the mug from him. The simple brush of her fin-gers shot tingles through his arms, and he pulled back, clinging to the cup. He then motioned to the picture on the white marble.

"Thank you for my painting." Perhaps someone else drew it and not her. "Did you paint it?"

She nodded hesitantly.

"I love your art." He managed, meaning it because the two he'd seen had powerful inspirational messages.

"Thank you." She gathered up his painting. "Did you already eat lunch?"

"Yes. I even took the medicine. Did you eat?"

She nodded again. "I brought some Valentine's Day decorations. Is it okay if I hang up a few?"

"Of course." He needed a moment to compose himself. "I'm going to apply some more cream."

And probably change too. The little episode had dampened his shirt beneath the sweater he was wearing.

"Would you like to watch a movie this afternoon?" she asked as if she had one in mind.

"A movie sounds great."

As Joy's songs played in the background, he ambled past her. She was in the kitchen hanging up heart-shaped decorations, the vibrant reds almost garish against the classy white-toned rooms. But maybe the place needed some color—some Joy.

In his bedroom bathroom, he slid off the sweater and the dampened T-shirt.

Looking at his reflection in the mirror, he touched his flat stomach. The rash was clearing, just the way it was on his face and his arms.

How could he smear his back? He could ask Sabastian, but he handled food. No need to traumatize him with his scabs anyway.

His feet felt weak after a few seconds of standing, so he sank onto the bench. After reaching for the cream from the cabinet under the bench, he twisted open the lid.

He rubbed the cream on his arm. His brain spun, suddenly fuzzy and dizzy.

A flame flashed in the mirror before it crept up to the wall.

Oh no! "Fire." He swallowed, struggling to breathe when smoke clouded the room.

"Fire!" He stood as the flame drew in on him. Then, somehow, he sprinted out of the darkened, hot bathroom. His vision blurring.

He slammed into something hard, hitting his head. "Aaa!"

He bounced back, landing on the floor.

With his heart hammering, he touched his achy forehead.

"Eric!" The faint sweet voice soothed him. "I'm here."

His lips parted and he gasped. "Joy."

He savored her gentle touch on his shoulder, then his forehead. "Let me call 911."

"No!"

He was panting. It wasn't the first time he'd had this episode. "I'm okay.... I just need a moment."

"You're shaking." Like her touch, her gentle voice calmed him. "Let me get you a blanket."

She left without insisting on calling 911. Soon a warm fur swept over his shoulders, and she tucked it around him and shoved it down to his back. It reminded him of the way Mom used to swaddle his baby sister.

Joy's hair tickled his face when she propped a pillow beneath his head. The subtle scent of her conditioner—and whatever soft perfume she had—was refreshing.

He opened his eyes briefly to take a glimpse of her deflated face.

"Thank you." He breathed out the words, more grateful when she kept her hand on his shoulder.

"Dear Lord, please remember your servant, Eric." Sweet words fell from her lips. "Show him that there's a God who still cares, that he's not forgotten." With her plea so fervent and loaded with anguish, he could almost imagine she could feel his pain.

A hot tear puddled and fell, and he wiped it away.

"Take him away from that dark place and into Your light, Father...."

Eric's parents prayed for him—friends and many others, too, no doubt—but he hadn't heard a prayer with words that seemed to point to his condition in a long time. Barely did anyone pray for him right to his face, but he'd not given them the satisfaction that he needed prayers.

When she finished praying, a silence stretched between them as she pushed his hair from his face.

The flesh beneath her fingers made his skin feel amazingly alive, and her gentle touch left him longing for more.

"I need to get an ice pack for your forehead."

He already missed the warmth radiating from her nearness. She soon returned, and Eric winced when the cool ice hit his forehead.

"This is so cold."

"I don't want your face to get swollen."

Having someone, a woman he admired, besides his mom, take care of him was nice.

"Should I call Sabastian to help you to the sunroom?"

"No." He kept his eyes closed. She was already giving him the attention he needed.

"Tell me the meaning of your pictures." Perhaps starting with... "The tunnel."

She could give him a hint of why her art seemed to speak to him.

"I once was in a dark place." She slid her hand off his forehead and stayed silent so long he thought she wasn't going to talk anymore. "During my radiation therapy for Hodgkin's lymphoma."

He sucked in a quick breath. She'd survived, thank God!

She then put the ice back on his forehead.

"The lymphoma was gone, but on my eighteen-month checkup, they found a new growth outside my stomach. It needed to be removed."

That breath left his lungs when she mentioned the infection she'd developed after the procedure. "They didn't think I'd make it."

*Oh Lord, Joy didn't deserve to be sick.* Was she going to be okay? Despair wrapped merciless hands around his heart. His chest tightened, and he struggled to speak.

"I was living in suspense and fear for a while." She sighed and rubbed her forehead with a shaky hand. "I got back into drawing about that time. It was relaxing, and since then, scenes of redemption have been my inspiration."

He could sense her nearness and guessed her to be leaning over him while she rolled the ice pack on his injury. A brittle laugh escaped her. "It's been almost five years, but I still get nervous whenever I have my follow-up blood tests and physical exam."

His heart ached for her. While he masked his fear to anger, Joy masked hers with happiness. Her name suited her perfectly.

"How often do you go to your appointments?"

"Used to be every three months, but it's just going to be once this year."

He wanted to encourage and comfort her, the way she did for others. "When is your next appointment?"

"In April."

He had no idea how to help, but he was compelled to do something. Eric kept his eyes closed when she took the ice pack from his skin.

"As for the tunnel, I was thinking about you."

She was such a selfless soul. Making valentine cards for patients and creating pictures for him and everyone who needed them. "For some reason, I pictured you in a dark place. Stranded, looking for answers, and yearning to see the light again."

Who was this woman?

She brushed a finger across his forehead, wiping away moisture the ice pack left. "I know you have more going on than just the sickness. I can't take away your illness or your physical and internal pain, but I'd like to be your friend. I'd like to know more about you."

Eric relaxed in her presence. His heart rate had slowed from the earlier attack. "What exactly do you want to know?"

"You don't strike me as an angry person. There has to be a reason why you act the way you do."

He almost argued with her to justify his anger, but he didn't have it in him. Who knew what other picture she would paint next?

A picture that would speak to him. There was no reason he shouldn't tell her about himself.

"I get nightmares."

"I know."

"Sometimes hallucinations," he added. "You don't have to call 911 as soon as I pass out."

"I didn't know that."

That had been one of the reasons he didn't want caregivers around. The idea of them rushing him in an ambulance whenever he passed out... Well, he couldn't bear to deal with that.

Joy was different. She'd been through pain, sickness, and loss. As much as he wanted to keep his demons to himself, the least he could do was to reveal more.

"Now if you can help me up." He finally opened his eyes. Joy was kneeling on the floor beside him in the hallway.

"I noticed you had cream on your arm." He must've left a smudge when the fire ambushed him. "Do you need help smearing it on your back?"

She'd already seen his scarred chest and experienced his episode. Hiding his back from her was no use. It wasn't like they'd ever be a couple.

If his illness and appearance hadn't kept her from being attracted to him, surely both of them wouldn't get past his looming loss and nightmares. What would a girl like Joy want from him? Sympathy was the reason she took care of him. The awful reality—Eric needed help.

"Let's use the cream you got today." He accepted her offered hand and pulled up to sit.

As she went to retrieve the cream, he draped the blanket down to his stomach. When she returned and dipped her finger in the jar, he turned and hunched his back to her, then winced when she smeared the cool cream over his scaly skin. While her hand worked in slow circles over his back, every nerve in his body seemed wide awake.

"There." She scooted away.

He picked up the cream from the floor, his voice hoarse when he thanked her.

"Any time."

"I'll go get a shirt and meet you in the sunroom?"

"Yes. So you can tell me the rest of your story."

She was persistent. Eric could only shake his head. He might first need to take a nap if he were peeling off more layers of himself.

ERIC SETTLED ON THE chair and pulled the throw up to his waist. He was hoping Joy would pursue the movie, but she moved the recliner closer to him and sat there, twisting her fingers in her lap waiting for him to speak about himself.

"You're sure this is how you want to spend your Valentine's Day?"

"I'm sure."

Well... He drew out a breath and tilted his chin to the bookshelf, to his New Living Translation from his teen years. "Can you please get the Bible?"

Joy's eyes widened, and seeming confused, she walked to the bookshelf and returned with the Bible.

"My biological mom was a single mother." He vaguely remembered how she looked. "She died when I was four." He couldn't remember what surgery she'd had, but the oxygen mask, the tubes, the monitor, and the antiseptic scents were still engraved in his mind. "Regina was my counselor."

Thank God for kindhearted therapists like her.

"Oh, Eric." Joy set the Bible on her lap and put both hands on her cheeks.

If she was almost breaking down over that, how was she going to handle the rest of his story? "The picture..." He gestured to the Bible. Surely, she remembered the photo that had fallen from it the night she'd stayed. "It's my kids.... They died." He wasn't there to save them or die with them. His chest felt so tight it hurt. "And my wife."

Joy gasped.

The lump of emotion grated like shards of broken glass in his throat. He didn't trust himself to speak anymore. He pushed the lever and leaned back, closing his eyes. Joy's sniffles and deep breaths didn't help his already emotional state.

"Read Lamentations 3," he spoke between shuddering breaths, "1–20. It sums up my life."

The soft pages rustled. She then cleared her throat. "'I'm the one who has seen the afflictions that come from the rod of the Lord's anger. He has led me into darkness, shutting out all the light....'"

The fulfillment he'd once had vanished within five years.

"'He has made my skin and flesh grow old. He has broken my bones, besieged and surrounded me with anguish and distress. He has buried me in a dark place, like those long dead.'"

How could God blame Eric for doubting His love and goodness? The loving God who'd placed him in Regina and Kyle's family and given him kids and a wife was the same God who'd stripped most of it away.

He still had Regina and Kyle and his siblings, but why not his wife and kids? *Why, God?*

Joy's soothing voice continued, crackling as if she were fighting tears.

"'He has bound me in heavy chains, and though I cry and shout, He has shut out my prayers.... He has made me chew on gravel and rolled me in dust.'"

That was where he wanted her to end, but she kept reading.

"'I will never forget this awful time, as I grieve over my loss. Yet I still dare to hope when I remember this; The faithful love of the Lord never ends, his mercies never cease. Great is his faithfulness, his mercies begin afresh each morning....'"

She blew her nose. Good thing there were tissues on the coffee table. "I had to read that last verse," she whispered. "I needed to know there's a promise, some light at the end of the tunnel."

Eric didn't want to take that away from her, the hope since she'd already come out of a dark place and, somehow, she was managing to pull him back into the light. He'd better pull himself together and not ruin her day. "What movie do you have in mind?"

"You want to watch it now?" Her voice trembled.

He couldn't think of a better way to get back the normalcy they'd had before he broke down three times. When she'd given him the painting, then the fire dilemma and talking about his past.

# CHAPTER 12

Spring brought more hope and inspiration, a lovely reminder of how beautiful change could be. Joy was looking forward to the unknown. Maybe she wanted to make Pleasant View her permanent home, as long as Eric lived there. He could die, or she could die before him. She shook her head to fight the dark thoughts.

She would live. And Eric would recover. He just had to. That was her prayer, a plea lately.

On a Wednesday afternoon, Joy's mom called, wanting to know how Joy's follow-up appointment went.

"Everything's still normal." Joy closed her eyes and tilted her face to the sun, remembering her relief when the doctor called her two days ago. Then she leaned against the railing of the apartment patio. "I want to hear more about you and Alex."

Her mom's soft laugh whispered through the phone, and the lightness of her voice as she talked about her date with her fiancé warmed Joy's heart. "He's so silly...."

Mom hadn't talked about a man with such fondness since Dad died. The afternoon breeze lifted Joy's hair, and a couple of tendrils fell on her forehead. "You should marry him."

Mom breathed sharply. "I'm not ready."

Likely, she wouldn't ever feel ready. She'd accepted his proposal, but she kept putting off any talk about a wedding. Thankfully, Alex was patient and made himself available to love Mom as well as offering help with Grandpa or whenever they needed a hand with house projects.

"Life is too short." Was all Joy could say.

"How about you?" Mom diverted the subject. "How are the triplets... and Eric?"

Joy had told Mom to pray for Eric to recover from Lyme disease, but she didn't tell her about his nightmares and hallucinations.

"The kids..." Joy smiled when she relayed the boys' backyard adventures. "They want to build rocket ships to put in the garden...." That's what they'd said when Joy was helping them plant seeds in the pots that they would later transfer in the garden.

Mom laughed but then wanted to hear an update on Eric.

Joy gazed at the green grass and bright flowers shooting from the ground. It reminded her of his journey. He was on the mend and showing glimpses that he could be the healthy man he used to be. "He has good and bad days."

She tried not to dwell on the days when he woke up with throbbing headaches or the sporadic fevers that drained his energy throughout the day. On some good days, she succeeded in getting him to go on a drive with her around town, sit on the back porch, or walk to the gazebo in the front yard. "He came with me to my appointment the other day."

A soft gasp whistled through the speakers. "He came with you?"

His offer to go had surprised Joy too. In his condition, she'd thought he was kidding, but he wanted to support her.

"He stayed in the car...." Self-conscious about his appearance, an appearance that didn't bother her at all. Her chest squeezed. If only he didn't have those bad days. "He's a wonderful person."

"I can tell he is." A moment of silence passed before Mom spoke again. "You're talking about life being short, when are you going to start a family?"

Joy suppressed a snort. She needed a husband first. "After I travel."

Mom chuckled. "That may take forever—after all, your Colorado trip turned into a whole year's stay rather than a summer visit.

I would love to have grandkids someday, but you kids aren't getting married."

Joy didn't blame Mom for being worried about her extended visit in Colorado. Joy had probably given her the impression she was setting down roots, but she'd only transferred her medical records to Pleasant View, so she didn't have to drive back home and return in a couple of days.

She couldn't set down roots, not yet. She had so many things she wanted to do before she died, and she'd lost so much time being sick—time she could never regain.

Time. God had given her the gift of more time when she survived cancer. A shiver coursed through her. Despite her checkup showing things were all right, she still feared...

She stiffened her spine and refocused.

As for her romantic life, she'd had a boyfriend in Uganda, but that relationship ended when she left the country. After Dad died, Joy spent the following three years adjusting to her new job in the US. She'd met a guy in her Bible study, but two weeks later, she found out she had lymphoma. The last thing she needed then—or even now—was to nurture a relationship.

Mom went on to chat about Joy's brothers, then Grandpa who was happy that Mom was living with him.

When they hung up, Joy returned to the kitchen to touch up the painting she'd been working on. She stroked the brush against the canvas, and her mind wandered back to Eric. The day he'd passed out in the hallway outside his bedroom.

The white cream on his arm had shown he'd been in the middle of applying the rash cream. After one look at the full rash on his back, she'd offered to help, and since then, he'd come to the living room and asked for her help.

Between that and him opening up about his loss, she felt a deeper connection with him—feelings that caused her to long for him whenever they were apart.

She smiled at the sound of chirping birds. Outside the kitchen window, they sang their afternoon lullaby. Hints of something green budded on the branches. In less than a month, the tree will be lush, just like the one she'd painted on the canvas. After dipping her brush back in green paint, she added extra texturing to the brown twigs for the nest. The birds flying out of their nest perfectly defined new beginnings.

Littered paper on the floor crumpled under her flip-flops as she carried the easel closer to the window. The picture needed some of the spring afternoon sun streaming through the window. She wanted it ready by tomorrow so she could give it to Eric.

Hmm... She stilled her brush, stepping back from the canvas. Maybe she should've painted butterflies since she'd be releasing them with Eric tomorrow.

After cleaning the papers from the floor, Joy tossed them in the recycle bin. Thankfully, Ruby rarely used the kitchen. Otherwise, she would go ballistic with the papers and paint projects Joy had on the counter. Even if she gave away most of her paintings, she still had plenty of them eating up space in the tiny living room and kitchen walls, not counting the ones in her bedroom.

It was almost four when she looked at the microwave clock. Ruby would be home in an hour. Oops. She hadn't even started dinner. She'd just swung open the refrigerator to assess the cooking options when the doorbell rang. She was expecting a package for the bridesmaids' necklaces, but she instead opened the door to a couple of men in their early twenties, selling sports magazine subscriptions.

If they were like the salesman in Uganda, then she couldn't give a satisfactory explanation for them to let her off the hook.

Overcome with compassion at their dedication to earn a living, she held up one hand to stop their spiel. "Let me give you a donation."

The men looked at each other before one shrugged and the other nodded. "Thank you so much."

"You might need a coffee to get you through the day." God knew how many more doors they planned to knock on before calling it a day.

She closed the door and went to retrieve the twenty-dollar bill she'd set aside for main street parking. Their smiles were worth sacrificing her trips to Main Street for the rest of the month.

Before she could return to the refrigerator, the doorbell rang again.

Huh? Had they forgotten something?

She regretted not looking through the peephole when she swung open the door.

The daunting familiarity of the handsome man teased her memory.

"Hi, Joy!" His straight teeth flashed at her. His hair was slicked to the side, and he'd clasped both his hands behind him.

"Um..." She frowned as she scrambled to remember who it was.

"Nate. Ruby's—"

Joy slapped a hand over her forehead. "Of course. I'm sorry." She shook her head, then wondered at the nature of Nate's spontaneous visit. "Ruby's not here."

He pulled out his hands from behind his back, revealing a bouquet of yellow tulips in clear wrap. "I'm here to see you."

Joy stared at the flowers as if they had claws. "You don't need to get me flowers."

"You left in a hurry last time. I want to apologize if I was too direct and chased you off."

"It's not you at all." She'd told Ruby not to do this to her! Now the wedding weekend was going to be awkward. "I had things to do."

How did he even know where they lived? Maybe he'd been here to visit Ruby before Joy had moved in.

"Did Ruby tell you that I'm home today?"

He winced, still holding out the bouquet. "Please take the flowers so I don't feel humiliated."

All right! "Thanks." She took the flowers, but she didn't feel comfortable inviting a stranger into the house while she was home alone.

An awkward silence passed as Nate tinkered with his tie. The snazzy black shirt tucked into his jeans suggested he came for a date. She'd better kindly send him off. "Listen—"

"I wanted to see if we could grab a coffee or dinner. We can pretend Ruby didn't set us up."

His serious expression sent Joy's stomach churning and made it hard for her not to edge back a few steps. Instead, she fiddled with the tulips. They *were* lovely. It certainly wasn't the flowers' fault that she didn't want them. Keeping her gaze on them, she shook her head. "We'll see each other at the wedding soon."

"You seem to be the type of woman I'd enjoy talking to." He blew out a breath and shifted his feet. "You might enjoy my company, too if we got to know each other."

"I have a boyfriend!" Whoa. The lie flew out of her mouth.

Nate blinked, lifting his brows. "I guess Ruby doesn't know."

She would see Nate at the wedding. How awkward that would be if Joy didn't have a boyfriend with her. The cellophane crinkled as she twisted her grip on the bouquet. It was all Ruby's fault.

"Ruby doesn't know a lot of things—I mean I don't tell her everything."

Lies... lies. She stared at a woman who passed carrying bags of groceries up the stairs behind Nate.

"If things don't work out with your boyfriend"—Nate lifted his hand in a salute, taking a couple of steps backward—"maybe you can text me."

Unease swept over her. Nate would find out her lie during the wedding weekend. She hugged the flowers to her chest, wishing she'd never accepted them. Then she let out a long low breath. She may not want them, but she also didn't want them dying. So she carried them to the kitchen and put them in a vase that she poured water into, then rummaged around for dinner ideas.

That evening as she ate noodles with her friend, Joy tried to convince Ruby she didn't want any more setups.

"Do you see what situation you're putting me in?"

Ruby's long hair danced in a messy ponytail when she shook her head. "I didn't tell you to lie to him."

Joy shoved the half-finished plate to the side and folded her arms on the table. "Ugh."

"I don't see why you're frustrated." Ruby waved her fork. "You spend your free time with kids and hospital patients. If I don't play matchmaker, you'll never meet anyone."

Joy's temples throbbed, the pressure turning into a full-on headache. Couldn't Ruby understand how Joy hated the awkwardness of setups? That and her hidden reasons to not bond with more people. She massaged her forehead. "Seriously, this has to stop."

Ruby rolled her eyes, then twirled noodles onto her fork. "You and Nate would make a great couple. You should give him a chance."

This girl could be nice yet infuriating.... "Maybe I'm already in love with someone."

Snorting, Ruby nearly choked on the bite she'd just taken. She reached for her water to chase it down, then folded her arms, and gave Joy a *look*. "You can pull that stunt with Nate, but not *me*. The only man you spend time with is Eric, and from what I can tell, he's not into..."

Eric. Hmm. Joy tapped a finger on the table, her whole body heating. She could invite Eric as her wedding date! That could get Ruby and Nate off her back.

Eric would think she was crazy, but at least he would laugh about it. She liked seeing him laugh.

"What are you smiling about?"

Was she smiling? She took a quick look at Ruby.

Her friend's eyes widened. "Oh my! You're falling for Eric, aren't you?"

It didn't matter how Joy felt—besides, it was too early to assume she was falling in love. So, feigning innocence, she dismissed Ruby with a wave of her hand. "Me? No way."

She could try to convince herself, but deep down, she knew it was the yes way.

# CHAPTER 13

Like a child in anticipation of his birthday or Christmas, Eric woke up early on Thursday morning. He felt better than he'd felt that week, if not the best he'd felt in the last nine months.

Joy was coming. Restless and giddy, he wiggled into a seated position and tried to slow his excited breathing.

When Mom came to check on him, he'd already done his stretching exercises with the therapist, showered, and changed into a T-shirt and jeans that used to fit him and now hung loosely on him.

He'd also eaten Cream of Wheat as opposed to the protein shake with his morning medicine. Lately, he'd diligently taken his medicine, except for the days he forgot—good thing, Mom still came and double-checked to make sure he didn't skip a dose.

"You look, well, different this morning," Mom said as Eric stared through the window.

Dew kissed the fairy slipper and early meadow rue blooming in the distant wild grass. The sun just rising above the tree line promised a perfect morning. In a few weeks, even more abundant wildflowers blooming throughout their expansive property would make it the ideal time of the year to hit the trails in Pleasant View.

"It's a beautiful day." He then glanced at the two clear wide jars on the mantel. Ten days ago, Joy brought the cocooned caterpillars so he could watch them transform. "We're releasing the butterflies today."

Mom peered at the jar, the flapping butterflies only contained by its lid. "It's amazing how an ugly caterpillar can turn into a beautiful butterfly."

He had to agree. "I see why Joy likes butterflies."

127

Among the many redemptive images of living things she was inspired to paint.

After Mom left, he made himself tea in the guest kitchen.

With his mouth sores gone and the dietician expanding his meal options two days ago, Eric requested a bran muffin for his midmorning snack.

The morning dragged on as he sat, tapping his knee. He ambled to the window closer to the front door where he could see the driveway, in hopes that Joy's green Sentra would emerge soon.

It was only eleven thirty when he returned to the kitchen and looked at the stovetop clock.

Blowing out an exasperated breath, he entered the sunroom and flopped into the couch, then stared at the orange and blue butterflies. The next minutes stretched on like hours.

When the front door opened, he all but leaped up to stand.

"Eric!"

Joy's smile warmed his heart. It was so genuine he could believe she was as glad to see him as he was to see her. "It's so sunny. It's starting to look like spring."

His palms were sweaty, and his knees wobbled as if they could buckle as he walked toward her. The excitement had more to do with releasing the butterflies than Joy's presence.

"What do you have?" He motioned to the yellow bag in her hand. Concentrating on the butterfly print flitting over her yellow dress was easier than holding her gaze.

"I have something for you." She rummaged through the bag and handed him a canvas. This time, she didn't have it wrapped.

Just like the other two paintings, the blue sky painted on the canvas relaxed him. The spreading green tree with free birds flying out of their nest offered another glimpse into his life.

Yes, he breathed out deeply. He felt as if he were flying out of the nest after the many months of cocooning in the house. Thanks to Joy forcing her way into his life.

She'd brought meaning into his dull life. She was the inspiration and reason for him waking up each morning as if he had a purpose again.

"This is amazing," he said. "Thank you."

"You like it?" She bounced a little on her toes as if trying to see the painting over his shoulder.

"It's going next to the others on the wall." He'd had to take down the paintings from an artist he'd never met and replace it with Joy's meaningful art. Later, he'd move Joy's photos to his bedroom when he resumed sleeping there—if and whenever that might be.

"Have you dreamed more about the tunnel?"

He'd told her about the tunnel nightmares after her previous painting.

"I think the light in your picture keeps the dark tunnel away."

She then rubbed her hands. "Would you like to eat lunch before we release the butterflies?"

He wasn't hungry, not with her around anyway. "Butterflies first."

She carried her basket to the kitchen counter while he spread out his painting on the sunroom table.

Joy joined him. "Can we take the butterflies in the front, by the flower gardens?"

He didn't care. "Sounds good to me."

She handed him one jar and carried the other. Three butterflies fluttered in each of the mason jars with holes poked in the lids.

When she asked if he needed his cane, he told her he was fine as long as they walked slowly. His feet weren't as swollen as they'd been in December now that he was taking medicine.

Outside, he breathed in fresh air that smelled like rain, like Joy. When they opened the jars to free the butterflies, he struggled to watch the colorful butterflies. He ended up dividing his attention between Joy's vibrant smile and the butterflies that flopped and landed over the yellow and purple tulips.

"Tell me this is one of the best days ever." The corners of her eyes and mouth crinkled, and as he gazed at the beauty and genuineness in her eyes, his answer was automatic.

"Yes. It is." His gaze followed hers to the two butterflies flying toward the gazebo. "Butterflies are surely beautiful."

"How they represent change and life is captivating." She gave him a sideways glance, and her eyes sparkled in the midafternoon sunshine. "I like how their short life serves to remind us that life is short."

His breath caught when he held her gaze before he averted his attention to the garden.

"Is it okay if we have our lunch out here today?"

He wanted to stay outside. So he dipped his head. "I would love that."

Between the flower gardens, Joy spread out a picnic blanket on a stretch of grass. She'd brought her own blanket as if she'd planned to have a picnic.

Eric flopped on his stomach on the sun-warmed yellow blanket. After he'd downed a few grapes and cauliflower florets, his stomach felt full, and he was uncomfortable sitting. Wanting to know about her childhood, he plucked a blade of grass and rubbed the green life between his fingers, enjoying the stain it left behind as he asked about her.

She switched onto her stomach too, kicking her feet up behind her as she braced her chin on her hand. "I didn't have the four seasons like you do here, but I always loved to play in the rain." She smiled as if transported back in time. "We had to put buckets out for water, so that was a good excuse for me to get wet...."

She chatted, moving her hands as she described the long walks they took to fetch water from the well and the midnight dinners they ate. Her family always stayed up late. She shared memories of the orphanage her dad had started.

With her smile so infectious, Eric's cheeks lifted into a grin when she talked about the mud fights she had with her brothers.

"If you think that was bad..." Her shoulders shook, and she threw her head back laughing. When she settled down, she flipped onto her side, propping herself up on one elbow facing him. "Once we brought a poisonous snake into the house as a pet!"

Whoa. "I'm glad you figured it out and took it back before anyone got hurt."

She shook her head, her free hand covering her mouth, and whispered, "The snake vanished, and we *never* found it." Her nose wrinkled. "Don't ever tell my mom when you meet her someday."

*When*, not *if*. Did she intend for him to meet her mom someday? The statement did something to his insides.

She was one happy woman, and he told her. "Your name suits you."

"Oh." Her round lips parted, and she shifted to sit up, tucking hair behind her ears in a sweetly uncomfortable gesture. "I didn't know that."

Thankfully having her sitting made it easier for him not to look at her. "Musana." Since his African friends usually had names representing something, he'd wanted to ask the moment she'd told him hers. "What does it mean?"

"Sunshine." Sitting cross-legged now, she rocked her knees a little like the butterflies flapping their wings. "It was my dad's idea. My brothers have different last names too."

Eric learned they didn't use family names for their last names. Her parents did a great job choosing their daughter's name. She was the joyful ray of sunshine in his brooding cloudy heart.

"I wanted to ask you something." Her soft voice pulled him out of his thoughts.

"What's that?"

She reached for a handful of grapes from the bowl and tossed one in her mouth, then spoke over a mouthful.

With her words muffled, Eric stifled a chuckle. Memories of the day she'd stayed at The Peak and spiked his smoothie with meds came rushing back. How she'd acted was strange.

"Don't tell me you drugged my water." No reason not to tease, even though he doubted she would do anything of the sort. Not after how distraught and guilty she'd felt that day.

Joy swallowed and shook her head, wafting her sweet fragrance in the air. "Will you be my date at a wedding?"

It was Eric's turn to swallow. He gulped hard. Good thing he hadn't had a grape in his mouth, or he might have choked. He was as far from boyfriend material as could be. Didn't she notice the marks on his face? Even though the skin rash cleared, remnants—scars, in fact—remained and would likely always mar him.

"Why?"

"My friend is getting married."

"Your roommate?"

She looked surprised that he remembered. "Yes. I'm the maid of honor."

"It's good that your friend is getting married. Congratulations." He wasn't sure why she needed a date though. He dipped his head, encouraging her to go on.

"Ruby keeps fixing me up with all her fiancé's friends, and this time it's her future brother-in-law." She talked about the best man, who would be hard to ignore during the weekend at the ranch. "He seems like a nice person, but I don't want to complicate my job as maid of honor."

She was too stunning not to have a boyfriend. They'd not discussed her love life, but surely...

"You could ask Sabastian." He was more presentable than Eric. "Or you could contact a dating service."

"I want you." Her voice was soft.

At her soft words, his chin jerked up, and all the air rushed from his lungs. She'd ducked her head and was tucking hair behind her ears again—a fruitless nervous gesture. She raised her head and met his gaze, and the breath whooshed from his lungs again.

She was serious, he realized when her deep eyes pinned him with intensity.

"I'm not boyfriend material, you see." Had she forgotten his hallucination episodes? He didn't go anywhere except for the few drives she'd made him take. "Why me?"

"Because..." She rolled her eyes and then picked another grape from the bowl. "I enjoy your company. You're single and"—she shrugged, then tossed the grape in her mouth and, as she spoke over it this time, he could hear her words—"good-looking."

Eric rubbed at his chin, letting her sincerity soak in. She thought he was good-looking. Nothing would make him move, not even the annoying fly zipping by his face. "What if I'm sick that day?" he asked, not meeting her sweet gaze—too terrified to, intimidated by the way she already made him feel.

"It's a weekend, actually. We stay over on Friday and Saturday night. Or we can stay on Friday night and return on Saturday if you want."

Even worse if he had to stay for a night. If it weren't for the nightmares, he could consider her request—after all, the thought of her going out with the best man didn't sit well with him either.

"Hmm." What a tough choice for the wrong time in his life.

"The wedding is in roughly four to five weeks, so take your time to think about it."

Through the corner of his eye, he could see her hand reach out and touch a lock of his crazy long hair. "It might not be a bad idea to think about getting a trim too."

He managed a glance at her. "Is that so?"

Her long lashes flicked up, and she bit her lower lip. She was understandably shy, and he found himself unable to look away. Her round cheeks were spotless, no doubt smooth to the touch, and her mouth demanded his attention. But he'd better stop staring because the more he looked at her, the more she was starting to become familiar to him.

EITHER HIS STOMACH or the solid food his body was adapting to woke Eric up the next morning with a runny stomach and nausea. It was hard for him to sit in his usual spots in the house while frequenting the bathroom.

He didn't hide his discomfort from Joy when she showed up, and after he'd puked in a bucket twice, she'd moved his chair closer to the bathroom hallway. She'd also brought her chair and stayed close by. She'd held his hair back and out of his face whenever he threw up.

As if that hadn't been enough, Joy talked to him when he was awake, and whenever he drifted off and reawakened, she was still there drawing in her book.

Or on his palm. He noticed when he woke to an inked palm. He'd felt as if it were a dream of something tickling his palm, but he grinned now at the picture of an eagle and the familiar Bible verse written below it.

"'You will soar high on wings like eagles.'" Lifting his palm closer, he strained his eyes to read the tiny print. "'You will run and not grow weary.'"

Lowering his hand, he eyed her. "Why do you like to write in your hands?"

She lifted her gaze from her sketchbook to meet his before she closed her book and ambled toward him. She squished her face, lifting her clean palms—apparently, one of the few times she had them ink-free. "I don't have anything written in my hands."

If his head hadn't hurt, he'd have rolled his eyes. "You spent more time tattooing *my* hands, I see." He didn't mind it. He'd think about her when he looked at the smudged ink later.

"It's relaxing to write in my hands." She brushed a stray curl from her face. "I thought of that verse for you."

"It's perfect." He wasn't going anywhere soon, so the ink was just fine.

Joy patted his shoulder. "I'm going to get you some tea." She left and returned with his tea.

"This goes to show you I'm not dating material." Eric pulled the lever to take the steaming cup from her.

"I'll not have a date if you don't come."

He had no idea how he was going to feel in several weeks. With his body this weak, simply sitting up still felt strenuous.

The afternoon went fast as she asked about his favorite places to travel.

"Anywhere with a beach." He told her and learned it was her favorite destination trip too. Beaches and tropical destinations reminded her of her home country.

Joy gasped when he told her about his scuba and skydiving adventures. "That's terrifying."

"That's what made it fun."

Shivering, she covered her face. "I hope I'm never put in a situation where I'm forced to use a parachute."

He couldn't stand the thought of her getting stranded if she flew and the airplane had issues that could force passengers to evacuate. "It would be nice to learn out of fun, rather than necessity at least."

She shrugged. "I might consider it if you were my instructor."

He would train to instruct if it meant spending time with her. *Fat chance of that.* "You're lucky I'm confined in this house."

"I think we can change that."

She'd already changed a few things—well, his whole life—but he doubted he'd ever feel well enough for adventurous activities.

It was almost the end of the day, and Eric hadn't thrown up or used the bathroom for two hours. So Joy helped him move back to the sunroom.

Maybe he was on the mend after all. He relaxed on the recliner with his hands tucked under the soft throw while listening to Joy's soothing voice. She'd read poems from the book she'd brought and was now reading a psalm.

As much as he liked to close his eyes, he kept them open to savor her beauty, to study her while, intent on the leather-bound book, she wasn't aware of his scrutiny.

She was such a calming presence and so beautiful she stole his breath.

A commotion sounded in the hallway from the house, and keeping a finger on her place in the book, Joy peered toward the booming male voices. "Looks like you have company."

As feet shuffled and Eric glanced toward the living room, something tightened over his heart. His friends had come here against his will.

"Eric, darling." Mom's shoes clicked against the tile while four men followed her. "You've got visitors."

# CHAPTER 14

"What are you doing here?" Eric eyed Brady in particular. Why had he flown thousands of miles? "Shouldn't you be in Uganda?"

"I'm where I'm supposed to be." Brady gave Eric's shoulder a gentle punch, then motioned to the rest of the guys. "I met up with these guys so we could give you a surprise visit."

Joy was shaking hands with Eric's other friends as Mom gave introductions. "Bryce Solace, an investor and friend to the family."

Bryce, the only one in the group not married, was looking well. Too well with his muscular build and flawless skin. Eric ground his teeth, the taste of bile still strong in his throat as he wished Bryce hadn't come.

Mom kept smiling as Bryce clasped Joy's hand longer than necessary, paying Joy too much attention. "Ryan Harper and Lucas Matthews, both doctors in Denver."

Eric let out his pent-up breath when Joy moved on to shaking their hands, but Bryce was still studying her appreciatively. Not that Eric could blame the guy.

"Lucas moved to Virginia," Brady said, introducing himself to Joy.

"Brady lives in Uganda," Eric added, knowing Joy might strike up an easier conversation with Brady and hoping the happily married man would monopolize her attention.

"What part of Uganda do you live in? Why did you move there?" Good. Joy was hounding Brady while the rest of the guys, Bryce included, surrounded Eric.

"How did you all meet up to plan this ambush?"

"We figured if we showed up together"—Lucas moved his hand between the guys around him—"You'd be less likely to kick us out."

Eric stared at the trio. Ryan and Lucas, especially, were the last people he'd expect to come to his hometown. Eric saw them once a year at the Christmas fundraiser for the Colorado hospital he sponsored.

"You're the reason I have a job." Ryan lifted his hand, his blue eyes sparkling. "I want to make sure I still have work."

Some of the tension left his muscles as Eric appreciated their light tones, rather than pity. "What makes you think I'm not going to kick you out?"

Bryce crossed his arms over his chest. "Logan said you would for sure."

Eric's brother Logan was Bryce's best friend. Being an only child, Bryce spent a lot of time with Eric's family.

"Doesn't seem Logan's warning kept you away." Eric pulled the throw over his shoulder.

"I'm here to run some investment ideas by you."

Eric had started in investments before he ventured into his own financial company. He'd also trained Bryce the ins and outs of stock trading.

So, investments he could talk about—really, anything that didn't involve his health.

"Before I go," Joy's soft voice interrupted, "can I get you anything?"

"We're fine." The guys spoke collectively. "It was nice to meet you."

To Eric, she smiled warmly, making his stomach bubble. "Stay out of any mischief."

"That should be easy," he said, already missing her. Monday was too long before he could see her again. He could only hope his disappointment didn't show. "You're taking all the mischief with you."

He then looked at his palm where she'd left a mark for him to think of her while they were apart.

"What's with the ink in your hands?"

At Brady's voice, Eric slid his palm back under the throw. After being alone so long, he'd almost forgotten he had company. He swallowed, trying to squelch any fondness in his voice. "Joy wrote a verse when I was sleeping."

Brady gave a slow nod, prying for information. "She's nice." He then sank into the armchair Joy had been sitting in. "How long have you known her?"

Like Ryan's, Brady's eyes were blue, only now laced with curiosity.

"A few months."

"Caregivers are troopers." Lucas lowered himself to the tile while Ryan sat on the floor not far from Lucas.

Bryce claimed a couch cushion and outstretched his arms, making himself comfortable like he'd almost done with Joy. "While we're here, we're going to execute a plan on where we're going this weekend."

"If you haven't noticed, I look like a dying man." Wait a minute. He blinked as Bryce's words registered—*this weekend*. "How long are you guys staying?"

"My flight to Uganda leaves on Tuesday." Brady crossed an ankle over his other knee.

"We leave Monday morning."

"You may want to let Sabastian know if you plan on eating—"

"Regina is on it," Bryce said with a knowing look.

Yep, Mom had been in on this plan.

The moment his friends insisted on camping out on the sunroom floor and slept in sleeping bags right there close to him, any hope of solace for this weekend flew away like those butterflies.

"Guys, we have guest rooms, remember?" Eric reminded them on Saturday morning when Ryan complained about his back hurting.

"We're here for a short time," Brady said. "We might as well utilize every minute together."

Not wanting to focus all his friends' attention on him, Eric asked about work.

Lucas and Ryan spoke about their days in the hospital, Bryce gave an update of business news he'd read from the *Wall Street Journal*, and Brady talked about his charity and then Eric's he was overseeing.

"I've learned so much from managing your organization...." Wow, Brady went on to explain how funds had doubled from donors after word had gotten out about Eric's illness. "There's your annual speech in Ukraine in December. I'm confident you'll be well enough to go in person."

No sense in reminding his friend how uncertain Eric's future was.

They dragged him outside on Saturday afternoon, and he watched them play tennis and basketball. Saturday night after dinner, they settled into the same positions in the sunroom again and wanted more health updates, so Eric detailed what he was dealing with and which medicine he was taking.

"I knew it was Lyme disease." Ryan slapped his knee.

Eric twisted his lips. It seemed one negative test should've been enough. At the time, he'd been too discouraged to get poked and prodded at the hospital. That was around when he'd chosen to move back to his childhood home, hoping some rest would ease his discomfort. "I should've listened to your advice to get tested again."

"I'd steer clear of any depression meds," Lucas added. "You don't look like you're depressed."

Eric told them about his nightmares.

"Has it crossed your mind that your God could be punishing you?" Bryce, never interested in God before, was suddenly giving his analysis.

"Of course, God isn't punishing him." Brady furrowed his brows, giving Bryce a death glare. "Why would you even say that?"

Bryce shrugged. "Eric probably got on God's wrong side. That's why I stay clear of the Man upstairs." Bryce continued pointing out all the reasons he'd never want a relationship with God. "You're the godliest person I know, yet you're being crushed from every angle."

Eric had done his best to live for God, help the needy, pray without ceasing, and seek after God through thick and thin. But this blow had hit hard.

Maybe Bryce was right. Maybe he'd done something wrong. "I wish I knew what I did."

"God doesn't operate on paybacks." Brady's drawn brows were visible under the light. "Your love for your family and friends, your generosity to those in need, your faith and confidence in God were the reasons many people believe in God." Brady let out a huff and eyed Bryce, who was perched on the floor, hands dangling over his knees.

Then Brady lowered his voice, his gaze moving to Joy's tunnel painting on the wall. "Because of Eric, I became like that boy there, reaching for the Light. If it weren't for him, I'd still be far from God, trapped in the dark tunnel that boy emerged from."

Brady pressed his lips into a thin line. "I'm not going to tolerate the idea that God is punishing someone who has selflessly served Him."

Waving both hands, Bryce edged backward, fake cringing. "Hey, man, don't shoot the messenger. I'm just pointing out facts."

"Please stop." Lucas lifted his hand in Bryce's direction. He wasn't too far from him on the floor. "We get your opinion already."

At last, Bryce did as asked and kept the rest of his thoughts to himself.

Tension wasn't what Eric had expected from his company, but everything about the visit was a surprise—a bonus surprise on how the three had connected with Bryce in the first place.

A silence passed with everyone lost in thought until Ryan cleared his throat.

"My kids lost their parents in a car crash." Ryan spoke about his niece and three nephews he'd adopted. "They were innocent and hadn't done anything wrong." He reached over and clamped a hand on Bryce's shoulder. "I get your perspective. I was there, feeling the same thing, angry that God would do that—until I understood a glimpse of His grace."

"My wife, Brit"—Lucas dangled his hands over his knees where he sat on the floor—"lost both her parents while she was still a student. But God has been there for her."

"The point is, we all have struggles in this life," Brady added. "God never promised smooth sailing but—"

"A safe landing." Eric finished the familiar words he'd used to encourage so many people who had doubts in God. Including Brady when he'd called and asked how Eric was holding up after his family died.

Brady gave a slow shake of his head. "Whatever God is doing has nothing to do with your sins."

"Life's a journey." Ryan stretched out his legs and crossed them at the ankles.

"God's got your back." Lucas let out a heavy breath. "Even if you feel like you're on your own right now, He's got you."

Eric's heart felt light as Brady reminded him of Job from the Bible. A righteous man who God allowed to suffer because God knew what Job could handle. Eric was no Job, but if God let a righteous man like Job deal with such tragedies, He wasn't punishing Eric after all.

"You should honestly think about searching yourself to see if you did something wrong." Bryce dampened Eric's hopeful thoughts. "Even with all your good deeds, you're not too perfect."

Bryce always knew how to put Eric in his place. Surely God put Bryce in Eric's life for that sole purpose. A typical skeptic who seemed to know all the arguments against God. "Why else would God be punishing His own?"

As the three men tried to debate their reasons for faith in God with Bryce, Eric partially listened while he considered Bryce's comments.

"If Eric ever recovers from this blow and still clings to this God," Bryce spoke to the guys, "then maybe, just maybe, I might believe there's a God."

*You hear that, God? I'm being put on a pedestal. If not for myself, please strengthen my faith and make me well for Bryce to see You are a God of miracles and wonders—a God who cares more than I ever needed.*

While heavy breathing filled the room that night, Eric stayed awake, whispering conflicting prayers and questions.

He eased himself onto his left side and peered at Bryce in the sleeping bag across the room. Could Bryce be right about God punishing him? With his breathing shallow and his heart thudding, Eric tried to reflect on the verses he remembered from the book of Job, just random paragraphs memorized over years of reading and rereading the Bible from cover to cover.

"Oh God, remove your heavy hand from me and don't terrify me with your awesome presence. Can you at least speak to me? Please tell me what I've done wrong and I'll try to right my wrongs." Why would God keep him alive and hopelessly in agony?

"Why do you turn away from me? Why treat me as your enemy? Is it something I did in my youth? As a young child?" He doubted God would trace his past and punish him.

Confusion was his companion, and despair gripped him tightly. He closed his eyes, stifling a cry so the guys didn't hear him. This was worse than the tunnel nightmares!

He was grateful for Joy's call the next day. Mom buzzed on the house intercom for his call.

Eric left for his bedroom and took the call on the landline from his nightstand.

"How, um, are you feeling?" Joy spoke breathlessly as Eric sank onto his bed. He didn't trust his knees since they felt weaker. What a night it had been!

"The worst is behind me."

She'd taken good care of him, perhaps the reason he felt better already. He gripped the cordless phone close to his ear. The room felt warm. Or maybe it was just him.

"Are you enjoying your visit with your friends?"

*I like your visits more. I wish you were here.* "Yes."

He could hear her rapid breathing through the phone, so he was breathing hard too. He gripped the back of his neck, mashing the tension there. "What did you do today?"

"I went to church earlier, and then came home to rest. Ruby is away visiting her fiancé's family, so I have the apartment to myself and no one to complain if I make a ghastly mess with some project."

He'd never seen her leave anything messy. But then he'd never seen her with her paints—and suddenly he wanted to hear more about her than anything.

"Tell me more." He relaxed as he asked about the details of her service, needing the secondhand message from what her pastor taught and the songs they sang. When she finished, he couldn't let her go. So he asked, "What did you do yesterday?"

"Called my mom, cleaned the apartment, and cooked some meals."

"Here I was thinking my life was boring, but goodness... you spend your Saturdays cleaning?"

She chuckled, and heat flowed through Eric's body at her sweet laugh. "In my defense, I'm still new in town."

"Okay, I'll let you off the hook. For now."

They chatted for a bit longer while she teased him over his reluctance to show her around his hometown.

"I'm sure you wouldn't want an ill man to accompany you anywhere." Even as the words came out, her invitation to her friend's wedding nagged him. She didn't treat him as a patient, wasn't embarrassed by his appearance, and that alone evoked an emotional connection with her.

"I'll let you get back to your company," she said, reeling him from his wandering thoughts. "I just wanted to see how you're feeling since you'd been so sick."

"Good." With his mind suddenly blank, he had no clue what to say—and if he didn't think of something soon, he was going to lose her for the rest of the day. "Glad you called."

"See you soon."

"Okay." He waited for her to hang up, but he could still hear her breathing through the phone.

"I'll hang up now." She stifled a chuckle.

Wow, did that mean he wasn't the only one struggling to end the call?

"You're not hanging up."

Eric broke into laughter, feeling giddy like he was a normal teenager for once. "Okay, bye."

"Bye... for real this time." The line went dead when she hung up.

Eric was on an emotional roller coaster when he rejoined his noisy friends in the living room. Should he be bothered that the rest of the evening and night Joy consumed 80 percent of his mind?

When his friends left Monday morning, Eric was so worn out he turned down physical therapy. "I worked out all weekend."

Plus, he needed to sleep all morning to be refreshed enough to keep up with Joy's cheerfulness that afternoon.

When Mom came by and told him Joy wasn't coming until Thursday, Eric's whole body deflated, and it must have reflected on his face.

"Honey, I thought you'd need to recover from having company all weekend." If Joy hadn't called last night, maybe Mom wouldn't have canceled her visit.

Eric's chest rose as he tried to draw some air back into his lungs. "She could use a break too." She probably needed it with everything she did for everyone.

With no Joy to keep him company, he'd nap and then make arrangements to be her date.

THE MORE ERIC THOUGHT about it, the more he liked the idea of passing as Joy's date. If Joy didn't mind his scars, for one blissful moment, he could let himself forget he was a patient, the sullen useless man who sat in the guesthouse every single day without a plan.

In his bedroom, he rummaged through his drawer for his cell phone. It was no surprise when the thing didn't turn on. He hadn't turned it on since he got home months ago. It probably needed to be charged. So he reached for the cordless landline instead and scrolled for his driver's number.

He answered on the first ring.

"Hello, Terrence."

"Mr. Stone?"

Eric laughed at the man's obvious surprise. "How is your family?"

"Oh man, I'm so happy to hear from you." Terrence wanted to dwell on Eric's recovery so Eric had to keep his conversation brief. He'd see him soon enough. Although Eric's driver and bodyguard, Terrence did more work for Eric than the two main jobs.

"Any chance you can send a barber over tomorrow?"

"Of course."

Sensing questions in the way the man breathed heavily through the phone as if he was holding something back, Eric spoke first to best utilize his time on the call. "I'll need you to drive me somewhere on the twenty-fifth next month."

"Yes, sir! I'm ready to get back to work."

"Don't get too excited. It's just for one day."

"So good to hear from you again."

"Me too."

With the busy life Eric had lived, he'd spent more time with Terrence than anyone else. When Eric returned home, he'd given his driver paid leave until further notice. The man had insisted on following him to Pleasant View, and knowing his wife homeschooled their two kids, Eric suggested Terrence move his family to the cabin Eric rarely used.

With the grooming resolved, he'd have to check with his tailor to get some clothes tailored on short notice. He'd lost too much weight to fit in any of his dress pants and suits.

If God would grant him mercy and keep him from getting sick before or during the weekend, Eric would consider it a win. Joy needed him. No, it was the other way around. Eric needed her.

After his grooming the next day, Eric felt as if he was missing something on his face. When he looked in the mirror, his scars were more visible with his beard gone. He felt almost... naked as he touched his cool chin.

When he joined his family for dinner, Mom eyed him oddly. "Honey, you look handsome."

"I always look handsome," he quipped, even though he hadn't felt handsome in a long time—probably never would again.

"What's the occasion?" Dad tipped his head to one side, curiosity etched in his graying brows.

"Can a man look nice for no occasion?"

"Of course, he can. I look nice all the time." Dad tugged at his T-shirt and grinned at his wife. "Don't I, Gina?"

"Joy has invited me to a wedding." Eric might as well let them know since it was an overnight trip.

Mom's lips curled into a smile. "Has she now?"

Eric felt like a schoolboy, but it wasn't a real date. "I'm a buffer to keep away the unwanted guy."

He wasn't confident about faking a relationship. Maybe he'd once been capable of nearly anything, and business-wise, investments and mergers could be a lot like faking a relationship. But now? He probably couldn't pull anything off while he had his own baggage.

Still, anticipation coursed through him. He was going somewhere and doing something different.

When Joy showed up on Thursday, Eric was in the kitchen fixing himself a cup of tea.

She didn't hide her surprise, letting her jaw drop as she looked him up and down. "You got a haircut?"

Was that admiration? Sure looked like it. Heat tingled up his neck and seared his ears, leaving him blushing like a schoolboy with a crush just because she liked his haircut.

He dropped the tea bag in the steaming mug of hot water and leaned against the counter, then touched his jaw. "I thought I'd clean up a little. Needed to look more like a boyfriend than a man you snatched from the street."

Her smile was shy, and she was fiddling with her curls again, brushing them back from her face. "You look... handsome."

Finding himself standing up straighter, he blossomed under her praise and gripped the back of his neck. Man, it was burning. "Glad you approve."

Her eyes lit up, and her smile widened. "So you'll do it?"

"Unless you changed your mind."

"I was hoping you would say yes."

His chest puffed, and when she ate up the space between them and threw her arms around him, Eric felt like he was floating. The embrace ended before he could wrap his arms around her, but she lingered long enough for him to take a whiff of her intoxicating scent.

Eric composed himself fast when he retreated for his tea and lifted the tea bag. "I'll be your date on one condition, though."

"Yes?" She beamed at him.

"I will pick you up."

Her nose crinkled, and her lips flattened together as if she were trying to register Eric's words. "Okay."

She was probably wondering why he hadn't offered to drive her before, yet she didn't ask. She must trust him, or she was a naturally trusting person.

He handed her the cup made from one of the teas she'd brought and left in the guesthouse kitchen cupboards. "Would you like some turmeric tea?"

"I'll make my own."

"I got it."

"Thank you."

A zap zinged through his arm when their hands brushed. He needed all the distraction he could get. The least he could do was microwave another cup of tea.

# CHAPTER 15

In the final week before the wedding, it was a Tuesday afternoon when Joy sat with Ruby at their kitchen table.

"Don't you think this is backward?" Crinkling her pert nose, Ruby stuffed a king-sized chocolate bar into the gift bag. "I should be the one getting presents, not giving presents."

Joy had come up with the idea to surprise Ruby's out-of-town guests with a little something. "Imagine how your guests will feel when they arrive at the hotel and have a package of wedding excitement waiting for them."

Rolling her eyes, Ruby gathered up a handful of bags and stood to take them to the dark marble counter. "I guess, since they're coming from out of town, it's okay."

Joy reached for another empty bag from the pile in the center of the table. "On the bright side, you're getting all this attention from everyone that weekend."

The two continued to stuff the bags as they discussed what they needed to do before Friday.

With the final week of wedding prep ahead, Eric had suggested Joy take time off from The Peak. Despite her initial disappointment, she was now grateful since she needed time to make her follow-up calls to vendors.

"The coordinator said we can take some of our things to the ranch tomorrow."

"Yes!" Ruby gave a triumphant fist pump. "Then we won't have to lug a bunch of items on Friday."

When the doorbell rang, Ruby shoved aside her half-finished gift bag and dashed out of the kitchen. "That must be our food."

Continuing with her task, Joy ignored Ruby's muffled conversation with the food delivery person since she'd already paid for the food and tip when she'd ordered online.

"Oh my world!" Ruby shouted, then came scuffling closer. "This is for you, Joy."

Joy blinked, dropping the trinket in her hand as she gasped at the enormous gift basket blocking her friend's face. The chair scraped the tile when Joy stood.

"Nate again?" How clear was she going to have to get?

"I doubt it's Nate." Ruby set the basket on the counter and yanked the card from the ribbon tying the yellow-tinted cellophane into place.

"Um, you said that was for me." Joy stole the note from her friend and ripped it open, and her hands shook as she registered who sent it.

> Thank you for everything!
> Hope you can get a new sweater to replace the one I puked on.
> Your wedding date,
> Eric

Squeezed by the memory and grateful that Eric was happier nowadays, she let her finger trace the lines of his signature.

Ruby snatched the card.

"Wow. Looks like you make this man happy or vice versa." Ruby then studied the clear wrap protecting the basket. "Any man you approve of as your weekend date has to be special."

"He's special." Joy nearly whispered the words, the depth of their meaning catching in her throat as she already imagined the lake and trails through the ranch where she'd be walking with him.

Ruby untied the ribbon, taking over the way she did with almost everything. "Come on. Let's see what he sent."

Joy's heart was racing as if Eric himself had delivered the basket.

"I've never seen so many gift cards and chocolates." Ruby held a boutique gift card in one hand and an art supply card in the other. More Visa cards lay nestled between chocolates and boxed teas and decadent snacks.

"That's the fancy boutique on Main." Ruby clutched the card. "What did you say Eric used to do again?"

Joy still had no idea what he used to do, besides his mention of being in the financial industry. Since they had so many things to talk about, it hadn't crossed her mind to ask what financial industry he'd worked in. "I think an accountant or something like that."

His career was an irrelevant topic, anyway.

IT WAS JOY'S JOB TO make sure nothing stressed Ruby before the wedding, and that kept Joy busy the rest of the week. In the mornings, she worked at Tao's and took the triplets to school. In the afternoons, she made calls to vendors. She'd had to schedule another mani-pedi artist since the one she'd booked three months ago couldn't afford the rent for the building and decided to move to another city.

Joy had checked in with the bridesmaids to see if they had any last-minute questions, and she'd helped Ruby pack for the weekend. Thankfully, Ruby's honeymoon was a few days after the wedding. So Joy would help her friend pack for the trip next week instead of squeezing in another job this week.

When Friday rolled in, she was ready for a break and looking forward to seeing Eric.

As she waited for his arrival, she repacked her luggage. It was only two nights, one if Eric decided to leave once the wedding was over. But she still packed carefully and added extra clothes.

She glanced back in the closet. The orange frill-neck top with its flowered print called to her. Silk and long-sleeved, it was perfect for the mild spring weather. She then rummaged through her chest of drawers for a pair of jeans. That would be her outfit for tomorrow's activities.

She stood aside, fanned herself as she stared at her open luggage, then the list written in her palm.

First aid kit—check.

Underwear—check.

She continued to the bottom of her list, then rubbed at the ink. Whew! She had everything ready to go.

Before getting dressed, she checked her phone for the time—three fifteen. Eric should be arriving in ten minutes or less.

Ruby had left three hours ago with her fiancé. They'd wanted to stop for horseback riding on their way to the wedding venue.

Joy flung her V-neck top over her head and tucked it into yellow denims. Just as she scanned her shoe rack, the doorbell rang.

A thrill rushed through her as she ran for the door and swung it open.

Even if she was expecting Eric, her breath caught at the sight of him. It seemed like she hadn't gotten a better look at him since he'd shaved. His jaw was more defined than it had appeared while hidden in scruff for all those months.

"You look lovely." Eric's eyes danced as he looked down and then up at her.

Joy swallowed. Her heart was pounding beneath her ribs. What was she wearing? She couldn't even remember and had to look down.

"Am I too early?" he asked. His eyes were even brighter today.

*Thank You, Lord, that he's feeling better.*

"Um..." Joy nodded, then shook her head, suddenly unable to put two words together, not with him dressed so handsome in an olive-green dress sweater that brought out the green flecks in his hazel eyes.

"Can I come in?" Amusement lifted the corners of his mouth.

Good grief, where were her manners?

"Of course." She slapped her forehead, then shifted her feet to step aside. As soon as he walked in, she closed the door.

"Nice place," Eric said, once he was in the center of the main room, his hands thrust in his jean pockets.

"It's small." Compared to his parents' mansion.

"It's cozy." He gazed at the paintings taking up the space on the wall. "Looks like a gallery. I like it."

Joy walked closer, needing to explain why she was obsessed with painting. The spicy fragrance of his conditioner lingered in the air, and all else vanished from her thoughts. Um, what were they talking about? Her art.

"Ruby thinks it's like a gallery too."

Eric was quiet, soaking in the paintings before lifting his hand to point up. "I like the flitting birds." He then pointed to the lion limping out of its cage. "Can you draw me something like this?"

"Which one?"

"The lion." He rubbed at his chin, his gaze wandering to the bald eagle escaping a loose chain. "All of them when you have time. I'll pay you."

"You can take all of them if you want to." She only hung onto them because she kept painting and had no idea what to do with what was left after she gave some of them away.

She usually gave away the small canvases. Who would want a giant painting of some art that didn't make sense?

"How long does it take you to create something like that?"

She shrugged, surprised he was making a big deal about her paintings. "If I focus, I can finish it in a day."

Not wanting to talk much about her art, she told him, again, that he could take whatever he wanted. "I should pay you to take them off my hands."

"Your work belongs in a gallery."

At the awe carried in his voice, her cheeks heated. Unsure of how to handle the praise, she asked if she could get him something to drink, but her voice came out weak. Thankfully, Eric didn't seem to notice when he responded.

"Like your unique tea?"

"If you'd like to."

"I'm good, thanks."

At least she'd composed herself and managed to usher him to the black faux leather couch. "I'm just going to get my shoes and luggage."

"Your art should keep me occupied."

When she returned to the room, Eric didn't seem to hear her footsteps. His eyes were strained, and the corners of his lips curled as he stared at the open book in his hands.

Joy had left her sketchbook open on the coffee table last night. She'd started sketching out Eric's face, but the oven timer had gone off for the muffins she'd been baking.

The paper rustled when he flipped to the next page. *Oh no.* He was flipping it forward as if he'd already seen all the drawings.

Cringing, she cleared her throat to announce her presence. "Ready to go?"

"I am." He flipped back to the sketch of his face, the way she'd left the book before, and set it back on the table.

As they moved toward the door, his hand brushed against hers when he reached for her luggage. "I've got this."

"You're..." She stopped herself from reminding him of the status of his illness. Not wanting to make him feel inadequate, she said instead, "My guest."

"Your date," he corrected as he swung open the door and held it open for her to go first. Then he asked if she needed to lock the door.

"It has an automatic lock." She folded the chain around her clutch handbag, and the door clicked when he closed it.

*What a gentleman!*

With no elevator to her apartment, she was grateful they were on the second floor since Eric paused now and then while they descended the stairs. The sun warmed their backs as they walked toward the half-empty parking lot.

"Thank you for the chocolate... and the gifts." She hoped it wasn't payment for her volunteering at The Peak.

"You're welcome."

Her lips parted with the complaint that it was way more than she could ever expect, but he spoke first. "There's our ride."

The black limousine took up two spaces of their guest parking. As if on cue, a husky black man jogged toward them and took the luggage.

"Hello, Miss Musana." He smiled as he put out his other hand and she took it. "I'm Terrence."

Eric must have told him about her.

"Call me Joy." She didn't need formalities. "Nice to meet you, Terrence."

"Nice to meet you too."

She was about to ask how he knew Eric, but Terrence started back to the car. Eric's free hand hit her lower back, and her body set off a chain reaction of some sort. His hand felt warmer and stronger than she'd expected. Then Terrence swung open the back door for Eric and Joy to enter.

"Just because I've been down, doesn't mean I can't open a door." Eric spoke with fondness to Terrence.

Either he was their family driver and showed up in the mornings before Joy arrived, or he was a friend of Eric's. With his fancy black suit and tie, perhaps he was a friend who owned the limousine and had offered Eric a ride.

Joy hadn't done an internet search on the Stones because she didn't feel right invading their privacy, especially since Regina had considered asking her to sign an NDA. What if she learned more information than she could keep to herself? Was Eric someone important? A movie star or congressman? She barely watched movies or followed politics to know the faces of famous figures.

"Everything okay?" Eric's gentle voice pulled her back to the present.

"I've never ridden in a limousine before." She fastened her seat belt and settled deeper into the leather seat so soft and comfortable.

"It's not much different from a usual car." Eric buckled his own seat belt. With the empty seat between them, she felt the urge to scoot closer. She was still pleased that he sat with her in the center bench seat rather than the two seats on the side.

The privacy window went up, and Terrence drove them out of the parking lot.

"I didn't give Terrence directions."

"You told me the venue last time. Pleasant Lake Ranch?"

Wow, such a sharp memory for someone who took so much medicine. "You remembered?"

"Try staying in the house all day, and you'll cling to everything you hear."

Eric reached to the shelving area and pulled out a drawer. "Would you like anything to drink?"

Joy scanned the glasses slid into holders and the sink. It looked like a bar area. Instead, the drink options offered lemonade, sodas, and water. She accepted the small bottle of Simply Lemonade Eric offered her.

"Thank you." She twisted open the cap. After taking a couple of sips, she set the bottle in the cupholder by the armrest.

"I saw your drawings." Eric gave her a knowing look.

"I know." Joy popped her fingers, feeling exposed.

"There's more of me in your book than any other drawings."

The back of her neck burned, and she bit her lower lip, staring through the tinted window. The distant horses munching on the lush green pasture should be captured in paint. They made it easy to pretend this conversation was not happening. But it *was* happening. She glanced at Eric, who was staring at her with a softness that made her toes curl in her sandals.

"Why's that?"

He wasn't one to give up easily. Joy glanced at her palm, and the fancy ceiling radiated decent light for her to see her scribbled packing list.

"I've been trying to figure you out."

"And have you figured me out?"

She managed to hold his gaze, though she swallowed a few times since her mouth felt dry.

"I'm hoping to." Perhaps this weekend. And even if it was a fake date, she'd fantasized about him and what their weekend would be like at The Ranch.

"When did you start drawing pictures of me?"

At least he kept his voice gentle, seeming more curious than bothered that she'd drawn him. It didn't stop her from feeling as if she'd stolen something by sketching him without his permission. "The first or second day at The Peak."

That was when, right? She couldn't remember clearly.

"You missed adding the rash to my face."

She gave her eyes a soft roll, struggling to maintain eye contact.

"The rash doesn't define who you are." Whenever she pictured him, the skin rash never came to mind. She shifted and brushed at his fingers. "You barely have the rash left."

And his illness would heal. He was better already.

His eyes locked with hers before he said, "You haven't figured me out because you already know me. More than you think." He then reached out and took her hand, stared at her palm. When his fingertips brushed the center of her palm, her heart lurched, missed a beat, and then started to thump wildly.

"When did you start this terrible habit of writing in your hands?"

"When I was little." It had to do with boredom, stress, or just the art skills. "It's been too long to remember."

"You're a natural artist. You just can't help it whenever you have a pen or paints."

There was truth in that, perhaps.

"About this fake date." He released her hand, and she longed for his hold already. "What are my expectations this weekend?"

Expectations... Joy needed to reach for her lemonade from the console. What was a date like? She hadn't been on one for a while. She didn't have to prove to Ruby that she was in love with Eric, but if Nate still showed interest in her, he'd need proof. "We'll play it by ear."

# CHAPTER 16

The 250-acre ranch had potential, based on what Eric had seen throughout the evening. Tucked twenty miles outside Pleasant View, the peaceful location showcased Colorado's natural beauty, and spring brought the land to life, scattering stunning wildflowers throughout the property. The peaceful atmosphere could relax anyone used to the city's bustle, but the rustic building with chipped wood needed some upgrades. So did the clean, but dated bathrooms and their rusty sinks.

Upon their arrival, they'd done barrel racing and random activities involving moving and running. Eric had steered clear of that, but he'd gone on a tractor ride with Joy and the hayride they'd taken with the entire wedding party. They'd returned to their respective rooms to clean up and change for dinner.

While everyone got bunkmates, Joy ensured Eric had his own room in the men's cabin across from the ladies'. Since Eric sent Terrence back to his family for the night, Joy had emphasized he could call her anytime—even in the middle of the night—if he didn't feel well.

If he hadn't been dealing with his health, Pleasant Lake Ranch was the kind of investment he'd normally support. He loved to see small businesses thrive, but unless the old couple did something soon, their business may not last for another five years.

Now seated with fourteen people at the long table, Eric should feel out of place, yet he was anything but. Joy was sitting to his right, her shoulder brushing against him while she laughed at what someone said.

The server passed fluted glasses with liquid that reminded Eric of the amber medicine canisters.

"I'd requested two sparkling ciders." Joy spoke to the server, and from what Eric gathered, the drinks were for toasting the bride- and groom-to-be.

Soon, another server showed up with two glasses, one for him and one for Joy.

"No drinking for you?" the woman on Eric's other side asked.

"You don't want me drinking." He lifted the glass, clinking it with the woman who looked older than his mom. Not that he drank, for more reasons than his well-being.

When he turned to Joy to toast, she had her full attention on him and lifted her glass to clink against his.

"To a perfect evening," he said.

"To a perfect evening."

Joy was the perfect distraction and stunning in her elegant maroon dress with a high-laced neck. The simple gold stud earrings gleamed beneath the lights. Besides her comforting presence and appearance, she made him feel like a normal person.

Whenever someone asked him a question, Joy kept her gaze on him, her hand resting on her chin as if clinging to his every word.

"Joy." The man she'd introduced as Nate leaned closer, and his brown eyes glowed the way they did whenever he spoke to Joy. Eric didn't have to ask to know this was her pursuer. He'd caught Nate's wandering gaze lingering on Joy more than once during the hayride.

Since she'd suggested they play the evening by ear, Eric had draped a protective hand over Joy's shoulder as if he needed to stake his claim.

"We're thinking of dancing all night." Nate lifted his fluted glass with the wine. "Will you and your date join us?"

Something tightened in Eric's stomach when Nate winked at her.

*She's my date!* Eric wanted to shout out, but thankfully, Joy turned toward him.

Something in her gaze caused his breath to catch. The golden flecks in her brown eyes sparkled beneath the light, transfixing him. And then she shifted closer, her small hand sliding up to his shoulder, and he had to remind himself to breathe.

"What do you think, honey?"

With the warmth of her hand seeping through his button-down shirt, Eric couldn't remember what question he was answering. "Um..."

Joy turned to Nate across the table from them. "It's going to be a long day tomorrow."

"We'll dance a little," Eric said when his mind registered Nate's question.

*Am I jealous?* No.

He lifted the glass to his mouth and took a sip then another. He then stared around the room.

The strung lights and white linen draped around each wooden pole gave the interior a fancier look than the exterior. The enchanting wildflowers on each table were a great complement—beauty and rustic. Eric assumed the vacant tables in the room were set up for tomorrow's reception.

Soft music played in the background as chatter continued around the two tables. Waiters passed trays of decadent finger foods between Eric's table and the other table seating about the same amount of people as Eric's.

Eric declined the appetizers each time they presented a platter to him. His nutritionists had approved his return to a normal diet, but the last thing he wanted was a runny stomach. What kind of date would he be?

He liked being surrounded by people who didn't know his background, thank goodness. Or at least he thought they didn't until the groom-to-be pointed it out for what seemed like the hundredth time since Joy had introduced Eric.

"I knew it!" Hudson said, and as all eyes on the table turned to him, he pointed at Eric. "I knew I'd seen you somewhere."

Everyone's focus moved to Eric.

*Please don't tell me that he knows my family, he knows my status.* His heart beat against his ribs. "I probably resemble someone you know." That's what he'd told him earlier.

"You funded the recreation center in Pleasant View."

Whew. At least it was something in his hometown.

Hudson snapped his fingers. "That's where I saw your photo—highlighted in the lobby."

Ugh, they'd put up his photo? Eric hadn't ever gone into the recreation center. He'd thought adding activities to the recreation center would give the low-income families a chance to enjoy amenities that were not overly priced.

"You were also the main speaker at the small businesses' conference in Vail. Two years ago."

He couldn't deny it. The tattletale almost needed an award in journalism as he went on to mention Stone Park, which had been named after his family name in Pleasant View. As Hudson pulled out his phone to share whatever else he knew, the servers returned with salads and placed them in front of each person at the table.

It didn't seem like a spiritual event, and no one offered to pray. So Joy discreetly took his hand and clasped it with her soft ones as she bowed her head. Eric did the same and listened to her whispered prayer through clanking forks.

"I NEED TO GO TO THE bathroom," Joy whispered halfway through their salad. "Will you be okay?"

No. But Eric nodded. He missed the warmth of her closeness the moment she left.

Suddenly cautious around the strangers, he found himself holding his breath. Was Hudson going to blurt out more about him? Maybe not. He was feeding his fiancée, his eyes glowing with affection. Thank goodness.

"So, Eric..." Nate set his fork on his salad plate and rubbed his hands together. "How long have you and Joy been together?"

"A few weeks." The vague enough response, not too specific to corner him, should pass.

"What do you do again?"

Perhaps due to his long long-term self-isolation, Eric seemed to have lost his social skills. He could easily see why Joy was avoiding the guy. He was pushy, like the groom. Come to think of it, he was the groom's brother.

The fire alarm went off, and the disc jockey shouted, "Fire!"

"He's joking!" someone at the table said.

Eric peered at the double doors where servers were running out in a frenzy.

Beyond the glass, smoke engulfed the room.

"Fire!" Someone shouted, and while the room erupted in panic, Eric's heart rate sped as he stood. Joy!

He ran as fast as he could toward the hallway where the bathrooms were.

If the women's bathroom was like the men's, there was only one stall.

Someone inside the room was pounding on the women's closed bathroom door.

"Joy!" Eric's breathing quickened.

"The door is stuck." Her voice was strained. "I can't open it."

With everything rusty, no wonder the doors couldn't open. Eric gave it a shove, but the tall door wouldn't budge. If only it had space below, she could at least crawl her way out, but not this door.

As adrenaline surged through him, Eric spun around in search of anything he could use to hit the door open.

"I'm going to get you out." Even if he died in the process.

Now how was he going to get her out? He wasn't as strong as he used to be, or he could knock the door down. There was another door next to the men's bathroom, likely a supply closet.

The broom and vacuum cleaner wouldn't do. *Oh Lord, please don't take Joy away from me.* He scanned the wooden shelving, and his focus narrowed on one of the few tools strewn on the shelves. A sledgehammer?

It was much heavier than he expected, and as he panted his way back with it, he was blurred by all things going wrong with his mission. His feet felt heavy with each step forward. He was wheezing and dizzy.

The smell of smoke engulfed his nostrils. The flames... The blood drained from his face, and a heap of dizzying images fluttered through his mind. Images of his kids struggling and trapped in the house, his in-laws. "This is a dream," he said, struggling when flames engulfed his surroundings.

Joy! He ran through the fire, heat burning him, as he fixated on the burning door.

"Step back. I'm going to hit the door."

"Okay." Joy's voice was panicked.

Eric groaned as he lifted the heavy hammer, swinging it once, and the door fell. Wait—was it him that fell or the door? His cheek hurt, and his head pressed against some sudden coolness.

"Eric!"

Joy's voice was faint, and he could hear distant sirens blaring.

Oh no! Were the sirens rushing Joy to the hospital?

"Please, Eric, stay with me."

Darkness blanketed the fire, and his mind went blank.

"JOY!" WAS SHE ALL RIGHT? Eric eased open his eyes.

"I'm okay."

The tension seeped from his shoulders at the sound of her sweet voice.

"I'm here, Eric." Someone squeezed his hand. The softness was familiar, Joy's.

He opened his eyes from his trance, relieved to see her radiant face. Then he winced at the brightness of the light. Where was he? He took in the narrow space and frowned when a man in a navy uniform knelt beside Joy. A stethoscope hung around his neck as his thick fingers pressed Eric's pulse.

Eric's lips twisted when his eyes roamed back to Joy.

She smiled fondly. "We're in the back of an ambulance. The firefighter wanted to see if you're okay."

As long as Joy was unharmed, he was more than okay. "Like I said, things like this happen to me." He meant the hallucinations. Apparently, that's what had happened since he wasn't burned up in the fire.

"Your blood pressure is normal." The man touched Eric's head. "Do you have a headache?"

"Story of my life."

"I have his medicine." Joy told the fireman, who finally took his hand off Eric.

"You need to take it easy for the rest of the night."

He had a vague memory of people evacuating the building.

"Did you put out the fire?" Why was he focused on Eric instead of, well, the burning building?

"Steam from the dishwasher and something burning triggered the smoke detectors." The fireman gripped the flat bed to stand.

Eric let out a breath and pulled up to sit. He needed to get out of the tiny bed.

"I'm glad you didn't rush me to the hospital," he said to the man.

"Your girlfriend told me not to drive this ambulance away." The man opened the first aid box and closed it.

*Your girlfriend.* That had a good ring to it. Eric was Joy's boyfriend for the weekend after all. He winked at Joy, who squished her face. She was so adorable. "I'm ready to return to the festivities."

She gave a slow nod and handed him the button-down shirt he'd had on before the debacle.

"You don't think I look presentable?" He tried for a joke as he pinched his white undershirt, holding it out for her inspection.

"You look perfect, but it might be a bit cold out there."

Outside of the ambulance, the building's security lights lit the expansive compound—making it easy to see the people hovering by the door. Joy, having climbed from the ambulance alongside him, waved at them and cupped her mouth, then shouted, "He's okay."

To emphasize Joy's point, Eric waved at the group, and they waved back before going back into the building.

"Such great excitement for the wedding eve!" The DJ's voice boomed through the microphone, enough to be heard outside.

"Would you like me to call Terrence?" Joy asked.

Eric reached for her hand. "You of little faith." He swung both their hands. He needed to sit, but he forced himself to trudge further. "You're not getting rid of me until the wedding is over." Unless something major interfered.

She stopped walking and eyed him. "How's your head?"

"Not too bad." He winced at the throbbing pain.

"I'll get your medicine." She then suggested they hang out at the main cabin.

"I promised you a dance tonight."

"There's tomorrow."

Since she didn't look disappointed missing tonight's dance, he'd best postpone the dancing to tomorrow. After seeing him safely to the welcome center, she left to fetch his medicine and returned minutes later.

# CHAPTER 17

"I warned you." Eric shifted his foot on the love seat he shared with Joy, a whisper apart. "I'm not dating material."

"You didn't tell the cooks to burn their food or their dishes to trigger the fire alarm." Joy bent slightly toward the metal fire stove and lifted her fingers close to it.

"Thank you for coming after me." She leaned back and turned to look at him, her face serious. "If the fire was real"—she swallowed—"I could've been stuck."

"You scared me." He couldn't handle another loss. "When everyone started running, I didn't know..."

His family was gone, and if he were to lose Joy too... His chest tightened. The ache bloomed until it pressed against his lungs, making his breaths quick and shallow. He kept his gaze on the metal stove, not daring to look at Joy for fear she'd see his every thought.

"But you came after me." Gratitude whispered through her words. "Did your family die in a fire?"

*How did she know?*

As if his question reflected through his face, she continued. "Your dream about the fire in the tunnel, the fire incident you had at the house, and then today..."

Emotion tightened his throat until he couldn't speak. He nodded instead.

"Oh, Eric!" Joy touched his shoulder. "I'm so sorry." Her voice trembled as she repeated the same word a few times.

Then she closed her eyes and breathed out as though exhaling a lungful of smoke. "You came after me. Even when you're scared of fire."

170

He'd do that for anyone but somehow, losing Joy... He shivered, shaking off the crippling images that threatened to skim through his mind.

"How many kids?"

He struggled to speak, wanting to be back in the comfort of the guesthouse, left to his thoughts. But he wasn't home, and he wasn't alone. "Ten."

"Ten kids and your wife died in the fire?" Her hand on his shoulder seemed to tighten on reflex, the grip almost painful.

"The kids... and my in-laws." He and Josie had gone to the Bahamas for their anniversary. "My wife died later." Josie never was the same after their kids died. "She went driving one night and slammed into the bridge." Either she'd done it on purpose, or she'd been out of her mind. "She never drank, but the officers said she'd been drunk while driving."

He shouldn't have let Josie go when she said she needed time alone a week after their kids died.

Eric's entire body shuddered, the throb in his head intensifying, and he eased away from Joy's touch and rubbed at his temples. He could've done something. He shouldn't have suggested they celebrate their anniversary out of the country. Perhaps then, they wouldn't have had Josie's parents watch the kids that week, and they wouldn't have been in the house the night of the fire.

Chilled, he started shivering. Even the heat from the stove didn't seem to keep him from shaking. Joy shifted, moving closer and taking his hands in hers.

"I wish I could take away your pain," she whispered. When Eric managed to stare at her, agony glowed in her eyes and tears streamed down her cheeks. Joy shuddered before she broke out in a loud sob, crouching as if in pain.

Eric pulled her to his side and draped his arm around her shoulder, rubbing her arm to comfort her. But as tears burned his eyes, he failed to keep himself under control. For several moments, they cried together, and it crossed his mind that it was the first time he'd let himself cry about his family in front of someone.

Eric let out a shudder. With her snuggled into him, he inhaled the sweet scent of her hair, now bothered that he'd caused her to cry. "I'm ruining your evening."

"I'm glad you're here." She sniffled. "Thank you for telling me."

Moments of silence passed as they listened to the crackling fire and humming soda machine.

It didn't make sense that she'd needed a fake date with a messed-up person like him.

"The man you're avoiding couldn't keep his eyes off you the entire time." So, Nate had acted pushy, perhaps fighting to have Joy—After all, what man wouldn't work hard to have her? Nate was also nice-looking and presentable.

Eric, on the other hand, still had scars on his face, and he'd aged like an old man.

"You're sure you don't want to change your mind and go without me?"

"I'm afraid I'm falling for my fake date." As soon as her words registered, she stammered. "I mean I'm happy..." She eased out of his arms and stood. "You know what I mean. I like you and we're..." She slapped her forehead. "Maybe you better get to sleep. It's going to be a long day tomorrow."

And a long night. Because Eric tossed and turned with sweet visions and dreams of him laughing and traveling and kissing Joy as cameras flashed over them. He, too, was falling for his fake date. He'd probably fallen for her before this weekend. And why not? What man in his right mind wouldn't fall in love with her? But what about her? Could *she* possibly fall for *him*?

SOMETHING HAD SHIFTED after he opened up to her and spoke about his family's death. Something he'd dreaded to say aloud since his family died four years ago.

What was it with Joy compelling him to rip off his bandages and expose raw flesh?

As if the fire hadn't interfered with last night's dinner, the wedding day dawned fresh with clear blue skies and mild sunshine—a perfect spring day in late May.

The ceremony was outside in front of the lake, and the bride and groom couldn't keep their eyes off each other during the priest's words of encouragement to the happy couple.

Eric struggled to keep his eyes off the maid of honor, standing next to the bride. Joy's cream-colored dress fit her in all the right places, and she was the most beautiful person in the tent.

He blushed when she glanced at him and caught him staring, and his body felt like he was on fire—a good kind of fire that left him heated but not traumatized. He needed to let Joy be. Seriously, he had enough issues to deal with without giving her false hope. She had a life and dreams to chase while he had no plans for life but death. Anyone he got attached to seemed to die, even when he was a kid before his parents adopted him. At least Regina and Kyle and his siblings had been spared.

Joy needed to live and pursue her dreams. With that in mind, he must keep his feelings for her back at the friendship level.

Throughout dinner, Eric made small talk with other people at the table while avoiding Joy. After dinner when the tables were moved to the side to clear the dance floor, Joy told him she needed to go find the wedding coordinator in regards to where they should store the wedding presents.

When the music started and after the bride and groom danced, Eric sought out an older man with oxygen tubes, who was in no way planning to dance. He asked about the man's relationship with the bride and groom and learned he was a family friend. They talked about horses, hunting, and all sorts of things as Eric managed to stretch out the conversation.

Surely Joy wouldn't ask him to dance while he was busy talking to a man who needed company.

It didn't seem she noticed how busy he was when she returned and greeted the man. "Hello, Theo." She bent in between Eric and Theo, her gentle flowery scent encompassing them. "Is it okay if I steal this gentleman for a quick dance?"

"Of course. Of course." Theo lifted his hands to the dance floor, then adjusted the tube in his nose. "It would be a shame if he turned down a beautiful lady for a dance."

"I'm just... I need a moment." Eric fumbled with his tie. It was suddenly stifling. The coat needed to go, but he kept it on for good measure.

He really needed a grip on his roller-coaster emotions. One dance. He'd promised her a dance yesterday. But a dance would be more intimate with her so close.

"Next song then?" Those doe-brown eyes twinkled beneath the string lights.

Eric didn't trust himself to speak, so he gave her a quick nod.

The moment she stepped on the dance floor, Nate, like a lion stalking its prey, rocked his way toward her and claimed her hand.

Keeping an eye on Joy in the sea of dancing bodies was easy. The sparkly lights gave her hair a glossy golden hue as it bounced above her shoulders whenever she sashayed from side to side.

Something tightened in Eric's stomach when she smiled for Nate. The pain grew worse when the man pulled Joy flush against him, then pushed her back, and spun her around.

Eric had no idea how to describe this feeling, but whatever it was, it compelled him to stand. Forget waiting for another song and forget the friend territory he'd wanted to put her in.

Cocktail dresses and jackets brushed against his fingers as he shoved his way toward Joy before the song ended. He was rarely rude, but Joy was his date, not Nate's. With the loud music, he didn't think Nate could hear him, so Eric tapped the man's shoulder.

"Can I cut in, please?"

Please was the least he could say after interfering with the man's dance, but he didn't intend to take no for an answer. He would stand there until Joy felt sympathy for him. Thankfully, Nate slid his gaze to Joy, who was smiling shyly at Eric. Then the man nodded and stepped away.

Eric took Joy's hand and pulled her in closer to him. The bold action left his body tense, but the song ended and strings to a modern slow song played. He relaxed when she melted into him.

"I'm glad you joined me," she said breathlessly as her soft hands rested on his shoulders.

"I bet Nate is hovering and waiting for me to pass out so he can take my place."

"He was only dancing with me."

Either she was clueless, or she had no interest in Nate at all. Nate had had his hands all over her back and her waist. "He likes you." He didn't mean to sound so gruff.

"He knows I have a boyfriend."

"Does he now?"

Joy nodded, her hair brushing against his chin, teasing his senses. She felt good in his arms as they swayed as if they had all the time in the world.

How could he blame Nate while Eric was now inhaling the exotic scent of her hair? He closed his eyes to savor the feeling and soak in the gentle rhythm of the song. With his heart beating wildly against hers, she had to hear it. But when she sighed and pressed her face into his neck, Eric knew he wasn't alone in this.

As soon as the song faded, he was ready to yank off his coat and breathe in the fresh outside air.

He looked into her eyes and barely held her gaze.

"I'm going to take a break."

"I'll come with you."

No. No. He didn't think he wanted her to come, but when her feet fell in step with his, his heart felt light.

Outside, the sky was darkening, but the twilit hue revealed the tractors in the metal building further away. Joy sat next to him on a bench in front of the wagon.

"This is the first wedding I've been to," she said. He could feel the warmth from her breath against his cheek.

"Really?" He'd thought he was one of the few people who rarely went to weddings.

"Uh-huh."

"We should go to weddings more often."

Did he just say "we," or was it his imagination? It must be the latter. As for weddings, none of his siblings were married, and after losing his family, Eric didn't want anything reminding him of what he'd lost. "I haven't been to many weddings myself."

"I don't believe you," she said. Her dress brushed against his slacks when she swung her feet. "You funded a recreation center. I'm sure you know enough people in town—"

"Pleasant View is expensive." He cut her off, needing to explain why he'd helped the community yet kept his status low. He didn't want to talk about his job or the memories related to what he should be doing. "It's nice to have the original residents stay in town. Makes it easier if they can afford to enjoy some extracurricular activities."

She seemed to understand his reason. Then her lips parted, and her face scrunched with questions. "We drove here in a limousine. Surely, you know a bunch of fancy people who've gotten married."

"The limousine serves everyone in the family." No reason to tell her he'd had it specifically built to suit their family needs. It was convenient for his siblings and his parents to ride together whenever they were all in town. He refocused. "Last wedding I went to was Brady's, three years ago. I was the best man. In Uganda."

Her shoulder brushed against him when she shifted to stare at him. "What part of Uganda? How come you haven't told me you've been there before?"

"I was hesitant to tell you everything about me." Just a little.

"Oh..." Her gorgeous brown eyes widened. "Is now a good time to tell me about your time in Uganda?"

He told her about his connection to the country. "I have a few orphanages I started there."

"I think it's wonderful that you're passionate about orphans too."

"I learned from Kyle and Regina." If they hadn't adopted him, who knows where he would be today. "I couldn't adopt all the kids, but I *could* help more by starting orphanages."

She touched his hand. "You're a good man, Eric Stone."

He felt an oncoming blush under her praise, but helping people was the right thing to do. That's what Joy did every day.

"So are you, Joy Musana."

It would seem like bragging if he talked about the other countries where he'd started nonprofit organizations. So he talked about his friend instead.

"Brady met his wife in Uganda, and now they've started a hospital in the village."

"Oh yes, he told me about the hospital." Joy relayed what Brady had told her during their brief introduction.

"My dad's orphanage was in western Uganda." Her words were clipped as she talked about the orphanage shutting down when he got sick.

"Thank goodness another orphanage was able to take the kids when yours shut down."

When she said the name of the orphanage that took in the kids, Eric was surprised it was one of the orphanages he'd started. He didn't point out that detail to Joy.

Uganda didn't have many orphanages, so it must have been easiest for Joy's family to seek out the main orphanage to take in more kids.

As the air turned crisp when a breeze stirred and Joy wrapped her arms around herself, he eased out of his coat and draped it over her shoulders. "Here."

"Thank you."

He shrugged. It was just a polite gesture.

"I really had a good time." The longing in her eyes reflected in his own. "Thanks for coming with me."

Eric's mind wasn't in the right state. He didn't think when he reached for her hand and lifted it to his mouth, then kissed the back of it.

"You're welcome." He put her hand back to her thigh where it'd been.

His heart soared when their gazes held. She was staring at his mouth. The bench was suddenly burning as if he was sitting on a live wire.

He should look away, but why wasn't he?

Her round lips called for his attention. Eric fought the urge to cup her cheek and brush his lips to hers.

He was feeling things, things that shocked him. How could romantic feelings, once long dead, revive? Not good. He stood, taking her hand in his. "We better go back inside."

He knew one thing for sure. This weekend was more than a fake date.

# CHAPTER 18

"**H**ave you had another dream about the fire since the wedding?"

"No." Eric rubbed his hands on his thighs, his palms sweating as his counselor, Ian, typed something in the tablet he'd braced on his lap.

It had been four days since Ruby's wedding. Not long enough for Eric to declare himself free from nightmares and hallucinations.

"And no horrifying tunnel creatures?"

Seeing Joy every day and letting her dominate in his mind lately had kept depressing dreams and thoughts away. He looked at Joy's painting on the wall. Among all the other paintings from her apartment she'd given him last week.

"Whenever I see a tunnel, I try to envision Joy's painting." He'd stared at the tunnel painting long enough to master each detail in it. "I see the happy boy at its other end." Though the painting only showed the boy's back. "I picture his smile as he anticipates a day full of brand-new possibilities...." Life and hope.

Ian crossed one leg over the other, setting the tablet on the table. "That would be one week without having nightmares in a tunnel?"

"Three weeks." Except for the fire hallucination at the wedding that he'd told Ian about when their session began.

Eric's dreams lately had Joy scribbling in his palm, Joy riding the snowmobile with him, Joy making an appearance in all sorts of other dreams.

Ian glanced up at Joy's tunnel painting. "How did you feel being in public? At a wedding?"

179

Eric closed his eyes to reflect on the heartwarming memories. Joy's tenderness and compassion when she felt his pain and cried with him was so touching. Eric sighed, trying to get past the tears and to the dance. A thrill of warmth coursed through him as he almost smelled her sweet scent on him like when she'd melted in his arms. She'd stuck with him, even when he'd been indecisive, yet there was a handsome man she could've easily danced with. Not that Eric had given Nate the chance.

"I'll take it that you had fun?"

At Ian's query, Eric opened his eyes. Eric's lifted cheeks must have matched Ian's smile. But he tried to play dumb when he remembered the fire.

"Besides my dilemma of playing the hero?"

"That was a brave thing you did. Facing one of your greatest fears to save a loved one."

*A loved one.* Joy was becoming a loved one, and he cared about her.

"I told her about my family." Eric swallowed. "We cried together."

Ian nodded his approval. "How did you feel after?"

"Free." For the most part.

"The best way to overcome grief and fear is to talk about it."

Maybe the counselor was right. He was an excellent shrink. Mom had chosen the perfect psychiatrist. Although it had taken Eric two months to open up to Ian, the young man had been patient with him until Eric felt comfortable pouring out his darkest secrets.

Eric was glad that he'd argued and won with his parents where it involved him paying for all the people they'd hired to take care of him.

Except for Joy. Right from the start, she'd offered her time freely without expecting anything in return. Still, he owed her his devotion, money, and time. He was sure she'd be offended if he paid her.

If he sent her gift cards in baskets more often, she'd realize he was trying to pay her.

"I think right now it's safe for you to cut down your antidepressants." Ian pulled Eric out of his thoughts.

Eric grimaced, hoping he didn't insult the man by not following through with the prescription. "I stopped taking them a long time ago."

"You also haven't taken the haloperidol for the last six weeks?"

His hallucination medicine.

"Music has helped. The one at the wedding was the second hallucination I'd had within the last five weeks."

After moving back to his bedroom two weeks ago, Eric still kept his lights on at night. "I've resumed reading my Bible as well." Reading the psalms, like he'd done before his illness, relaxed him.

"How do you feel in Joy's presence?"

Eric had to close his eyes again. Joy was the kind of person he needed to visualize before he spoke about her. That radiant smile always warmed his heart. "She's easy to talk to."

He liked the smooth way she approached every topic. She wasn't pushy, yet her gentleness and availability made it easy for anyone to share their inner secrets. "She's kind and selfless and when she enters a room—"

"You're drawn to her." It wasn't a question.

Eric couldn't argue, so he kept his eyes closed to avoid looking at Ian's knowing eyes. He might know Eric had almost kissed her on her friend's wedding day. And he was sure she'd wanted him to.

"I think she is drawn to me too."

"But?"

At this, he opened his eyes and straightened on the couch and peered at the swaying grass beyond the flower garden. "She wants kids and a family. I can't give her that."

"Is that her priority to fall for someone?"

He hadn't asked, but... "Everyone I get close to dies."

Ian had his thick eyebrows lifted, waiting for Eric to continue.

He wasn't even sure if he was ready to move on. "I can't do that to her."

"You should let her be the judge of that."

What a simple statement for a complicated problem!

Would Eric love her the way she deserved? Would he be betraying his wife? He hadn't been the greatest husband as far as dedicating his time to Josie. Running a billion-dollar company, meeting presidents and leaders in other countries where he had charities, had kept him away from his wife and kids often.

"It's been five years since your loss." Ian kept his voice low as if aware of Eric's inner struggle. "We all need someone to mourn and cry with us."

The genuine way Joy had thanked him for telling her about his family was probably why Eric felt the action so freeing.

Joy was a stranger he'd met less than six months ago, yet she didn't feel like a stranger anymore.

"I'm glad to finally see some progress." Ian slid his tablet from the coffee table, grinning like he'd reached the peak of his career. "Keep doing whatever you're doing with Joy. Our next session will be virtual."

Now that the wedding was over and things weren't fake anymore, Eric wanted Joy to stay a lot longer.

He wasn't ill, but he wasn't back to his normal self either. He would be taking Lyme disease antibiotics for years before they eradicated it from his system—*if* it ever left his system.

His feet barely hurt the way they used to. He had the PT to thank for that, but mostly Joy. He looked forward to taking walks with her on the 200-acre property.

He had no idea how long she intended to stay in Pleasant View, and he was afraid to ask, afraid she might say goodbye soon. Joy had taken care of him and so many other people. Now that he was better, it was his turn to take care of her.

SATURDAY MORNING DAWNED sunny and bright as Joy hugged Ruby in the complex's parking lot.

Ruby eased out of the embrace. "Are you sure you don't want me to tell you what I know about Eric?"

Joy motioned to the 4Runner running its engine. "Your husband is waiting. Shouldn't you be dreaming of your honeymoon instead of gossiping?"

"You're the least curious person I've ever met." Ruby waved her hand in the air before heading to the car.

They'd waited almost a week after their wedding before taking their honeymoon to Belize. Joy had offered to drive them to the airport, but Hudson wanted to drive his bride and didn't mind paying for airport parking.

As the car reversed and vacated the parking lot, Joy waved. Even though she'd had the apartment to herself for the last week, it felt like the final day that she would see her friend for a long time.

At least she would see her when she came to collect the rest of her belongings. Joy could also visit Ruby in their new home in Carbondale, but it would be different with Hudson there.

Having another four months left on the lease, Joy had decided to extend her stay in Pleasant View. She still had unfinished business. If she'd learned anything from her illness, it was not to make plans that would tie her down from things that mattered. In her case, Eric mattered. Getting attached to him was one risk she'd decided to take. The triplets were fine in their grandma's care, but Joy wasn't ready to walk away from them either.

A lawn mower sounded in the distance, and as she stared at the clear blue sky, she was reminded of her surprise adventure with Eric and her need to get ready.

The memory of his touch, his warm embrace during their shared moment of sorrow made her feel closer to him than before. He'd almost kissed her at the wedding, or so she'd wanted to believe. Since his hesitation stemmed from pain and inner struggle, she could be patient.

As she climbed the two flights of stairs, she retrieved her phone from the pocket of her dark-red leggings. It was five past eight.

Eric or Terrence or both of them would be here in ten minutes.

*Dress comfortably* was what Eric had told her. T-shirt comfortable.

All she needed to grab was her mini handbag backpack. It was comfortable and complemented her casual appearance. Flip-flops were comfortable, and she could only hope the adventure didn't include a hike. Not that Eric hiked, not in his condition anyway.

By the time she made it back down to the curb, she was breathless and had seven minutes left. She took a deep breath, inhaling the scent of freshly cut grass lingering in the air.

Even though cars filled the rest of the parking lot, the four visitor parking spaces were vacant. She waited, anticipation surging as she peered over the complex's entrance.

It felt like an eternity by the time the black limousine pulled up.

Her heart soared when the car parked and Eric stepped out from the front seat. The sweetness of his smile weakened her knees. Perhaps that's why she wasn't moving, but how could she when Eric was striding toward her with his gaze fixed on her?

Dressed in a short-sleeve button-down and jeans, he looked relaxed with the shirt untucked. No more shadows smudged under his eyes, maybe a few scars lingered from the rash, but they were barely noticeable. His cheekbones seemed to have some flesh over them, his neck less scarecrow-like. Yes, surely, he'd gained a few necessary pounds to fill out his usual lanky appearance.

"Nice shirt," he said.

Not remembering what shirt she'd worn, she glanced down to look at the pink T-shirt sporting the puff print of six different emojis—happy, sad, angry...

She was a jumble of emotions with Eric, hence the shirt. He was warm one minute as if ready to kiss her and pulling away the next minute. But she understood why. Knowing he'd had a drastic loss like that, she was surprised Eric still believed in God. Despite the seven-month faith crisis he'd shared with her, no doubt God understood the man's doubts.

"Ready to go?" Eric reached out and brushed an escaped ringlet from her face, his touch a flame that ignited a fire inside her.

"Do my clothes work fine?" It was the best distraction from her emotions again.

"Perfect." He slid his hand to the small of her back as they walked to the car.

"Good morning, Terrence," Joy greeted the man who held open the back door for them.

"Good to see you again," he said with a genuine smile.

Joy's heart rate kicked up when Eric's jeans brushed against her tights. This time there was no space between them.

"What's the plan?" she squeaked as she attempted to buckle herself the moment Terrence drove away from the parking lot.

"You're going to spend a day at an art studio."

She craned her neck to look at him. Oh my, he was a whisper away. "Really?"

Her excitement must have been painted on her face, if Eric's widening smile was any indication. When he nodded, she asked if they could return for her supplies.

"It's not exactly a studio. But it has everything you'll need."

Joy didn't have to ask any more questions and instead told Eric her plan to stay in Pleasant view for another four months or so.

"That's the best news I've had in a long time." A spark in his eyes accompanied his genuine words.

"Now that you're better, I'll be looking for a job." Another part-time job to sponsor the trips she had in mind.

"You're hired."

Joy playfully bumped into him. "You don't have any jobs at your house."

"Until my doctor clears me for work, I'm still in need of care." He smiled that loving sheepish grin.

Not ready to give up her regular visits with him either, she didn't want to get paid. Not that the tremendous gift cards he'd given her weren't worth an entire year of pay. She would stay until the doctors cleared him for work, which shouldn't be longer than three months. The Visa cards would sustain her grocery bills and more.

When they arrived on Main Street thirty minutes later, Terrence pulled into an employee parking spot before a boutique whose name she couldn't read without biting off her tongue. Although she'd been on Main several times, she hadn't seen a studio before.

She walked with Eric along the pristine shops, decadent coffee-houses, and austere bank.

The store at the end of the row, the biggest on Main Street, which had been vacant the whole time Joy had been in Pleasant View, was the studio Eric walked to and handed her the key to open.

"Why do you have the key?" Shouldn't the landlord or studio owner be the one to let them in?

"I'm temporarily leasing it."

The building had been vacant for a long time—probably no one could afford it. Renting a house in Pleasant View was crazy enough. A shop owner on Main was another thing entirely.

"It doesn't have all the windows an art studio should have, but for one day, I hope this will do."

As Eric apologized about the building not being perfect, Joy studied the vacant room. With the subtle scent of paint and the crisp white-painted walls, surely, the building had been painted before it was put up for lease. Along the wall was a desk and chair. Beyond that were three studio easels, lamps, and three full-size shelves stacked with art tools, canvas, paint—you name it.

Everything looked new, specifically planned for this day. Too overwhelmed by his generosity, she pressed a hand to her heart and fought for the breath she'd forgotten to take. "How did you get all this?"

"I had help from an artist." He peered through the big back window with a backdrop of Pleasant Mountain. "Terrence helped too."

Overwhelmed, Joy pushed her hands harder over her heart. Yes, it was still beating. But she'd better remember to breathe, or it might stop. "You did this for me?"

"You deserve it." He spoke simply without taking his focus from the window.

He needed to know that going out of his way and planning something this special for her wasn't ordinary in her life. Nobody ever did something like this for her. So she walked to him, catching him unaware, and threw her arms around him, squeezing him tight.

While his neck and shoulders stiffened, Eric didn't attempt to hug her back, which was fine.

"Thank you," she whispered against his ear, the scent of his subtle cologne adding sweetness to the moment. Then, just as she almost eased out of the hug, his arms slid around her back, and he squeezed her. She felt safe and secure with his arms wrapped around her. When she eased out of the embrace, she remembered to mention the gift cards he'd given her.

"I didn't want you to pay me."

His brows furrowed, and he gripped the back of his neck. His face was serious when he met her gaze. "No amount of money or gift will ever justify the time you invested in me."

Her heart twisted at his kind words. "That's a nice thing to say."

He shrugged, squeezing his neck again. It was time to switch the subject.

A mischievous grin tugged at her lips and rounded her cheeks as she wagged a finger at him. "I get to paint you first."

Eric shook his head. "No... no."

Her flip-flops crunched against the drop cloth covering the floor as she crossed the expansive room and carried one of the easels into its center.

"Yes... yes." She then went back to the chair, setting it closer to the window for Eric to sit.

On one of the shelves, she browsed through the clear container for HB and H2 pencils.

"How many drawings of me do you need?" He spoke with a light in his eyes, then flopped into the chair.

"This will be the first with your permission." She was already sketching his chin. "I'll be fast. I promise."

She drew him as quickly as possible. "This will do."

He stood and rounded toward her. "Can I see?"

Joy turned the easel away from him. "Not yet." It would be the best picture of him she'd ever drawn, now that she had an entire day. "I need to perfect it."

"I'll be back to take you to lunch." He was standing behind her, so close his warm breath tickled her neck.

"Okay." The word was barely a whisper as she fought the urge to turn around. Would he kiss her, or was he still too deep in mourning for his wife to attempt a relationship?

At the wedding, she'd thought he would kiss her, sensed he wanted to as much as she'd wanted him to, but he'd probably been terrified and opted to go back in the building.

"Goodbye, Joy." His voice was smooth and low as he stepped away and walked to the door without even a second glance.

Needing a moment, Joy walked to the wall and leaned against it. Next to the shelves, she noticed a mini stainless steel fridge. It looked new, and when she checked the inside, there were a dozen small bottles of Simply Lemonade and glass containers with vegetables and fruits.

Sponsoring orphanages in Uganda, funding the recreation center, riding in the limousine, renting an expensive building for her hobby, and sending gift cards? He clearly was a rich man, and he wasn't just using his parents' money to do all those things. Come to think of it, Regina said Eric redesigned their home.

Now that Joy was attracted to him, she was more terrified to find out who he was. What would she find out that she couldn't keep to herself? And what if he or his family assumed she was attracted to him because of his money?

Ugh, that could complicate things. She rubbed the crinkled lines that were suddenly pinching between her brows. She'd better just ask him who he was.

Joy took a moment to pray, to thank God for the day and for Eric's health. He continued to feel better each day since the wedding. *Have You healed him, Father?*

Something in her wanted him to be in her life, maybe hers forever, but it was hard to know how long forever could be. That could change the moment she went for her doctor's routine check. If her cancer returned, it could put a halt to her dreams.

She wasn't afraid to die, but maybe, just maybe, it wouldn't hurt if she had a spouse, even for the shortest time in her life, and started a family if that was what God wanted.

She prayed for inspiration as she moved the easel closer to the shelves containing the supplies.

After toning Eric's picture, Joy used a different easel to paint an abstract of the first thing that came to mind. Baby chicks, the perfect reminder of a new beginning. Perhaps her whole theme today would be images for a new beginning.

It was everywhere as she looked through the window, along the storefronts, up the mountains, in the blooms spreading along the countryside. Even the aspen trees in between the evergreens displaying a vibrant green after months of their dormancy during winter.

She drew a little chick popping out of its egg on another canvas. She drew plants and flowers budding with expectation for blossoming soon. Butterflies. Not only were they beautiful, but they represented hope and change. They had a short life span, yet they were a deep and powerful representation of life. Joy wanted nothing more than to start a new life with Eric, a family, regardless of how short their time on earth would be. That's if he was willing to start over after going through such a tragic loss.

She drew on big, medium, and small canvases. The small ones seemed to dry faster, so she used the brush pencils to write messages on those canvases. She would hand them to the patients sometime in the next week.

On one of the canvases, she wrote *Breathe*, on another one she wrote *Hope, Life, Relax*, and any other words that were soothing and breathed inspiration to the hopeless.

By the time Eric returned to take her to lunch, Joy had twelve canvases spread on the floor to dry.

"Joy!" His tone laced with admiration, he stared at the paintings. "This is amazing."

He was her favorite cheerleader of her art. "I'm hoping to use up most of the canvas you have here this afternoon."

"You can come back and paint any day." He lifted the picture of the chick popping out of its shell. "The studio is mine for a while."

After studying the picture, he murmured, "Life. A new beginning."

Wow. It was mind-blowing how he could interpret her art. "Do you like to draw?"

"Never drawn anything in my life." He set down the canvas, then brushed his hands together. "But I like art."

"I'd like for you to draw something with me this afternoon."

His brow arched. "What part of never drawing something didn't you get?"

"Everyone can draw or paint." She then carried the easel of his drawing. "I'll paint it, but this is the finished sketch."

Eric tapped his chin. "How come you put big ears on me?"

Did she? Joy bent, slightly leaning into Eric to study the picture. He glanced her way with an impish grin. Aha, so he was joking.

She playfully elbowed his ribs. "They're perfect."

His eyes locked with hers, his face turning a shade of pink while they drank each other in as if there was a quenching thirst that had been too long denied.

"You're hungry?" His voice was raspy as he straightened.

Joy straightened too. She wasn't hungry, but said, "I'm starving."

# CHAPTER 19

Eric's attraction to Joy was becoming more undeniable each day they spent together. The week that followed the studio, they barely hung out at The Peak. Joy had driven them to a music festival on one of the afternoons, a film festival on another afternoon, and a walk in the nearby town on another day.

With the kids out of school, one of the mornings she'd wanted Eric to meet the triplets, and she'd picked him up to take him with her to work.

The boys were so adorable.

Today, as he sat with Joy on a long flat boulder overlooking the valley, a peacefulness he hadn't felt in a long time enveloped Eric. The moist air hinted at rain, but it remained the perfect June afternoon.

The fact they were both content in silence, taking in the Peak River Valley, was a testimony in itself. He was comfortable around her. Whether they were talking or quiet, it didn't seem odd. The idyllic stream passed through the distant meadow. Various shades of green—God's own canvas—painted the expansive ranch where horses grazed.

"I bet this is where Pleasant View got its name." Joy finally spoke. "You can see mountains from every angle."

"I agree. I've always thought the name originated here." When he'd climbed the hills around The Peak, he'd come here as a child more often than not. "This was my favorite place to hang out." He told Joy about the good and bad days when he would come here to talk to God alone. He nodded toward the only house visible from where they sat. "I used to think I'd buy that house someday."

The breeze seemed to tickle her curls over her forehead as she nudged his shoulder with hers. "Why didn't you?"

Once he left, he didn't see the need to buy a home in his hometown. While he owned property all over the country, he'd settled for a cabin in Pleasant View because he wanted the kids to see their grandparents rather than stay in their own home whenever they were in town.

"After Harvard, I became a broker, then got into investing. I spent most of my time in New York, then got married before I started a financial business in San Francisco." It had been a small company when the owner sold it to him.

"What's the name of your company?"

"Stone Enterprises."

Joy's jaw dropped, and her breath whistled past her lips. "Wait a minute. You're the Stone from Stone Enterprises?"

Eric nodded.

"You have locations in different states!"

"And other countries."

She blinked as if soaking in the new revelation. She then said, "I never invest in anything. Otherwise, I would've put your name and the financial firm together."

Eric shrugged and rubbed a sudden chill from his arms. But, surely, this wouldn't change her attitude toward him. He knew her well enough by now to trust her. "I'm glad you didn't. I didn't want to talk about work."

While she nodded her understanding, her nose scrunched a little. "What exactly does Stone Enterprises do?"

"We provide several securities. Banking for one, money management, brokerage..."

He spoke about the ups and downs of his business and his thoughts to slow down the moment he recovered. "I might start simplifying my life." The way Joy was handling hers, with the flexibility to spend time with people who needed him and those he loved.

Then, as if sensing his willingness to delve into his past, she twisted on the rock, tucking a foot up beside her and hugging her arms around that knee as she fixed her focus on him like she was about to paint a picture of his past.

"Was The Peak your first home?"

"Sort of." He'd been four when Regina and Kyle adopted him. It seemed as if his life had started then, the memories of his mother and their life together so fuzzy he didn't try to bring them into focus.

"My parents used to live in Denver, but they had a second home in Pleasant View." He'd always looked forward to coming to the mountains, away from the city noise. "After they adopted my three brothers, they moved back to Pleasant View."

"It's a perfect place to raise a family." She picked up a stone and tossed it into the valley below.

"My kids barely spent time in my hometown." Josie's family lived in San Francisco, and it seemed they already had a set of grandparents close by. "We only came to Pleasant View for the holidays."

"San Francisco isn't too bad either." Probably not wanting him to dwell in regret, she then switched the topic. "I noticed the diversity... in your kids...."

Of course, she would hesitate. He hadn't made it easy to talk about his family.

"What countries were they from?"

"My oldest, the sixteen-year-old, was from Guatemala. He was seven when we adopted him. My fourteen-year-old was from China." Eric closed his eyes as he talked about all his kids, answering her questions when she asked about their personalities.

At some point, her soft hand curled around his. "It was wonderful that your wife was on board with the adoptions."

A lump formed in his throat. Josie hadn't warmed up to the idea at first because she'd wanted biological kids. However, they didn't have that choice unless she'd divorced Eric and married someone who could offer her kids.

He talked more about Josie and his in-laws who'd died in the fire with the kids. He was surprised to not break down or switch the conversation.

"Where did you bury your family?"

He shuddered as the tremor in her voice seemed to shiver over him. "San Francisco."

Josie had wanted the kids to be buried with her parents. After all, they'd died together, so it only made sense. "Josie is buried there too." Eric would eventually be buried next to his family.

Joy's palm was moist in his, and he opened his eyes. His body tightened at the sight of her squeezed eyes and the tears flowing down her cheeks.

"Hey." He slid his hand out of hers and draped his arm over her shoulders, pulling her to his side. Goose bumps were scattered over her arm. With her short-sleeved top, she must be cold. "I didn't mean to make you cry." He brushed her face with the back of his knuckles as he wiped her teary cheek. Her warmth seemed to curl into him and reach clear through him when she freely leaned her head on his shoulder, her curls tickling his neck.

Long moments passed while he kept his hand on her, and once her sniffles died down, he switched the conversation.

"Besides traveling, what are some of your long-term plans?"

She cleared her throat and sat up, peering at the darkening gray sky. "Marriage." She swiped the moisture away from her eyes and offered a wobbly smile. "Kids, maybe."

Now that he was feeling better, he could be marriage material if he opened up to it, but he still had major mountains to climb.

"I think you'd make an excellent wife." His face burned red when she peered at him with those bottomless brown eyes.

"You think?"

"To the right person, of course." Not him. "Yes... I mean..." What? His words were slipping off his tongue. And before he could make a fool of himself, he stood up and offered his hand to her.

"We better get going before the rain catches us."

THE PEAK SAT ON AN expansive mountain property with no neighboring structures in sight.

Joy pointed out all the things she liked about the property while they strolled through the meadow and wildflowers brushed against their ankles.

She ran ahead of Eric and outstretched her arms, walking backward. "Look at all the openness surrounding us." Her smile, as wide as the meadow, was heart-stopping. "I can live here forever."

"What happened to your grand travel plans?" Eric thrust his hands into his pants.

"Who says I'm not traveling anymore?"

He caught up to her as the trail curved to the right. Their hands combed through the tall western wheatgrass they passed. When they reached a boulder in their path, he sped in front of Joy, putting out his hand to help her climb up and then step down.

"Thank you." She bowed dramatically, and laughter bubbled in his chest.

The rain clouds seemed to be rolling in. "We better speed up." Eric clasped Joy's hand, and they sped along the trail. A dollop of rain hit him right in the forehead, and he blinked.

"Uh-oh." Joy gave him a sideways glance. "I think I felt a drop on my arm."

A second drop landed on his nose, followed by another on the back of his arm. In case they got a downpour before they made it to shelter, he eased out of the plaid shirt he'd worn over a white T-shirt and handed it to Joy. "Take this to cover your hair, just in case."

She stared at him with a quizzical brow. "I love rain."

He all but shoved the shirt in her hand. "I don't want you to get sick."

As she held the shirt in her hand, he took her other hand, clasping it in his. With a long way back to the house, he asked her to sprint. He wasn't back to his real self, but he used to love running—and there was no better time than the present to resume.

The gazebo came into view. Whew, they were close. A steady rain began falling, and he exhaled heavily. "We're going to be drenched."

Joy draped the shirt over her head. "You're going to duck a little so you can get under the shirt."

Using the shirt for an umbrella seemed like a joke. But he liked the idea of being closer to her, so he obliged. Although they were too close to each other and a couple of times he tripped over her leg, he'd held her back to keep her from falling. By the time they arrived at the gazebo, they were both giggling at the whole fiasco.

"We made it," Joy said, breathless as she used his shirt to wipe at his wet arms. His breathing quickened—it had to do with the running, of course.

Although her wiping water from his arms should be unnerving, she appeared relaxed as if she'd do it for anyone. She then started wiping her arms.

Eric walked to the railing and leaned against it. While rain thundered against the cedar shingles, he spoke over the pattering noise. "If you'd just listened to me and covered yourself instead of sharing the shirt, you may not have gotten so wet."

She swung the shirt at him. "It wouldn't be fair if I used your shirt while you got drenched."

As she wiped through the damp curls now clinging to her head, Eric almost swallowed his tongue. The urge to close the gap and run a hand through those locks intensified. He'd had a few fantasies of Joy. The fantasy of his hands running through her hair being one of them.

*Stop it.* He spun around to look at the creek trickling alongside the gazebo. He'd never been drawn to anyone since Josie died, but something about Joy awakened all his hormones. Feelings he had no idea he was capable of resurrecting.

"I didn't know you had a creek over here."

Sensing her nearness, he didn't want to shift and look, afraid he might put his thoughts into action.

"Your mom told me you built them a house?"

He shrugged, keeping his gaze on the dollops that landed over the creek's gentle trickle. "We rarely see each other, so it only made sense if we could stay together whenever we visited."

"Did they always have this big property?"

Eric told her about the neighbors who asked his parents if they wanted to buy their house when they moved. "When Dad asked me and my siblings if any of us wanted to own the property, I bought it to benefit all of us."

It was secluded. The east side was federal land, a national forest.

As Joy asked about his favorite childhood adventures, he told her the two times he'd snuck into the national forest with his brothers. Especially the last time. "I was twelve. Logan got stuck on a high rock, and when I got up to help him down, we fell." He rubbed his forearm as it twinged. "I broke my arm."

Joy gasped.

He may not have been hurt if he'd figured another way to get his brother down safely rather than curling his arm around Logan. "That was the end of my sneaky adventures."

But he'd answered enough, so he asked about her childhood and what it was like in Uganda.

"We were surrounded by bushes where the orphanage was. So, it was a national forest in itself." She talked about her brothers getting rid of poisonous snakes that slithered into their outdoor kitchen and their adventures bull riding.

Relaxing, he leaned against the railing and folded his arms over his chest as he laughed when she talked about a turkey attacking her.

They were both laughing. He realized when they stopped and held each other's gaze.

"You have something in your hair." She closed the gap between them and retrieved something. "Here."

She flicked a flimsy leaf over the gazebo railing.

"Thanks." His heart beat louder than he wanted it to. Could she hear it?

Perhaps she did now that she was staring at him with dilated eyes.

His gaze darted to her mouth. It looked moist and called for his attention.

Daunted by the thought of cupping her face, he took a step sideways to widen the gap between them.

"You shouldn't have invited me to the wedding." That had been the beginning of his deep fantasies for her. He'd had to trim his beard and hair, and that only made him feel like a normal person.

"Why?"

His jaw twitched. Why did she even want him while she could have a normal person who could give her the family she wanted? "You're young. You have dreams."

She swallowed. "Maybe you're a part of those dreams."

Eric gripped his forehead, rubbing it and dreading this exchange. "I'm fine today, but I'll be ill the next day. Is that what you want?"

"Yes." She looked at him square in the eye, not wavering for a moment. "I want you."

Assuming he got a clean bill of health from his next doctor visit, Eric still couldn't give her the kids she wanted. They could adopt like he and Josie had. But he had no idea how to go back to that place of running a company or starting a new family without feeling like he was betraying his deceased family. And what if Joy died because of him? He turned his back to her.

"You don't know what you want."

She grabbed at his forearm, her grip fierce. "How would you know that?!"

He glared at her hand on his skin, hating the feeling of fire shooting from it. "You should be married to someone by now, instead of spending your time with a dying man."

"You can use all the excuses about dying you want. You're still alive... today." Hurt laced her voice, and being responsible for it bothered him. Her hand slid away, exposing him to the damp chill. "But at least *I* know what I want."

It was still raining, but Eric didn't have to turn around to know she'd left. He fought the urge to watch her go. But his body had a different mind, and he spun around.

It felt like something had sliced through his chest when he saw her walking along the path toward the gardens. Her shoulders were sagging, and she didn't seem to care about the rain drenching her. Her hand moved to swipe at her face. *Please don't cry.*

How could he live with himself if he ignored her today? Without thinking any more, Eric was out of the gazebo and leaping down the four steps and to the path.

"Joy!" he called as she turned around the red shrubs and he couldn't see her anymore. "Joy!"

Rain poured over his head as if washing away his past for a brand-new start.

There was a rustle behind the shrubs, and he sighted her yellow top.

"Joy!" he whispered, relieved when he caught her jogging back toward him.

She wiped the rain—or was it tears?—from her face and frowned. "You shouldn't be in the rain."

He didn't care. He cupped her chin. "I'm so sorry...."

"Don't be."

With his other hand, he swiped away the raindrops from her soft face.

Uncertainty flickered in her eyes, and the corners of her mouth drooped.

"You know what you want. You also know that I'm falling in love with you...." It was past time to clarify his reservations to pursue a relationship with her. "I don't know what my life will be like tomorrow."

"Let's not worry about tomorrow."

He could barely hear her whisper, but he was able to read her lips with his eyes intent on her. Eric let out a breath. "I'm haunted with nightmares and loaded with baggage. How selfish would I be if I dragged you into my mess?" He closed his eyes briefly. "That must be very confusing."

The last thing she needed was his conflicting messages.

"It's not confusing."

His chest squeezed tight, and his throat constricted at the love glowing in her eyes. Oh well. Forget all the reasons.

He curled his hand around her neck, bent, and buried her lips beneath his. Her skin was hot from running, and her lips were so soft. Her kiss was so sweet and tender. He moved his hand to wrap around her middle to shield her from his weight.

She smelled so good, so fresh, just like the clean slate he could have with her. A small moan escaped her, and she gripped the front of his T-shirt, then deepened the kiss.

Their lips danced in the gentle rain, and for a moment, it was just him and her.

When they broke the kiss and kept their foreheads together, they were both panting as they stared at each other. Eric pulled tendrils of her hair from her face. The rain seemed to be turning into a drizzle.

"You're going to get sick," she said, her shaky palm rubbing at his cheek.

"That makes two of us."

He wrapped his hands around her waist and nuzzled at her neck, then brushed a fleeting kiss on her soft lips. A rainbow arched above, God's promise shimmering over them, and he breathed in deeply of the refreshed world around him, feeling God's promise for him as well.... The floods of tears and heartache were over, and his new life on earth was beginning.

# CHAPTER 20

J oy should've known better than to kiss Eric in the rain. She knew it would come down to him getting sick, but she'd lost any coherent thought the moment his lips touched hers.

Early the next day, she received a text from Sabastian saying Eric was sick and she didn't have to come to work. Just in case she'd gotten the fever from kissing Eric, she texted Tao to cancel her morning with the kids. No need to risk getting the triplets sick. Once she'd cleared with Tao, Joy showered and changed, then drove to The Peak.

She was now plopped on the chair by Eric's bed, reading one of the business management strategies books from his nightstand while he rested. Light from the hallway spilled through the open door, and the big window beyond his bed illuminated the room with brilliant daylight, offering some sunlit warmth.

Still, even with the extra wool throw she'd added to his comforter, now and then Eric's lower lip quivered from being cold.

When Joy had arrived that morning, Regina and the doctor were leaving Eric's bedroom. According to the doctor, Eric's fever should break within twenty-four hours. He just needed to stay warm.

Joy better make sure he did. She stood and reached for the Rubik's cube from his nightstand, putting it in the book. It wasn't the best bookmark, but it kept the book half-open. She then leaned toward the bed and pulled the covers to Eric's chin.

Her hands lingered on the faux wool, soft and warm in her fingers as she admired his handsome face. His chest rose and fell with a gentle rhythm. He looked so peaceful and vulnerable, her heart squeezed.

How did anyone recover from such a tragedy, the kind he'd been through? A shuddered breath escaped her, and she lifted her hand to touch his forehead. She kept it there a bit longer than necessary, but thank God, the temperature seemed to be subsiding.

Eric squinted and rolled open his eyes. "Hey there," he rasped.

Joy's smile was instant as she apologized for waking him.

"It would be a shame for me to sleep away my day." He swallowed, staring at her with such affection it stole her breath. "I'd rather look at you—after all, you're more refreshing than sleep."

Joy's cheeks heated, and without permission from her brain, her hand moved to his forehead to stroke back the hair from his face. "How are you feeling?"

"With this kind of attention"—a playful grin twitched at his lips—"I might fake my illness for quite some time."

Her stomach bubbled, and she was suddenly struggling to keep eye contact. She slid her hand from his face and knelt on the soft rug, resting her arms on the edge of the bed.

"Sorry I kissed you in the rain." And made him sick.

"Are you kidding?" He shifted, turning to the side and resting his hand on her shoulder. "That kiss is the highlight of my year."

Joy bit her lower lip and tried not to replay the softness of his lips against hers. The coldness had been replaced by warmth and—oh my!

"I can tell you understand."

Oh dear! He must be reading her thoughts. Needing a distraction from the kissing topic, she eyed the clock next to the phone on the nightstand. Hmm, one thirty. "Your temperature has gone down a little. I'm going to get your medicine and bring you some soup or something."

"Okay."

She bent down to place a chaste kiss on his lips, but he curled his hand around the back of her neck to keep her from standing.

Something flickered in the depths of his eyes, making her heart do a slow roll. With the pillows propping his head, Joy could almost feel his escalated breath against her face. She longed for a repeat of yesterday's kiss. But he was sick, and Sabastian could walk in on them making out.

A heartbeat later, he cradled her face, and she forgot all the logical reasons why she shouldn't kiss him when she brushed her lips against his.

Eric took things from there when he sat up and deepened the kiss. Joy's knees were wobbly, so she knelt, suppressing a moan as his lips moved against hers in a way she felt to the core.

She was gripping his T-shirt, savoring his warm lips, and inhaling his manly scent. Her hands drifted to his jaw, his scruff scraped the tender flesh of her palm, and they were both breathless when they tore apart.

"Now that..." With his voice hoarse, Eric cleared his throat and trailed shaky fingers along her cheek. "Is the kind of medicine I need."

She peered toward the door, fearing someone would walk in at any moment. "You're a terrible patient, Eric Stone."

"I blame my caretaker for my behavior."

His eyes danced with light as he released her face and lay back in bed. Joy stood and moved his feet, then pulled the covers back to his shoulders. He thanked her, but if she kept kissing him, it may take him forever to recover.

JUST LIKE THE DOCTOR had said, Eric's fever broke within twenty-four hours. He was back to his normal self, not the real normal of being free from medicine or exhaustion. He still had days and afternoons of sporadic fevers and headaches, but that didn't stop him from taking minimal adventures into the small town with Joy.

They went to one of the town's annual film festivals, free and held at the Opera House where they'd spotted a couple of celebrities.

Another day, they went to the classical music festival with live performers. Ever since she'd painted with Eric when he'd surprised her with the rented room, he initiated trips with her to the studio so he could paint. He loved abstract art once he learned that all it took was having an open mind and a big imagination.

They painted, made out, and kissed in her Sentra whenever she dropped him off at The Peak. One of those evenings, Eric brought up the need to tell his parents about their blossoming relationship before they walked in on them kissing.

"You're sure?"

"We can tell them together." Eric held onto the Sentra's half-open passenger door.

Joy shook her head. The thought of approaching Regina and Kyle and discussing her love for their son terrified her. "I'm not sure."

His face fell as if he misunderstood what she was saying. "I mean, you know I'm into you, but it's just... I'll let you tell them."

He drew out a breath, his grin returning. "I will."

Depending on the given day, Joy would sometimes walk him to the house and sometimes she wouldn't. Today was one of those days she didn't walk with him since the day had almost lost its light and his parents were home by now. Lately, she felt shy around Regina, especially whenever she walked in the room and smiled curiously between Eric and Joy.

Regina apparently knew about them, as Eric confirmed the next day, saying how his mom had smiled at him and simply said "I know, sweetheart," while his dad had given a gentle nod with a grin.

One evening when they were exploring the expansive Peak property, Eric paused to invite her to a charity ball in Vail. His family attended the National Cancer Society's ball on the last week in June every year. "My grandma died of cancer, so my dad honors her that way."

Surprised he was ready to resume some of the things he used to do—more so that it was a cause she was passionate about—Joy touched his shoulder, even as something tender touched her heart. "You would like to go?"

"Only if you go with me." His shoulders were stiff as if he were unsure of the request. He drifted his gaze to the skyline where the sun was tinting the treetops a pale gold.

"As your date?" Oh boy, she hadn't been on a date in like forever—unless their "fake" wedding date counted. Now she was acting desperate.

"Or my girlfriend, if that sounds better?"

Butterflies fluttered in Joy's stomach, and she felt a glow rise in her chest. "Yes. I'll go."

Eric's shoulders relaxed as if he'd assumed she would say no. "Good."

She'd been to fundraisers but not with rich people. At least, she assumed it was for rich people if the Stones were invited to a gala in Vail—the town wasn't for cheapskates, after all.

"What's the dress code?"

"Black-and-white formal," he said breezily. "I can have Terrence take you shopping."

"It won't be necessary." She still had the boutique gift card he'd given her and told him so.

The only formal dress she had was her bridesmaid dress, which was fine by her since she rarely needed a fancy dress for any unique occasion. Usually, she would've taken Ruby shopping with her. But she was still a newlywed, and lately, they only communicated via texts.

When Joy went shopping one Wednesday after volunteering at the hospital, the knowledgeable associate helped her choose the right dress—an asymmetrical satin evening gown. The black lace over the white bodice and sleeves fit snugly and complemented the flowy white bottom.

As Joy inspected her reflection, from the sleek silver heels to the silver clutch purse in her hands, she felt like she was walking down the red carpet. She'd done plenty of things to distract herself from worrying about life and health and a future, but this moment, she sensed the charity ball would be a day she'd never forget.

Still, she cringed while she handed the gift card to the cashier. There was a reason Eric had put a lot of money on the card. In fact, there was still enough for her to buy four more outfits like that. The boutique wasn't for cringers like her.

ON THE AFTERNOON OF the event, Joy forgot about the expense the moment she opened her front door and swept her gaze over Eric.

His tailored black dinner suit showed off the chiseled angle of his torso and the regaining width of his shoulders, while the black bow tie stood out against his crisp white shirt.

"You look, um, very nice," she said, but when she looked up at him, he was gazing at her with wonder.

"Joy—*you* look stunning." He stepped toward her in the doorway and kissed her forehead before claiming her hand.

She closed the door with her other hand, the same hand holding the chain of her clutch purse. When they joined Kyle and Regina in the limousine, their surprised appreciative expressions made her feel like she'd won the lottery. And she did, with Eric.

"You look sharp, Joy," Kyle said from the other bench seat, his arm draped over Regina's shoulders.

"Outstanding." Regina nodded, the motion making the diamonds in her necklace sparkle beneath the overhead lighting.

"Thank you." A glow of warmth wrapped itself around Joy as she ducked her head, giving herself a moment to savor their kindness and admiration. She then complimented Regina's elegant black dress.

At the event center's pavilion tucked into the mountainside, more lights shone on the dazzling attendees—all dressed in the themed black and white. The stunning timber and stone building aglow for the evening suited its Colorado setting as if part of the mountain itself. Soft music like a burbling mountain brook trickled over the gentle murmur of those socializing. People clustered in groups at each of the four doors, chatting, while others perused auction items at the tables lined to the side.

Joy felt warmed by Eric's gentle hand on her back as they looked at the gift baskets similar to what he'd given her with those gift cards. When guests greeted him and his parents by name, Eric introduced her as his girlfriend, and she felt like she was floating, perhaps in someone else's dream, rather than hers.

Eric *was* her boyfriend—a sweet and kind selfless man.

Servers in black-and-white tuxedos carried trays of fluted champagne glasses through the crowd, passing them to whoever wanted one.

Growing up in Uganda where life was basic, Joy had never tasted an alcoholic beverage. But she wasn't about to start now while she was not confident about her well-being.

At the end of the table was a printed list of items to bid on:

A ski trip to Vail for two ~ Mr. Magik

A weekend vineyard tour in Grand Junction ~ Ms. Juliet Jenkins

A Disney cruise for four ~ Mr. and Mrs. Greene

Four tickets to the opera at the Ellie Caulkins Opera House ~ Mr. And Mrs. Stone

A private two-way flight anywhere in the US ~ Mr. Eric Stone

What? She looked at Eric to ask, but a gentleman came from behind them. "Eric Stone." His white teeth flashed against his black skin as he shook Eric's hand. "I see you're feeling better."

"You could say that, Ledo." Eric shook the man's hand and introduced Joy.

Joy shook Ledo's hand. Then a regal black woman joined them with a champagne glass in her hand. Ledo introduced her as his wife, Cindy.

Cindy's long hair draped off her shoulder. Her white dress made her look like a bride.

"I love your dress," Joy said.

"I own a few boutiques in Downtown Denver...." Cindy seemed to love what she did since she went on talking about fashion and the story behind the designer of her dress.

When Eric's hand touched Joy's shoulders, she realized Cindy's husband had moved on, and Joy encouraged Eric to keep browsing the auction items without her.

"So anyway, I'm starting a new boutique in Boulder...." Over the next several minutes, Joy learned what the boutique industry currently looked like.

When she joined Eric, he took her by the hand and tugged her to his side, his tone teasing. "Did you get enough information about boutiques to start your own?"

Hah! She playfully squeezed his shaven chin.

Regina then ushered them to their designated table with the name *Stone* printed on the folded card in the table's center. Just like all the other thirty-some tables in the room, the linens were white with black napkins wrapped around silverware at each place setting.

Servers continued to pass trays from one table to another, offering nibbles and refilling people's champagne glasses. Regina took a bacon-wrapped something, and Kyle helped himself to a pastry-shaped appetizer.

Eric declined and so did Joy. She wanted to save her appetite for the gourmet food on the menu she was now studying. Lamb chops fondue, steak tacos, filet mignon, Vancouver Island salmon... Mmm, that sounded good.

"How are you doing?" Eric's hand slid around her waist, and he glanced at the table in the corner with a multitude of drinks. "Can I get you something to drink?"

Dinner shouldn't be too far off. It was hard to judge the time since it was still light outside beyond the window. However, it could be the summer's long days, so she asked, whispering into Eric's ear. "Are they serving dinner soon?"

"What are you going to eat?" he asked, then smiled when she pointed at the salmon. "That sounds good, actually."

Chatter continued along the table with the two gentlemen who joined them. Eric's uncles who were international businessmen.

Soon six servers, each holding a plate, stood between them on a silent cue, asking their food options and placing the right plate in front of each person. Another set of servers followed and placed salads beside their plates.

The salmon was the best she'd ever eaten. Again, she always ate tilapia in Uganda, but she enjoyed salmon once she'd first tasted it in America.

The microphone crackled, and everyone's focus went to the announcer on the stage. The disco ball glinted purple, yellow, and red against the man's face.

"All right. Good evening, ladies and gentlemen..." The man spoke through the microphone, introducing himself as the charity patron, a football player from the Denver Broncos.

"It's a shame that I didn't watch football this season." Eric's warm whisper tinged through her ear.

Joy didn't watch sports, so she cupped her mouth with her hand and whispered back to his ear. "You hated turning on the TV." She'd never pictured him as someone who watched TV, even without the headaches.

Regina winked at Joy from across the table. She'd better stop whispering.

"Join us in the ballroom after the president's speech," the patron said, and Joy's table joined in the applause.

At first, she had thought that it was the president of America, but it was the American Cancer Society president.

"Ahem." When the dark-haired middle-aged woman cleared her throat, the applause died down. "Thank you for being here tonight...." She relayed her gratitude for everyone's investment in the society that helped support cancer research. Seeing so many generous people come together for an evening of fun to support a great cause was, indeed, encouraging. "All proceeds from this event go to cancer research."

People applauded again.

When it was time to dance in the ballroom, Eric didn't shy away. Could be because his parents were dancing as well, but he spun her around with such ease as they sashayed from side to side.

"You're a very good dancer," she whispered, breathing in his fancy scent when he pulled her to him.

"I have a few hidden talents."

By the end of the event, Joy was still thrumming with adrenaline, and music was still pulsing in her ears when they slid into the limousine. She had fun with such a high level of service and friends.

Kyle was staring at the muted TV with the ten-o'clock news, while Regina sipped her water. Joy had her head leaned against Eric's shoulder, wondering how he was feeling after such a long evening.

"I'm sure I'll pay for it tomorrow." He rubbed her back. "But all good things come with a sacrifice sometimes."

"Everyone was so nice," Joy said, realizing she'd had no idea if everyone there would know her status, but no one asked what job she did, unless they preferred to talk about their careers, which she'd enjoyed learning.

"How could anyone not be nice to you?"

"And to you as well."

Eric had won two things at the auction. A luxury cruise for his parents and a Disney cruise for Terence and his family. He hadn't told either yet, but he'd told Joy while they cooled off from the final dancing session.

As the car moved for another forty-five minutes, Regina was yawning, and Kyle was already leaning back to rest. They still had another hour and a half drive to Pleasant View, and Joy was concerned about Eric as he massaged his temples. "Do you need more medicine?"

He'd already taken ibuprofen an hour ago, but she doubted it had eased his headache.

"Don't worry about me." He reached for a remote and pushed a button to dim the light. Then he pulled her closer to snuggle. At some point along the drive, almost everyone drifted off to sleep. Joy closed her eyes, letting her body relax.

Her phone rang. Ruby must be wanting details about the ball. She'd probably texted several times, but Joy hadn't taken time to check.

When she retrieved her phone from her clutch purse, Joy squinted at the unrecognizable number. If she wasn't afraid it would wake everyone else in the car, she'd have ignored it.

"Joy?"

"Grandpa?" From years of speaking to him on the phone while abroad, she'd know that voice anywhere.

"It's your mother."

At his clipped words, her heart leaped into her throat. "Is she okay?" she asked, even though she knew the answer—otherwise, Grandpa wouldn't be calling her this late.

"She's had a heart attack."

Oh no, not Mom.

# CHAPTER 21

"Is she alive?" Joy was shaking and doing her best to clutch onto the phone so it didn't slip out of her hand.

"I hope so." Grandpa's voice trembled. "Alex called me. She was taken by ambulance."

"What hospital?" Joy's throat closed over the words, thick with unshed tears.

"UCSF."

"I'll be there soon."

"Please"—Grandpa's throat must have been just as constricted as he choked out the rest—"pray she makes it."

The line went dead.

A warm protective hand was around her, and Joy hadn't noticed until Eric spoke.

"What happened?" With the dimmed light, she couldn't see his face clearly, but panic laced his voice—the same panic that now flooded her bloodstream.

"My mom." She relayed the words, barely pausing to breathe. Then, when Eric pulled her into him, she all but collapsed in his comforting arms.

"Oh no!" Regina leaned across the space to rest a hand on Joy's knee.

"What can we do to help?" Kyle asked.

"We need to get to the hospital." Eric spoke as if they could just barge in and take the flight. He planted a kiss on her hair and lifted his hand from her back. He then reached for the phone in the back of the limousine.

"Terrence," he said on the speakerphone, "call Kremley and have him get the jet ready for San Fran right away."

"Yes, sir."

Joy could barely think and process things as she took a deep steadying breath, but if she understood right, it seemed Eric had his own airplane.

"Let's head to the airport and wait there." Eric pressed the button to end the call and rested his comforting hand on her shoulder right away.

She tried to listen to Kyle and Regina execute ways they could help, but thankfully, Eric was talking to them since a dark moment had seized Joy.

"You're shaking, sweetheart." Eric's voice was gentle as he slid out of his coat, then draped it over her shoulders.

When the car stopped, Joy's teary eyes peered through the window. Lights blinked back. They were at the airport.

*Please, Lord, let Mom be okay. Please.*

Eric offered her something to drink, but she didn't want anything.

The lights in the back turned on, and he reminded her for the umpteenth time as he rubbed his comforting hand on her back. "Your mom's going to be okay, sweetheart."

She hoped Mom would be okay. Even if Eric's voice didn't sound too convincing.

While they waited, Kyle offered to pray and voiced a short prayer for the doctors working on Joy's mom, for strength for Joy, and for a safe trip.

"I'm going with you, if that's okay," Eric said, but it seemed he'd already made up his mind to go and wasn't asking if he could go.

Joy nodded, grateful for his support.

"We'll come too," Kyle suggested.

"I'll keep you posted on how everything goes," Eric said. "You need to be at work on Monday."

Terrence's voice sounded as if he was talking with someone on the phone. As soon as he hung up, the window slid down, and he announced, "The plane is ready."

FIVE HOURS LATER, JOY sat in the waiting area with Eric's comforting hand on her shoulder.

Grandpa was seated on the vinyl-covered chair across from them. Having a private flight sped up the trip and helped ease the stress Joy might have undergone while navigating the details of booking her last-minute flight.

Mom was still in surgery, an emergency coronary bypass that could take up to seven hours, from what Grandpa had said.

Alex, Mom's fiancé, was relaying the events that led to Mom collapsing on the dance floor. "The song had just ended, and we were walking back to our table...."

The pain etching his pale face and the panic in his strong voice was almost her undoing. Joy struggled to maintain her composure in Eric's arms.

Alex buried his face in both hands, giving up on relaying the incident.

In the far corner, Terrence sat with his head down as if lost in thought.

Eric handed Joy a tissue from a conveniently placed box, and she wiped at her tears.

"Sally will be okay." Grandpa's gentle gaze found hers. "She knows you need her. I need her, and she and Alex have to get married, you know."

At that, Alex stood and walked toward the window.

"Don't cry, sweetheart." Eric stroked her hair, and Joy wrapped her arms around his neck, inhaling his sweet scent, and wept.

Why was it that everyone she knew had a threatening illness? Was this God's way of drawing Joy closer to Him? It meant she would constantly be on her knees praying for healing. Was she going to lose Mom as she'd lost Dad?

Moments later, Eric took Terrence with him. When they returned, Terrence was carrying a tray of steaming Styrofoam cups, and Eric handed the hot drinks to everyone. He then sat back down by Joy and handed her a cup, trying for a lighter tone. "It took me a while to find Simply Lemonade and a microwave. I hope now would be a good time to take your unique tea."

Joy couldn't help but chuckle as she lifted the cup to her mouth. "Thank you."

He was sweet to remember when she'd told him a long time ago that she only drank the hot lemonade when she was upset.

It felt like forever before the double doors opened and a woman in bright-blue scrubs with a surgical cap on her head called Grandpa's name.

Joy leaped up, almost tripping over with her heels, but Eric caught her in time.

When the other men stood too, the fortysomething woman introduced herself as one of the attending doctors during Mom's surgery. "The surgery was successful."

Joy breathed out, low and deep, the tension easing out of her shoulders with the same speed the pent-up breath left her lungs. She wobbled a bit on her feet before Eric squeezed her hand.

"But?" Alex asked.

"She's stable but still under anesthesia."

"What's the prognosis?" Eric tightened his grip on Joy's hand, drawing her into his side.

The doctor went on to further explain the post-surgery risks. "Stroke, kidney problems, heart attack..."

That wasn't good. Joy touched her forehead, her knees buckling, only Eric's supporting arm prevented her from falling.

"What do the risks mean...?" *Would* her mom be okay?

The doctor stepped closer and rested her hand on Joy's forearm. "Based on how well the surgery went"—she gave Joy's arm a gentle squeeze—"Sally should be fine."

"Sorry I already signed the waiver." Grandpa waved his hand up and scratched his frail golden hair. Regret twisted up his face. "It was either that or have her die."

Joy gave Grandpa a reassuring smile. "I'm glad you signed it."

"Can we see her now?" Alex asked.

"Yes." The doctor told them the room number. "They've taken her to the ICU on the fourth floor. Until she's stable, we'll allow one person at a time in the room."

As much as Joy wanted to go first, Alex was about to yank his dark hair out. So she suggested he go first.

"Glad you let him go." Grandpa grinned, then reached to shake Eric's hand once again. "I'm sorry we didn't get time to introduce each other when you arrived. I'm Flynn."

"Eric."

"Eric is my boyfriend." Joy glanced up at him, catching his impish smile. "Sorry you had to meet during a family crisis."

Grandpa's shoulder shook with his rich laugh while he tucked in his T-shirt. It didn't matter where he went or what shirt he was wearing, he always kept his shirt tucked in. He looked strong for an eighty-year-old.

"A crisis is the best time to know if someone loves you." Grandpa winked at Joy before sitting down and mouthing to her. "In your case, I approve."

She then introduced Terrence. "He's Eric's friend."

Driver would be demeaning. Although he was Eric's bodyguard, Joy didn't want Grandpa to look at Eric any differently.

Eric sat next to Grandpa and asked how long Flynn had lived in San Francisco.

"Born and raised in Montara." Grandpa boasted about how he'd met Grandma and how much he missed her.

As their conversation flowed, they laughed about all sorts of things, and at some point, both learned they shared a passion for chess. Joy blinked at the revelation when Eric said he used to play in chess tournaments. Then Eric and Grandpa promised to schedule a time they could play.

When Alex returned forty minutes or so later, his dark hair was still disheveled, and a broad smile lit his face when he glanced at Joy. "She's asking for you."

A thrill coursed through Joy, and she touched Eric's forearm. "If you need to go—"

"I'll be right here."

Grandpa gave Joy a curt nod, and not caring what anyone thought, she took off the high heels and handed Eric his coat. She all but sprinted for the elevator, halting when the door opened and three people exited before she got in.

By the time she made it to Mom's room, she was breathless and panting. Her heart was beating louder than the sound of the ventilator and the heart monitor above Mom's bed.

Seeing her with breathing tubes constricted Joy's chest. Memories of her time in the hospital hit her, but she didn't have time to wander back to memory lane while her mom was on the hospital bed.

Suddenly hit with a new wave of tears, she fought them back. She needed to be strong for her, the way she stayed strong around all the patients.

"Oh, Mom." Joy touched the hospital gown on Mom's shoulder, and Mom rolled her eyes open.

"*Hon–neyyy!*" Her speech was slurred, but her flushed cheeks lifted in a smile. "How... did you get here so fast?"

"Eric brought me in his jet." Well, she assumed it was his after his directions to get it ready for the trip.

"I can't wait to... meet him."

Joy moved the tendrils of brown hair from Mom's forehead. "When you're rested, I'll bring him."

That was if he didn't get sick from missing hours of sleep.

"I'm so glad... you're here." Mom struggled to keep her eyes open. Even with the tubes, she looked strong, the kind of mom Joy always remembered her to be.

Except for the change in her appearance. Mom seemed to have gained more weight since Joy had last seen her. Always slender, she stress ate high-calorie snacks after Dad died. With the surgery, there'd likely be major changes to her diet.

Since she was closing her eyes, Joy clasped Mom's hand in hers and whispered a prayer, a plea that she didn't get any of the risks the doctor pointed out. Then she stood and placed a kiss on Mom's forehead. "I'm going to let you rest."

Eric and Grandpa stopped talking when she returned to the waiting room.

"How is she?" Eric and Grandpa asked simultaneously.

"I talked to her a little bit." Joy breathed out her relief. "I think she's going to be okay."

Eric walked to her and swept her in an embrace. "Yes, she will."

After the embrace, Grandpa asked if Mom was awake, and Joy told him that she was sleeping.

"I'm just going to give her a kiss for now." Grandpa stood. "Thank God, she's going to be okay."

"She's surely going to need plenty of rest," Alex told Joy. "If you want to settle in at home, I'll stay here with her."

It was four a.m.—five in Colorado. After being away from Mom for so long, Joy felt the need to stay until morning, but she told Eric, "You need to get some rest."

He ran a hand over her back. "I'm exactly where I need to be."

When Grandpa returned, he insisted they go home. "So you can at least change."

Joy finally glanced down at her black-and-white cocktail dress. "And shower probably."

"Let me take you out to eat something," Eric suggested, but Joy wasn't hungry.

"Since your mom was on a date, I only ate cereal for dinner." Grandpa patted his round stomach. "I could use something to eat."

Eric asked if Terrence could find out what restaurants were open for twenty-four hours, but Grandpa immediately chimed in. "IHOP will be fine."

"I'll go pull up the car to the urgent care entrance," Terrence said before leaving.

"Please join us, Alex." Eric nodded to the dark-haired man, who was now pulling out his phone from the pockets of his cargo pants.

At the front, they waited less than five minutes before Terrence pulled up in a black Escalade. It had enough seats for all of them and two extra people.

Eric seemed to have cars waiting for him everywhere. As soon as they'd landed at the airport, Terrence left to retrieve the car and returned almost immediately with this to drive them to the hospital.

At IHOP, Grandpa, Terrence, and Alex ate pancakes while Joy and Eric sipped their tea. Terrence talked about his family, and their excitement to spend their summer in Pleasant View. Alex talked about Joy's mom, wishing and hoping she'd accept to get married soon since he'd almost lost her.

After dinner—or breakfast in this case—Terrence drove them back to the hospital. Alex, who'd been sitting next to Joy, stepped out. When Joy asked Grandpa where he'd put his car, he was leaning back in the front passenger seat as if ready for a nap.

"I took a taxi." He explained his fear of driving while he'd been frantic, then the hospital parking being a nightmare.

"We'll drop you off." Eric clasped Joy's hand in his, giving it a gentle squeeze.

Still, she couldn't help protesting. "I took so much of your time—"

"Don't even think about it."

There was no sense in arguing at that.

With Grandpa's directions, Terrence dropped them off at their cottage.

While Terrence held the passenger door for Grandpa to exit, Eric cupped Joy's face. "I'm so glad your mom is okay." He then brushed a kiss on Joy's lips.

"You were so wonderful." She clasped her hand to the back of his neck. "Thank you for getting me here early." Resting her forehead against his, she exhaled, relieved the procedure was over and she'd made it in time to see Mom right after surgery. "Thanks for coming with me."

She brushed her lips to his to give him a chaste kiss, but he kissed her back. She almost melted into him, but they tore apart when Terrence shut the front passenger door.

"Oh..." Joy said, touching her lips.

"I don't make a habit of making out in the car," Eric whispered.

Hah! She squeezed his hand and leaned in to whisper. "What about all the times we kissed in my Sentra at The Peak?"

"You don't make it easy for me to resist you." He winked, his voice light as he swung open his door and stepped out, then held it for her.

The porch light was bright in the driveway, and crickets sang in the distance as Eric shook Grandpa's hand and waved away his thanks for the early breakfast. Eric then turned to Joy and brushed a soft kiss on her cheek while Grandpa started up alongside the green shrubbery path to the ranch house. "Do you need a ride to the hospital tomorrow?"

"Grandpa will drive me." It was nice of him to ask, but... "But where are you staying?"

He tucked a springy coil of hair away from her brow. "At my house."

Joy shook her head. She'd forgotten this was where he used to live. The city with his company's corporate offices. Something twisted inside her as she imagined him going back to his house with all the memories of his family there. It was probably another big mansion like The Peak. "Will it be hard for you to stay at your house?"

The light illuminated the thin line of his lips. "I lived there before I got sick."

That made sense. He'd sort of moved on after his family died, but the illness interfered with his progress. Which reminded her. "We forgot to bring your medicine." He didn't take hallucination medication anymore, but he would need his antibiotics.

"I'll email my doctor and have my prescription sent to the clinic by my house."

Good thing, it was easy to transfer prescriptions.

"Thank you for dinner—and for everything." His presence had helped her not think the worst while Mom was in surgery.

"I'm glad your mom is okay."

With one more kiss to Eric, Joy cupped her mouth to shout to the driver. "Good night, Terrence. Thanks for driving."

"The pleasure is all mine, Ms. Musana."

AS PROMISED, ERIC HAD joined her at the hospital the following day and the next. Today was the third day after Mom's surgery when Joy showed up for her daily hospital visits along with Grandpa.

Mom had been moved into a spacious step-down unit where she was still closely monitored.

When Joy and Grandpa stepped out of the elevator, she struggled to keep the get-well-soon balloons in place, yanking a string to keep one wayward yellow balloon from getting stuck inside the elevator as the doors closed. At Mom's room, she stopped in her tracks, and the balloon strings almost slipped out of her hands at the sight of Eric seated next to Alex beside Mom's bed. Eric's eyes were glowing, and Mom was all smiles now that her breathing tube was gone.

"That looks like my lovely child." Grandpa ambled forward to hug Mom.

When Mom greeted her, Joy lifted the balloons. They were too big to tie to her bed. Then she glanced at Eric, his soft smile warming her insides. Somehow, she managed to look around for a better place to tie the balloons. The counter by the sink was dominated by a vase with a wide assortment of mixed flowers and another single red rose in a skinny glass vase. The single rose was probably from Alex since he knew Mom's taste with flowers.

Joy crossed the room to tie the balloon strings on the cupboard handle. She could easily move it to one of the chairs later.

Eric vacated his seat for Grandpa to sit, and his eyes shone with something like admiration when he strode to Joy and wrapped her in his arms. "Did you sleep well?"

"I did." She breathed in his sweet scent. "You?"

He shrugged, and when they returned to the bedside, Alex stood to let Joy take the seat, then left to grab himself a cup of coffee.

"You scared me." Joy scooted the chair closer to the bed, her body tense as she leaned toward Mom and touched a strand of her rumpled hair. She then shook away the dark thoughts of what life would've been if Mom had died.

"I called the boys last night." It had been morning for her brothers in Africa, but Joy assured them Mom was going to be fine.

"I don't want them to worry. I'm not going anywhere." Mom winked and touched Joy's cheek. "Not until you get married. I have to hold my grandbabies first."

"That may be a long wait."

"Because of your travels, I know. But you can be married and travel too."

If Eric would be willing to join her on her adventures. Joy had no idea why she chose that moment to crane her neck and eye Eric. He was also staring at her, and her stomach flopped. When he squished his face, she turned back to Mom.

"Eric brought me flowers," Mom said. "You chose a good one."

Craning her neck again, Joy mouthed a thank you to him, and his sheepish return smile warmed her clear through.

"This world is so big yet small at the same time." Mom cast a sweet glance at her. "Eric and I have met before."

Whoa. Joy jolted a little in her chair, jarred by that. Gripping the chair arms with both hands, she managed to keep from springing up in her excitement. "What do you mean?"

"When you had your surgery."

That didn't make sense. She scrunched her brows, twisting toward Eric for clarification.

He shrugged. "I didn't recognize her, but she has a good memory."

"Sally still prays for the kind stranger who comforted her when you were in the hospital," Grandpa added.

With her curiosity piqued, Joy asked Mom to just speed up with the details. If it involved Eric doing a good deed, he would in no way feel comfortable to offer information.

"Remember I told you how God provided for your medical bills?"

Joy nodded, her grip tightening until the vinyl chair arms pinched her fingers. She didn't have health insurance at the time of her surgery and therapy.

"I was in the hospital chapel crying my heart out when Eric walked in and knelt beside me." Mom closed her eyes as if taken back into a memory. She then opened them and sighed. "Eric prayed with me. He came back to the hospital the next day to check on you. Of course, you were still in the ICU on life support." Joy shuddered, not wanting to imagine what her mom had been through. She'd had a terrible infection after the surgery, and the doctors had told Mom that Joy's organs had shut down. She wasn't supposed to make it. She let out a shaky breath and refocused on Mom's response.

"Long story short, in the three days he stopped by, he asked how he could pray for me."

Mom peered at Eric and so did Joy. He was shaking his head as if not wanting Mom to say anything more about the bill he'd paid for her to get out of the hospital.

Gratitude swelled through Joy's heart, and she couldn't begin to describe the burning sensation of warmth in her. She pushed back the chair to stand and went to him. He'd shifted and was now staring through the window to the city buildings.

"Oh, Eric." She threw her arms around him and squeezed him. He hugged her back, and they held onto each other in an emotional silence while she listened to his rapidly racing heart.

How in the world did God coordinate their chance meeting in Pleasant View? There was no way God didn't have something to do with such an encounter. She'd met Ruby who was on vacation, Ruby invited her to Pleasant View, and Joy volunteered at the hospital where Eric's mom worked.

"Thank you," she finally whispered.

"You do that every day."

"Not really." She stepped out of the embrace, and Eric captured her chin in his palm, probably so she'd look at him.

"With your time."

Grandpa stood to shake Eric's hand, praising God for bringing a stranger from Joy's past into her life. "Thank you, son."

Eric gripped the back of his neck, understandably uncomfortable.

"You know what the funny thing is?" Mom asked. "I prayed that God could give me another chance to see Eric someday so I could thank him face to face."

"It's not necessary." Eric leaned against the wall.

"And look how God answers the prayer with bonus points." Grandpa lifted his hands. "He gives you Eric for a son-in-law."

"Oh, we're not—"

"We're just dating," Joy finished for Eric. But were they even dating? Okay, they had a few blissful weeks of attraction, kissing, and mushy feelings. He'd been hesitant at first, but the last few weeks, he didn't seem bent on reasons why he couldn't fall in love, which had been nice.

When Eric said good night to her that night, he said he was going to let her spend the next two days with her family while he got a few things done at his house.

"I totally understand." She tried to hide her disappointment, but it'd be two long days without him.

# CHAPTER 22

What were the odds and chances that, out of the thousands of people Eric had helped, he could run into someone who recognized him?

Since Alex had been walking into the hospital the same time as Eric and asked him to go with him to see Sally, Eric had agreed. Once he entered her room, Sally had blinked twice, smiling in recognition, before reminding him of that agonizing moment in her life. When she mentioned the chapel, memories rushed back into his mind.

To the woman he'd thought about and prayed for... for months about her daughter. He'd prayed until the time he was physically attacked with seemingly endless diseases. Then, angry at God, he'd stopped praying for all the people he usually prayed for. After all, if God wasn't answering his prayers, how was Eric to trust He would answer other people's prayers on Eric's behalf?

As Terrence drove through the heavy San Francisco traffic the next day, Eric thought back to that morning when he'd gone to one of the three hospitals he sponsored in the city.

He'd lost his family a mere four months ago, but his particular visit at that hospital was to one of his Stone Enterprise employees. Eric had then gone to the chapel to pray for him while he was in surgery, and there, he'd encountered a distraught woman. Her pain was too intense, and she was sobbing violently as she attempted to pray.

Eric felt an instant connection to her agony. He was already feeling the same, and that was why he'd decided that month to pray for others. It helped him not focus on his pain.

"How can I pray for you?" he'd asked, touching her shaky shoulders.

Her eyes, swollen and red, blinked up at him. "The doctors don't think my daughter will make it." She'd blown her nose, "If she lives, she may not be the same. She could need therapy, and we don't have insurance...."

To ease her from financial worry, Eric told her to give him the documents saying who she owed and how much and said he'd take care of it. "I'll have your hospital bill sent to me, and if you need to follow up, from now on, it'll be under my name."

Her relief had been expressed through her shoulders when they loosened. She'd swiped at her eyes and asked, "Just like that?"

Eric gently squeezed her shoulder. "Do you believe in God?"

When she nodded, he told her she could glorify God for answering her prayers about the hospital bill. Then he'd promised to pray for her daughter, a promise he'd kept whenever he prayed for all the other patients.

Before he left, he'd given her his accountant's email and told her to forward the extra debtors she had. That accountant had retired since, but it was still unbelievable that Eric had helped someone not knowing he'd later come to care for her daughter.

The wailing sirens and honking horns pulled him out of his thoughts, and he stared at the homeless people they passed on their drive through town.

If only he could take care of the whole world!

Thinking Joy was the woman he'd seen surrounded by several beeping machines hooked to her body was still surreal.

His heart cringed. How could he not recognize that lovely nose that crinkled when she smiled? Well, that woman hadn't been smiling, and the tubes obscured her dainty lips.

Eric barely slept over the issue last night, which wasn't unusual for him, but lately with Joy in his life, he got his six hours of sleep unless a night terror chose to visit.

Making a stop at the pharmacy for his medicine was inconvenient, but he wanted to feel better. He wanted to be the boyfriend dating a beautiful and loving woman.

Just like Joy, her mom expected kids, though. Maybe Joy would be okay taking him as is.

As far as he knew, Joy was the reason he was making this morning trip to the cemetery. It was high time he paid his respects once again. Perhaps that would clear his doubts about moving forward.

Eric had bought an entire section, one-tenth of an acre, exquisitely landscaped at the end of the cemetery.

As Terrence parked and Eric stepped from the Escalade, moisture-heavy air greeted him, the day seeming to seep into him, the sky weeping with unshed rain, like parts of his soul had for years. He tilted his face toward the heaviness and oppressive thick gray clouds, then leaned back into the vehicle and told Terrence he didn't have to stay. After all, Eric had no idea how long it would take him to mourn and pay his respects. "Come back in three to four hours."

With scarcely anyone at this end of the cemetery, Eric was alone among the tombstones once Terrence left. He touched the engraved words on his wife's tombstone, flicking away the moisture gathered in the crevices: Josie Stone. Beloved wife and mother.

His heart was wrenching, and his knees buckled as he dropped his hand from the words, his fingers coiling into fists. "Why did you have to do this?" He shuddered. "You could've stayed with me. We could have cried together, mourned together, and overcome depression together...."

So, he hadn't had the best life after Josie died, but maybe he wouldn't have gone into depression or gone hunting because he was lonely, only to end up being bitten by a tick. He put his hands on his head. It was throbbing as if it was about to explode with pain and regret.

He moved to the next two tombstones—Josie's mom and dad.

Josie was an only child. Now, the three of them had left the world with no one to carry on the product of their parenting.

"I'm sorry I left you to watch the kids." If they hadn't been watching the kids, they may not have been too exhausted to hear the flames engulf their country farmhouse.

Eric could have worked harder to talk them into moving out of the secluded area to the city where they had close neighbors. Maybe then, someone could've seen the beginning of the wildfire and called 911.

At his kids' graves, he drew out a breath. "I shouldn't have pulled you out of your orphanages." Even if they had sad lives there, they could've had a chance of staying alive.

He sank onto the grass and groaned in anguish, racking his mind for what he could've done to stop all the bad things from happening.

A squirrel scampered in front of him, staring at Eric as if he would hand it something to eat.

If only food was the major problem in his life, then things would be easier.

"Do you even know what I'm going through right now?" he asked the critter as if it would solve his issues. "Just leave me alone." Eric shooed it away after feeling creeped by its sniffling nose. It was probably laughing at him.

Eric's gaze followed it as it scampered further into the bushes without a worry or care. The birds sang on flowery pink shrubs and from the trees lining the edge of the cemetery. It had been a long time since he let himself sing and relax. Except these days, maybe he'd been distracted by the happiness and sunshine—the *joy*—Joy brought into his life.

*Look at the birds of the air.* The verse from the book of Matthew rang in his mind. *For they neither sow nor reap... yet your heavenly Father feeds them. Are you not of more value than they?*

Something along those lines. Yes, the verse talked more about food, but there was comfort in knowing God valued Eric and would take care of him if he could quit worrying about things he couldn't change.

Eric felt lighter. By the time Terrence returned to pick him up, Eric was eager to see Joy.

But he'd promised to give her time with her family. Two days he'd said. He could do that, so he hoped.

THAT EVENING, ON THURSDAY, Eric ate grilled salmon and roasted brussels sprouts. One of his favorites his chef made.

During his absence, Eric still paid his household employees. Even with the six of them moving back and forth managing their duties, the house felt empty. The table was too lonely.

He'd been fine eating alone before he got sick. After all, he worked and ate in his office sometimes. But, after days of shared meals with Joy, it was hard not to think about her.

Despite the delicious dinner, he barely ate half of it and went to his lounge slash library to text her. He still hadn't turned on his usual phone. The idea of being bombarded by texts and emails had terrified him so much he'd gotten a new phone so he could keep in touch with Joy.

Eric: How's everything?

His fingers hovered on the screen as he reread the text. Was that romantic enough? What should he write now? He clicked the screen, intending to hit the backspace, but he somehow sent the message instead.

The phone chirped with a response as he was gritting his teeth and chiding himself.

Joy: Mom goes home tomorrow. She's doing really well.

Eric's cheeks lifted, and he whispered a prayer of thanks. She had to be well if she only needed two days of hospital therapy.

Eric: Need help to get her home?

Joy: You've done so much, but Alex is eager to step in. What did you do today?

Eric: I went to the cemetery

Joy: How do you feel?

At peace to move on without his family. He hadn't realized he'd been upset with Josie until his trip out there. Pouring out his heart to his deceased family and to God felt relieving.

Eric: Good.

Joy: Can't wait to hear about it

Eric: Miss you

Joy: Miss you too.

When he got off the phone, he asked the smart speaker on the coffee table to play gospel music before he entered his home office where he could hear the songs.

Clear tubs of mail were stacked on top of each other along the wall. The housekeeper wasn't kidding when he told Eric that the mail he'd received would take Eric a lifetime to go through.

He walked to his desk and reached for the frame with a picture of him and his wife and kids. He touched Josie's face. He'd almost forgotten the subtle freckles on her nose. Someone had to look intently to notice them.

Oh no. Her features were fading from his mind. Yet he remembered the birthmark on Joy's neck, her jolly smile, and the perfect proportion of her teeth.

"I think I'm falling for Joy." The confession was a betrayal. No. That wasn't true. He rubbed a hand over his burning eyes and swallowed down the bile rising in his throat, even as his stomach knotted. It was okay to move on. "I'm not betraying you," he whispered. "I would never do that."

When he went to bed, doubt about his blossoming relationship with Joy assailed him stronger than a panic attack. Was it the right thing? Was it not? He tossed and turned beneath the satin bed sheets until he drifted off to sleep.

And then, he was coming home from another long day at work. The tension of the day's exhaustion melted the moment he anticipated Joy greeting him at the door with a warm embrace and a melting kiss.

As he entered the house, Joy wasn't waiting the way she normally did. "Honey, I'm home," Eric announced his arrival as he peered over the pendant lights in the kitchen. "Hello?"

She wasn't there either.

Relief washed through him when he walked to the library and there she was, sitting in her favorite red X-base chair with a Bible in her hand. Her eyes were intent on the book.

"Hey, sweetheart."

She didn't move or respond.

Eric walked closer.

Blood drained through him when he saw her pale face.

"NO!" He knelt beside her, shaking her, but she was motionless. *Dead.*

"No! Joy!"

With a gasp, Eric flung his eyelids open and sat up, tossing the covers off the bed. The lamp on the nightstand cast light into the room. His vision brought to focus one of the pictures on the wall.

The Golden Gate Bridge with a quote: *God will walk beside you.*

It was a gift from Brady six years ago.

Wheezing with rapid, shallow breaths, Eric touched his chest to calm his breathing as he struggled for air. *It's a dream. Thank You, Lord!*

But what if it was a warning? A premonition that something had happened to Joy? He scrambled off the bed and grabbed his phone from the nightstand.

He had to call her.

The clock on the stand showed three thirty-eight. If she were alive, she could be sleeping, but he needed to know she was okay.

With his shaky hands, he didn't trust to scroll for her name, so he pressed on the call app and spoke through the microphone. "Call Joy."

"You've reached Joy. Sorry I missed your call...."

Her cheerful voice recording soothed him, but it didn't clear the panic coursing through him.

He tossed the phone on the bed and rubbed his hands over his moistened face. His shirt was damp from sweating.

Burying his face in his hands, he gasped. *Please, God, let her be okay.*

Dizzy and light-headed, he stripped off his dampened shirt and cast it to the tiled floor. He needed to see Joy. Tonight. Now.

After changing into another sweatshirt and joggers, he made his way to the garage and grabbed the keys to the Escalade instead of his Mustang. It would make his life easier since the navigator had already been programmed with Joy's address. Perhaps one could synchronize between the vehicles nowadays, but since he rarely did his own driving anymore, he wouldn't know how.

It had been a long time since he'd been behind the wheel. For more reasons than not wanting to think about his wife in a car accident. At least his driver's license hadn't expired, and he'd be back before Terrence realized he was gone.

Besides the few cars he drove past, the highway had little traffic. This one time, instead of driving ten miles below the speed limit, he was ten over, all while hoping and praying he wouldn't be stopped by the police.

Almost thirty minutes later, his confidence wavered when he pulled into the driveway and peered over the house. It looked dark inside. Perhaps Joy was alive and sleeping.

The garage light illuminated inside the Escalade. He'd just wait in the car, keeping his focus on the narrow path between the shrubs to the door. He turned on gospel music from the playlist on his new phone, then switched to the soothing classical, but it didn't feel relaxing.

He shifted in the chair, tried to close his eyes to pray, but he couldn't focus either. Soon, his thumping heart and the sound from his hands tapping on the leather steering wheel offered the only background noise.

By almost five thirty, the sunrise was coming into its glow when the lights turned on in the house.

Eric all but leaped out of the car and slammed it closed before sprinting down the path to the door.

If Joy was still alive, he wanted to spend each waking moment with her for the rest of his life.

# CHAPTER 23

Joy almost dropped her cup when a soft knock sounded on the door. Frowning over who it could be at the door this early, she set the empty cup on the counter and walked to the door. Despite the late night at the hospital, she'd had a fitful sleep and had woken up before six to make her tea to sip while she read her Bible. A glance through the peephole sent her heart into an uproar.

The porch light cast his deep frown into focus, and he had both hands on his head. She'd never seen him appear so distraught. Was he hallucinating? Or had something happened to his parents?

With her heart in her throat, she swung open the door before considering changing out of her pajamas. "Eric—"

"Oh, Joy." He emitted a long breath and wrapped her in his arms. "My sweet Joy." He was trembling as he squeezed her tight, pressing his nose in her hair, clinging to her like he never wanted to let her go.

He'd said her name, a good sign he wasn't hallucinating. So she savored his warm embrace as she inhaled his scent. But her heart twisted at the loud thundering of his heart against hers. She rubbed his back. "Are you okay, sweetheart?"

"I'm... so..." His words came out in gasps as he stepped out of the embrace and touched her hair, then kissed her left cheek and then her right. "You're alive."

A frown pinched her forehead, and she touched his sweet face. His days' worth of scruff scratched her fingers. "Did you have a bad dream?"

"The worst." His shoulders loosened from the tension as he took both of her hands in his, then squeezed them. "You... you were dead." He shivered, and her chest tightened at his panic.

238

Her tenderhearted Eric. After he'd experienced all the losses in his life, it would only make sense for him to worry about her.

She lifted their entwined hands to her mouth and kissed the back of his knuckles. "I'm sorry you had that dream."

"My life feels like a bad dream." As his gaze held hers, his eyes were so vulnerable. "You're a dream come true—the best reality I've had lately."

Warmth radiated through her. "So are you, Eric."

She then assured him that dreaming about someone being dead meant they'd live a long life. "God brought us together with a connection from our past. I don't think He's brought us this far only to let one of us die."

He didn't look convinced when he glanced up at the sun. The array of pink and orange streaks in the gray was the perfect painting of God's handiwork.

Wanting to comfort and assure him, Joy added, "With God's help, I'm going to be with you for a long time. Until you get tired of me and—"

"Never." This time he trailed his fingers on her cheek. Her body tingled, and she sucked in a breath. "I'll never tire of you. From this day forward, I want us to spend more time together."

Joy smiled. She saw him almost every day, but she was glad to know he also didn't feel like their time together was enough.

"I want to take you on a date, do things like a normal couple."

"We just had a date."

"A real date. Not a fundraiser."

"That would be nice."

His fingers trailed behind her ear. "I also want to travel. With you."

If he was better, he would soon return to work. His travel plans were probably long-term like hers. "I'd love that too."

The morning breeze seeped through her cotton top, and she asked if he wanted to come into the house. "I can make you some tea."

"As much as I'd love a cup of your unique tea, I'll pass. I probably woke your grandpa when I knocked."

He'd been considerate and didn't use the doorbell. "Your knock was soft. Not enough to wake Grandpa, anyway."

"I need to go before Terrence sends a search party." Grinning, he then asked what time her mom would be released from the hospital.

"Sometime after eleven." They hadn't been sure since Mom would need a few tests done. "I'll text you."

"I'll meet you at the hospital then."

As Joy walked him back to his car, she didn't feel ready for him to leave after he'd been so shaken up.

"I didn't know you drove yourself." She eyed the Escalade in the driveway. She'd assumed he was terrified to do so since his wife died in an accident.

"I only drive when it's necessary."

Like today.

His lips pressed into a thin line.

He pulled her again into his arms and nuzzled her neck. "I was so scared." His voice trembled as she held him tight, slightly panicked by his fear too. "I'm not strong enough to handle another loss."

Joy had her fears in the dark recesses of her heart. She didn't want to die before she spent time with Eric, married him, and maybe started a family if that was in God's plan. But their destiny was up to God. However, she had to remain strong for Eric, so instead of voicing her own fears, she rubbed his back. "God's got this. I'll be okay. We'll both be okay."

IN THE DAYS THAT FOLLOWED Mom's return from the hospital, Eric spent time with Joy and her family as her mom recovered. He sent his house chef to Grandpa's house, and for almost two weeks, they'd eaten healthy gourmet meals, which had been great for Mom's new diet regimen. He'd also hired an in-home physical therapist, which had sped her recovery a bit.

Mom and Alex loved Eric, but Grandpa took an extra shine to him after the chess games they'd played almost every afternoon, and the one day Eric had taken Grandpa and his buddies to play golf. Terrence had been patient and hung out with them each time.

It was mid-July on a Friday evening when Joy had her arm in the crook of Eric's as she walked him to his car. He stopped her, turning to face her. "Now that your mom is better, is it okay if you and I go out to dinner tomorrow?"

"That would be wonderful."

He eased out of their entwined arms, then retrieved his wallet. "I want you to go shopping tomorrow." He pulled out a silvery card and held it out to her.

No way! Not after everything he'd done for her family. She shook her head and folded her arms, then peered at the sinking sun.

Eric cupped her chin, his face pained. "Please. Let me do this. I let you help me all this time. Now it's my turn."

Looking into his eyes made it difficult for her to think, but she still managed to shake her head.

"If I love you, I want to share everything I have with you."

"Oh." He just admitted he loved her. *I love you too.* But her lips were left hanging as she nodded and he slipped the card in her hands.

"I'll send Terrence to drive you."

She didn't have her car, and she wasn't on Grandpa or Mom's insurance to be driving their cars.

It wasn't until Eric kissed her goodbye and left, that Joy looked back to the Amex card in her hand. Shopping for clothes wasn't her favorite thing since she wasn't knowledgeable in fashion, and neither was Mom or Grandpa. Hopefully, Terrence had a better idea of where she could shop.

SITTING IN THE BACK of the Escalade, Joy rested her head on Eric's shoulder. She was full and relaxed, and the soft classical music almost lulled her to sleep. She loved the restaurant Eric had taken her to. It hadn't been the luxurious type she'd assumed.

When he'd texted her earlier to ask her preference in food, she'd responded with "surprise me."

They'd ended up going to an Indian and Nepalese diner operated by volunteer servers and chefs. They'd paid nothing for their food since the person before them had taken care of their bill. Before they left the restaurant, they'd also paid for the dinner of whoever came after them to keep the chain of generosity going.

"Do you still want to come and see where I live?" Eric's gentle hand touched her shoulder.

"Is it still okay with you?" she asked in case he was having second thoughts.

He squeezed her shoulder and spoke without hesitation. "Without a doubt."

When he'd told her the neighborhood he lived in, Joy wanted to see his house. She'd always wanted to join the few tourists who took walking tours of the Pacific Heights neighborhood, but she'd never been able to.

When Terrence drove up the hill in the prestigious neighborhood, Joy gazed through the window at the largest homes and mansions she'd ever seen.

The homes were nicely lit as they passed the sign for Broadway Street. The homes there seemed bigger than the ones at the beginning of the community.

Mesmerized by the sweeping city view, she scooted closer to the window. With lights sparkling throughout the city, she could see the Golden Gate Bridge and the skyline at large.

"We're here."

At Eric's voice, she turned to him. The security lights from the house illuminated his sharp and shaven jaw. View forgotten, she was now entranced by the warmth in his eyes and the sweep of his combed-back hair—oh, how handsome he looked in his gray button-down shirt and dress coat. It wasn't as fancy without a tie, but he looked relaxed and stunning.

"Did I tell you how handsome you look tonight?"

He smiled shyly and squeezed her hand. "At least five times." The car drove into the garage while he commented on her dress. "Teal is one of my favorite colors on you."

Her heart warmed as she thanked him. She loved teal, too, among all the vibrant colors.

While shopping, he'd texted to remind her to buy whatever she wanted. Terrence had driven her to a luxurious shopping center where she'd relied on the associate to help her select a dress. Feeling guilty for spending a lot of money, she'd settled for one dress and had worn her heels from the charity ball.

Inside the seven-bedroom mansion, Eric gave Joy a tour and introduced her to the few employees they passed.

She slid off her shoes when they approached a nicely lit room with three bookshelves along the wall.

"This is where I spend most of my time at home. Reading, praying, and you name it." His hand moved along one of the navy accent chairs. He then pointed to the wall with two abstract paintings. "If I stay here, some of your paintings will be there."

Rubbing her bare arms, she suppressed a shiver. She still wasn't confident in her art, but he made her feel like the greatest artist there was. As he ushered her to follow, she ambled into another room with a desk and computer by a massive window offering a perfect view of the skyline.

"This is my office."

Her gaze darted to the framed photo on the desk—Eric and his family. Her heart constricted as she lifted the photo for a better look.

He joined her, his hair brushing against her chin when he leaned in to point out the names of his kids. "I put away all the photos, but I guess I hadn't gotten rid of this one."

"It's okay to keep it around and remember your loved ones."

He smiled sadly before setting the frame facedown on the table so the picture was hidden. "It's hard to move on when constantly reminded of the past you can't get back."

Facing him, she braced against the desk behind her, resting her palms against it. "Does it make it hard to move on when you stay here?"

"At first, it was, but I realized running away wouldn't erase the reality."

Unsure of what to say, Joy pointed her chin to the stacked bins along the wall. "What's with all the boxes?"

He ran a hand over his face. "Letters from people." He eased out of his coat and set it behind the leather swivel chair before moving to the bins. "They're probably well wishes."

"From work?" With the big company he had, he must have lots of employees who preferred postal mail to the internet.

"I don't have a clue." He bent and clicked open one of the tabs, then randomly pulled out a manila envelope. A fond smile curved his lips and softened the pain in his eyes. "This is from Indonesia. The orphanage."

Joy took a couple of steps to him, braced a hand on his shoulder, and studied the envelope. "Are you going to open it?"

Eric ripped it open, and when papers flew out and fell on the hardwood floor, she lowered herself to pick up the pencil and crayon drawings that looked like kids' artwork.

On the drawing with the rainbow, Joy read the scribbled note below it:

Get well soon Mr. Stone. Dewi

As her heart warmed at the tenderness of the note, she showed it to Eric. He gave her the paper from his hand—a drawing of what looked like a globe.

The words written below the picture read:

God loves the whole world, He loves me and He loves you too. Indah.

Eric sank down, glancing through more notes and passing them to Joy to read. She joined him, putting the opened bin in between them.

"How old are these kids?" she asked after reading a few heartfelt notes, more detailed than others.

"All the orphanages have infants to teens." Eric ripped open another envelope. "Those who don't get adopted, well, in some countries I've started businesses where they can work when they are older, but I haven't come up with a plan for that in other countries."

She read several kids' superhero drawings and adults' notes from orphanages in different countries. People and businesses he'd helped wanted to give Eric money so he could get treated if finances were hindering his recovery.

"They barely have anything." Closing his eyes, Eric scrubbed a hand over his face. "It's high time I schedule a virtual meeting and let people know I'm better."

He was probably anxious to get back to his normal schedule. "Are you thinking of going back to work soon?"

He dropped the mail on the floor and moved his hand to rub his forehead. "I'd have to schedule leadership meetings before I get to that point." He seemed hesitant to get back to work. "But that can wait until my next appointment."

They continued one tub after another, all from people conveying their gratitude and reminding Eric of their continued prayers for him. Reading these letters gave Joy a deeper understanding of his life before. He had a calling to help the needy, the hurting. How could God not be with this man?

"Oh, Eric." She looked up as he massaged his temples. His head always seemed to be hurting, even when he took medicine. Especially since they'd arrived in San Francisco. "I hope you can see why God still has you on this earth."

"I think you're right." He studied the San Francisco skyline photo on the wall. "These letters remind me I can still do something. I still have a purpose."

Glad he'd come to realize he had a purpose, she offered a silent prayer of thanks. He'd doubted the purpose of his existence for as long as they'd known each other.

After a moment, Eric stared at her, and his eyes sparkled. "Do you have your passport?"

Her heartbeat quickened. "Why?"

He shrugged. "Do you?"

"It's at my grandpa's house." With her not staying in one place, the passport was less likely to get misplaced if it, at least, stayed in one place.

"Besides Malaysia and South America, what states in America are on your list to visit?"

"Plenty. It will take centuries." Or may never happen.

"Name a few..."

"Hawaii, Florida, anywhere in the South—"

"We're going to Malaysia next week."

She blinked, studying Eric to make sure she'd heard him right.

"Or as soon as I make arrangements with my connections."

She tossed the paper toward him. "No way!"

"You wanted to see the butterflies, right?"

"Are you kidding me?" She crawled to him and threw her arms around him, knocking him over to the other side of the bins. When he called out ouch, she lurched back. Oops. He'd thwacked his head on the bin, and he was wincing. "I'm sorry."

"It's not you. It's the headache." His lips twitched. "But still, next time, I'll make sure there's a safe landing when I share exciting news."

"Yes!" She rubbed her hands together as exhilaration coursed through her and a happy laugh burst free. Penang Island!

# CHAPTER 24

Penang Island was like a scene in a movie. More picturesque than Joy had seen online. Even the butterfly farm seemed like a world of its own when she and Eric ducked under the splash of water to get to the enclosed garden. While pink, purple, and white flowers along the path brushed their feet, the waterfall's soft whoosh soothed her ears. Overtaken by a sense of wonder, she spun around, arms outstretched, and looked up at the dome sheltering them. A few butterflies flapped above, bouncing through the vines clinging to the roof, and her soul rose with them, floating on a prayer of gratitude.

Eric clasped her hand. "You wanted to take pictures?"

She spun to him. Oh how his face glowed! He looked relaxed.

Joy eased out of her backpack, a new one she'd bought when Eric took her on a shopping spree before the trip.

Once she yanked out her phone, he snatched it out of her hand and snapped a picture of her.

"Hey!" She tried to reach for it, but he pocketed it and looked back to the map in his hand.

"Let's start with the outdoor garden." He reached for her hand and clasped it in his.

Exhilaration coursed through her as blue and purple, orange, yellow, and black butterflies fluttered above their heads, while some flapped their wings as they rested on the green shrubs. Eric unclasped his hand from hers and then sprawled open his palm. A butterfly landed in it. "This sure is a good place to see butterflies."

"Yes," she whispered, too taken by the many magical creatures flying around freely. When one landed like a brooch on her yellow butterfly dress, Joy remained still. The blue butterfly stood out against the pattern on her dress.

The flash went off, and she looked at a grinning Eric. His smile captured her breath, and she smiled back. Then, rising onto tiptoe, she peered around in search of someone to take a picture of her and Eric, but besides the young man who greeted them at the entrance, she hadn't seen anyone else. It was ten a.m., and this place, based on her online research, tended to be crowded.

"Isn't it odd that there's no people around?" she asked as they strolled toward a waterfall.

"Hmm." Eric grinned at her, then snapped a picture of her. "The butterfly on your hair matches your dress."

It moved a little in her peripheral vision, a better crown than any queen could ask for. Surely, that would be a picture she'd treasure for years to come. "I need to find someone to take our picture."

"It's just us today." Eric shrugged. "The place has been closed for maintenance for the last week, and it reopens tomorrow." He told her about an exchange student, a family friend, who was good friends with the owner of the farm. "When I told him about our surprise visit, he made a few arrangements and suggested we come the day before the reopening."

Clasping her hands behind her back, she scooted closer to him. "Do we get to see your friend during our visit?" She would love to thank him in person.

"He's in Dubai for business meetings this week."

Inside, they walked through a funky tunnel with ethnic music playing. Dizzying neon lights flashed at them, and when Eric held his forehead and paused, Joy held onto him. "Are you feeling okay?"

"It's the lights," he whispered.

So she told him to close his eyes and held onto him as they sped out of the tunnel. "I was starting to feel dizzy myself."

They walked into the nature land featuring more waterfalls, a pond with red tail catfish, and butterflies seeming to bloom on the bushes or drift in the wind like displaced blossoms.

Joy took in the gigantic home tree, a perfect place for them to have their picture taken. Being taller than her, Eric lifted the phone and clasped his hand around her waist.

Their cheeks touched as they smiled at the screen. Snap and snap, they took two photos and another one with their silly faces before they resumed their walk.

Eric's arm stiffened around Joy's when they walked into the mysterious dark cave with big spiders against the glass. Remembering his recurring tunnel dreams, she slipped her arm around his waist and squeezed. "I don't like this cave," she said. "Let's go see something else."

"Are you sure?" he asked breathlessly.

The glass-covered roaches, caterpillars, and lizards were a contrasting sight to the beautiful flying butterflies—and certainly weren't what she'd come to see. And she was sure he shouldn't be in here. "We haven't been to the nature center yet."

When Eric checked the map, he directed them to another butterfly section. In the vibrant garden, he paused and turned to her. He then touched her heart, and a thrill ran through her body.

The look in his eyes—such love and admiration—made her swallow.

"Why do you like me, Joy?"

As his soft voice shivered over and through her, her feelings for him nearly overwhelmed her. "I love you."

"Why's that?"

She didn't have to think to respond. "You remind me of butterflies." Not only that, but he was kind and mysterious. Her new beginning.

He laughed, arching a brow as if needing clarity, so she lifted her hand to his heart. It was beating rapidly. Like her own.

"I love what's in your heart. Compassion," she said, then continued, "you're smart, competent..."

He snorted, so she pointed out the physical features she liked about him. "I like how you close your eyes when you're listening or talking, you're handsome, and I'm attracted to you."

He ran a thumb over her cheek, sending shivers down her spine. He murmured, his voice low, "I like your sunny outlook on life." His eyes burned with sincerity. "I love the way you make my heart feel. This love... it hurts at the same time."

He touched his hand to her face, leaning into her, his breath warm against her mouth. "I'd be lost without you."

His praise heated her belly. As his mouth touched hers with a simple but tender kiss that made her limbs weak, she curled her hand around his neck to deepen the kiss.

"Ahem."

They tore apart when a woman with an olive-toned face waved at them.

"Sorry." She spoke in an accent. Her blue shirt with a name tag indicated she worked here. "Would you like to release some butterflies?"

"Of course." His voice hoarse, he reached for Joy's hand as they followed the woman to a table nestled between the gardens.

When she handed each of them containers with butterflies, they opened them, and the butterflies flew toward the blossoms.

"The night before we released the butterflies at The Peak." Eric brushed his fingers over the back of Joy's hand. "I barely slept."

Joy felt as vibrant as the flowers when he confessed how he'd been anticipating seeing her the most. Still, she elbowed him. "I knew you always liked me."

"Really?" He arched his brow.

When he ordered their lunch, it was delivered to the café where they ate and watched the butterflies through the glass separating the café from the gardens. The slippery noodles in the fragrant sweet-and-sour coconut sauce were mouthwatering and filling. An hour later, they walked out of the building, and Eric tipped the three staff members who'd been on the premises.

"This has been the best day ever," Joy said when they stepped out into the glorious day with its blue sky.

"We still have a lot more to see on this island." He took her hand. They were staying for five days.

Terrence was waiting for them outside with the cab driver. For once, he sat in the passenger seat. Given the warm climate, Joy had expected him to dress in shorts and a T-shirt, but he still wore his dress suit. Perhaps it was easier to store his gun underneath the jacket or something.

Eric had told him to take a break this week, to go and be with his family in Pleasant View, but Terrence had insisted on coming, saying he'd had enough vacation time when Eric was sick.

They'd flown in a different jet than the one that they flew in from Pleasant View. Apparently, it was Eric's second jet, the one he used for international trips.

As the car drove through the crowded town, Joy took in the touristy place where vendors on each corner of the street sold coconuts and high-rises basked in the sun below mountains jungles.

When Eric suggested they take an art walk while they were still in town, the driver dropped them off at what he called the Old British Fort. Several people and ethnic groups, mostly tourists, strolled along with cameras in hand.

As Joy and Eric wandered the mural trail in George Town, Terrence followed discreetly. Murals and steel sculptures and wall paintings gave the town a different atmosphere.

"This is so fascinating," Eric said when they stopped before the mural on one of the wooden buildings. Two kids in a boat, sailing for an adventure.

"That little boy is you." Joy pointed to the picture. "And the little girl is me."

"Is that so?" A smile quirked his lips.

Pictures of children on bikes, motorbikes, or some sort of adventure beckoned their inspection, but either the heat or exhaustion caused Eric to find a corner in the alley to throw up a couple of times. So Joy suggested they call it a day.

Taking the boat to another island felt refreshing as she snapped a few pictures of the towering jungle they wove through. Thankfully, they had two men rowing the boat while they took in the view.

Nestled among the undulating palms and coconut trees, the boat dropped them off at a secluded island away from the tourist hustle and bustle. They were staying in a cliffside villa, facing the South China Sea.

"What would you like to do?" Eric asked, covering a yawn.

It had been a long day. Joy's flats padded as she crossed the light timber floors, and she pulled him into a hug. "Why don't you get some rest?"

"That's what I've been doing for over a year." He rubbed at his tired eyes.

Realizing he wouldn't rest, she said she needed a nap herself.

"Okay, I'll take a nap if you insist." He gave her a fleeting kiss before peering at Terrence. He was staring through one of the huge windows with views of the sea. Palm trees lined along the edge of the aquamarine water swayed, their shadows dancing on the shoreline.

"I'll stay right here." Terrence lowered himself into an armchair by the window.

With four bedrooms, Joy had her spacious room with a bathroom and kitchenette on the opposite side and assumed the other rooms looked like hers.

When she swung open the French doors, she walked out onto the deck and outstretched her arms to breathe in the sea. The view of the sandy beach was stunning. She hoped Eric had a good room like hers so he could enjoy the view, as well.

And that's what he did the next day when he woke up refreshed. The house belonged to a friend of his who used it as his vacation home. Eric seemed to know all the activities they were supposed to do and tons of water sports, none of which Joy had ever done before.

Watching him wakeboarding—an adrenaline-rush sport he'd loved when he was in his twenties—was thrilling. Her heart raced the entire time he stood on the board towed behind a motorboat. She was sweating and breathing rapidly by the time he rode back into view and the motorboat pulled off the shore.

On the third day, he was taken from the adrenaline spot. He had an intense headache and threw up.

"We should go home," Joy said, realizing they needed to see a doctor.

"No." He held up a hand. "A tour operator is coming to teach you parasailing."

As they sat on the balcony, Joy took in the expansive sea and shook her head.

"You'll be confident in case you're ever caught flying in a situation where you have to parachute on your own."

Her fear vanished when the confident guide took her on baby steps as he flew her like a kite on a parachute attached to his boat.

The more times they flew above the water, the more thrilling it felt. Still, by the time she was done, she'd concluded that parasailing was not for the faint of heart. She would only do it under expert supervision.

At the end of the day, they sat on the balcony for their dinner. Eric's friend had a chef who'd cooked their meals since the island offered minimal restaurants. Eric tried to convince Terrence to go wakeboarding on the next day, their final day.

Terrence shook his head. "If I die doing those things, who will watch over you?"

Eric scraped his hand over Joy and sniffed into her hair. "She's right here."

Terrence offered a shy smile as he moved his fork around the noodles. "I mean, who will watch both of you?"

"I see how you're trying to get out of this." Eric continued suggesting the lighter activities Terrence should try. He genuinely wanted his friend to have a good time during their vacation.

Way after dinner was dined and their plates cleared, Joy and Eric stayed and watched the sun sink below the sea, a beautiful orange beneath the palm trees.

"You make me so happy," he said after they shared a contented silence.

In such peaceful scenery, away from the noise and distractions, she was overwhelmed and deeply in love with him. "The feeling is mutual."

"I want to take you to Hawaii as soon as we leave here."

Although she wasn't tired of traveling, he needed some downtime since he'd had migraines and headaches, but when she told him so, he waved her off.

"I've had headaches and fevers for over a year." He took her hand in his and kissed the back of her knuckles. "You make me feel alive, and I want to catch up with what I've missed."

As long as they were flying in his jet and had medicine, Joy agreed to his plan. So they flew to the island Eric owned with his siblings. She regretted agreeing to the trip on the second day when Eric stayed in bed. He threw up a few times, and when he said he was dizzy, Joy called for a doctor upon Eric's approval.

Being a private island, there was only one doctor, a kind Filipino man Eric and his brothers paid to run the small clinic there.

"You need to get some blood work on the mainland," Dr. Reyes said in a thick accent.

"We need to enjoy our vacation." Eric's words slurred a bit as he rolled his eyes closed while lying on the bed.

Joy clasped his warm hand in hers. Her chest ached. And the same questions kept plaguing her. Were these ongoing symptoms of Lyme disease, or had he developed some new random disease?

She cleared the lump forming in her throat. "We need to go to the hospital." Getting him tested would only take seconds.

"Party pooper," he whined, but a smile tugged up his lips. "Let's go to Pleasant View instead."

Whew! *Oh Lord, please be with my Eric.*

# CHAPTER 25

I t was mid-August, almost a week since the vacation—not exactly how Eric had wanted it to end, but Joy had insisted on getting him to the hospital. Not that he blamed her after the way he'd felt, and he *was* glad to have gone.

During his twenty-four-hour admission, Joy had stayed at his side while they prodded and poked him for blood work and neurological exams and a CT (Computer Tomography scan). Although he'd had it done in the past, it had never revealed anything. They'd also done an MRI (Magnetic Resonance Imaging)—something he'd never had done before.

He'd felt better after the IV. With all the vacation excitement, he hadn't stayed as hydrated as he should've. He'd been okay since then, but as he sat in the sunroom for a follow-up call from the neurologist, the physician was taking his time relaying Eric's test results.

"There's an unusual growth in your brain."

Eric's stomach tightened in the silence passing before the neurologist continued.

"The good news is it can be removed. The bad news is it's dangerous if it doesn't get removed."

Eric froze as he stared through the window at the familiar scenery. The birds and flowers that had cheered him recently lost their appeal as he thought of Joy.

He'd given her false hope—hope that he could be a reliable spouse to spend the rest of her life with. His veins throbbed at the onset of a headache, and he massaged his temples.

"Hello?"

When the man's voice pulled him back to the vagueness of the conversation, Eric cleared his throat, but couldn't lessen the sharp ache in his heart. Joy. *Dear God, please be with her.*

And what about his parents who'd put in the effort for him to recover, only to have him end up in a worse condition than where he'd started?

"I'll send your documents to your doctor. He should refer you to a surgeon."

A surgeon. He knew an excellent surgeon, and the second opinion wouldn't hurt. "Can I, um, have those sent to my surgeon's office?"

"I'll email you a consent form, and once I receive your signature and the surgeon's address, I'll send your results."

Eric was enrolling Ryan Harper without his knowledge.

By the time Eric hung up, the tension building up in his shoulders pinched his neck, and he slumped into the chair. His mind worked on all the things he needed to do to prepare for the worst—death.

Earlier this year, he'd craved death in a heartbeat, but now, he had something to look forward to, something he couldn't comprehend leaving—a life with Joy.

He tossed his phone on the table and stood. Pacing through the sunroom, he thrust his hands into his pockets. He needed to call Ryan and let him know to expect an email about his test results. He also needed to call his lawyer, something he should've done while waiting for his results. It was important that Joy was taken care of for the rest of her life. She could travel and volunteer wherever she wanted to, without being tied to one place.

Eric now understood why Joy chose that path. Not planting roots.

He'd bought the studio from its owner and hoped to surprise Joy on her thirty-fifth birthday next month.

Why had he thought the results would show up normal? He let out a mirthless laugh. Everything he tested for in the past year was positive. He raked a hand through his hair, almost yanking it out.

His phone buzzed from the table, and he ignored it.

After minutes or hours—he had no idea since he'd lost all concept of time altogether—he wandered to the living room and reached for the laptop from the ottoman. He then returned to the sunroom and started typing emails, sending one to Ryan, then one to his lawyer. He also signed the electronic consent form from neuro and sent it along with Ryan's email address to the neurosurgeon so he could pass Eric's chart on to Ryan.

It was past eleven when Sabastian came to ask him if he was staying to have lunch at The Peak.

"I'm fine." Eric sucked in a breath to calm himself down. He didn't want anyone worrying about his new diagnosis.

"Are you okay, sir?" Sabastian's brows drew together. "You look pale."

"I said I'm fine!" Eric grimaced at the sharp tone he hadn't intended to use. While he worked on a comeback, he lifted his hand and pressed his lips, apologizing with a nod and saying gruffly. "Thanks... anyway."

As soon as Sabastian left, Eric was reminded of Joy. Whenever he wasn't ill, he and Joy went out for an activity. He checked his computer. It was almost noon. She would be arriving soon. She still took care of the triplets and intended to as long as she remained in Pleasant View.

It was too late to call and stop her from coming in today. But even if he did, she would ask why. It was also too late to escape The Peak and head for the cabin, but he hadn't made arrangements for that, either.

The only place he could hide might be his room. Before he could close the open window on the computer, a door closed. Joy had arrived.

JOY DIDN'T HAVE TO do more than look at Eric to know something was different. He had his stiffened back to her, and his gaze was intent out the window. He didn't turn around in his chair even as her strappy sandals clicked across the sunroom tiles.

"Hi, sweetheart?"

He grunted a response she could barely hear, evoking memories of her first week at The Peak.

The withdrawal she sensed terrified her as she stood in front of him. Eric was fully armed with a sternness she'd not witnessed from him, more intense even than when she'd met him.

"Any news from the doctor?" She'd asked the same question since his exam. At his silence, she edged closer and rested a hand on his shoulder, wincing when he stiffened. "Are you okay?"

"Why does it matter?" He crossed his arms.

Trying not to seem bothered by his gruff response, she knelt before him. "Because I care."

If she could try to read his face, she might identify the root cause of his mood. But he wouldn't look at her as he peered at her paintings on the wall.

"You were supposed to stay in Pleasant View for one summer." His gaze drifted back to her, his nose flared, and her chest deflated at the fury he displayed. "You're scared to put down roots. You're so busy taking care of others that you neglect your own needs."

She didn't appreciate his honesty. She shook her head to stop him from going any further, but he kept talking.

"You want to be the stronger one. You think it will take away the reality of your fears if you keep yourself busy with patients."

Reality bled in her consciousness, but she didn't need to be exposed. "Stop!"

He pressed his lips into a grim line, not seeming the least bothered.

Silence stretched between them as she waited for what to say.

"I stayed here because I love you." No reason not to voice the main reason she hadn't wandered off. After her sickness, she'd been so afraid of missing out on life, not getting to see all the world had to offer before she left it. That led to her wanderlust, her desire to travel. But in her wandering, she'd been missing out on life, never planning to stay in one place long enough to put down roots and grow through connections with those around her. In her struggle to experience all of the world, in her fear of creating attachments, she'd almost missed out on experiencing the normal parts of life right around her—on actually *living* her life. Eric changed all that.

"That's the problem." He was glaring at her. "I'm keeping you from going after your dreams."

Her dreams were meaningless without Eric in her life. She'd stopped worrying about things she couldn't control the moment she opened her heart to fall in love with him.

"You're right—I'm scared, but I thought maybe we could be scared together."

"No." His brows furrowed, and a tremor quivered in his voice. "Don't you see? I'm a sick man, always will be if I live to see another month."

Joy blinked as panic tightened her chest. "What did the doctor say?"

That had to be the only reason for his act. She reached to touch his hand where it was resting on his jeans, but he pulled away.

He rubbed his chin. "I don't need you to babysit me anymore."

Stung, she closed her eyes and breathed out slowly before focusing on him. "Do you think I've been babysitting you this whole time?"

Of course, he didn't mean it. He'd kissed her with tenderness and passion—like someone he loved rather than his pathetic caretaker.

"You shouldn't have volunteered to take care of me." Crossing his arms tighter over his chest, he turned to look through the side window. "You shouldn't have stayed in Pleasant View or fallen in love with me."

As the tears threatened to choke her, she managed to speak over the lump. "I... *love* you."

Perhaps reminding him how much he meant to her would compel him to share what was bothering him.

"I wish life gave us a choice to fall in love, but it doesn't." He clenched his jaw, then focused sad eyes on her. "You need to go home."

Was he breaking up with her? Yes, he had mood swings, but he was beyond reason right now.

A warm tear slid from the side of her eye as she wobbled to her feet. "I hope we're still friends."

"Goodbye, Joy." A muscle twitched in his jaw.

Yes. She needed to leave and would have left the first week she'd first worked at The Peak. Something was wrong with his medical exam. When she'd met him, he'd pushed all his friends away, and now he was doing the same thing again.

She had so much to say to him, and even with the uncontrolled emotion roiling her, she had to say something before giving him the space he needed.

"You told me you loved me." She wiped at her tears with the hem of her top. "Even if you think you're going to die, the least you could do is let me decide whether I want to be with you or not."

As his shoulders slumped, she continued to trip over her words. "You're not the only one scared. I'm scared to die and leave you behind, to miss out on having a family, scared—"

"Even if I was healthy, I'm incapable of having kids."

Was that the impression she'd given him? That it was all about her having kids? "We don't have to have kids."

He drew out a frustrated breath, and she suddenly struggled to breathe. With shaky feet, she found the strength to stagger and bolted to the kitchen for her backpack.

Sabastian, busy polishing the cabinet knobs, called her name in greeting, but she didn't have it in her to respond. She waved instead and left for the front door where she grabbed her keys off the hook.

The moment she made it to her Sentra, she felt as if she'd just lost a loved one. She didn't trust herself to drive. Still, somehow, after minutes of crying her eyes out, she drove away from The Peak.

Down the hill, she exited the metal gate. Instead of driving home, she took a side road to an open space where she parked as her mind replayed Eric's words. *Life doesn't give us a choice to fall in love. I'm always going to be sick if I live to see another month.*

Time to himself might not be a good thing. Their conversation about his wife drinking and driving into a crash came to mind. Joy tapped her chin while gazing at the deer that traipsed through the tall grass.

Eric never drank. He wouldn't take his life. He knew God had him on earth for a reason. *Didn't he know that?*

If he were going to end his life, he would've done so by now. But, just in case, Joy called Regina.

She answered on the second ring.

"How are you, my darling?" Regina was pretty relaxed for someone whose son was grouchy.

Joy clutched the phone tighter, her trembling fingers threatening to let it slip free. "It's about Eric."

"Is he okay?" Regina's voice was louder, panicked.

"He was acting differently today." Downright mean. "The way he used to be when I first started working at The Peak."

*"You want to be the stronger one. You think it will take away the reality of your fears if you keep yourself busy with patients."* His words ricocheted in her head. She shook her head, took a deep breath. She couldn't think about them now.

"He was in a good mood when I left this morning," Regina responded.

"Not when I got there..." Joy relayed her experience without sharing all the details of him breaking up with her.

Silence passed between them as Joy, and likely Regina, assessed their thoughts of what could be wrong until Joy said, "I think he heard from his doctor. Maybe you can talk to him."

If he would listen to and talk to anyone, it would be his mom.

"Oh, honey, don't be mad at him. I'm sure he thinks he's protecting you from his pain."

Joy pressed her lips together, then swallowed down her hurt. "I'll try to reach out tomorrow or the day after."

Even if she wanted to push herself toward him, she needed to respect his space to process the bad news. In the meantime, all she could do as she waited was pray.

# CHAPTER 26

It had been a long day for Eric. He'd had two virtual calls with Ryan Harper, going over X-rays—or whatever they called all the imaging and scans he'd had done—and making plans for Eric's next steps.

Like the neurologist had said, Eric had a benign tumor, non-cancerous which was sort of good news, but it could grow if he didn't have it removed. It was still a dangerous procedure, and that was made worse by his weak immune system.

Ryan had requested Eric discontinue using any more medicine, except over-the-counter medications if needed. He also wanted Eric in Denver tomorrow for an extensive test to determine the urgency of his procedure.

This particular Saturday Ryan wasn't scheduled to work, but he was making an exception for Eric.

"It's technically your hospital," Ryan had said when Eric object-ed, insisting Ryan spend time with his family.

Seeing he wouldn't win an argument with the surgeon where a tumor was concerned, Eric gave in. But in reality, he was eager to do anything to have his normal health back.

The whole thing would be easier if he didn't have to tell his par-ents. Ignoring Joy's calls and texts also exhausted him.

The pain in her eyes when she'd left lingered like a stark X-ray image in his mind. He hadn't meant to hurt her, but to save her from pursuing a wretched man like him.

To avoid Mom yesterday, he'd vanished into his room before she and Dad got home. Eric had almost forgotten how persistent she could be until she walked into his room and sat at the end of his bed, demanding an update about his health. He'd promised to talk to her and Dad once he heard from Ryan.

It still wasn't easy, even now, as Eric sat with both of them around the table in the living room. The popping in Mom's knuckles disrupted the quiet while Dad furiously raked through his gray-streaked hair as they waited for Eric to talk.

"I have a tumor." He said it. What a relief!

Mom's hands flew to her cheeks, and Dad swallowed.

"It's noncancerous." Eric needed to ease their worries, but how could he when he was terrified? He looked out the window into the growing darkness. The shrubs and jagged mountains ahead stood silhouetted against the starry sky, a full moon hanging over the mountains like an exclamation on the point.

"What's the worst-case scenario?" Dad asked.

"It has to be removed." No reason to go into detail on the risks Ryan had pointed out. Vision and speech loss, seizures, stroke... "Probably next week." As soon as Ryan got the tests he needed. Eric wanted it done right away.

Mom twisted her hands together, thankfully no longer popping her knuckles. "Does Joy know?"

Keeping his gaze on the darkness, Eric felt a black cloud looming through his mind and heart.

"No."

The ache and anguish hit him afresh for the woman he didn't deserve, couldn't have. It was best to let her be, so she could move on without him.

"She deserves to know, son." Dad's voice was low and gentle. "It'll only be fair."

Given the choice, Joy would end up choosing him. Her words rang in his mind— *"The least you could do is to let me decide whether I want to be with you or not."*

If the procedure wasn't successful, he could end up paralyzed for the rest of his life or worse.

If he let her make a decision, she would end up stuck with him. The same way she worked for free instead of earning money to pursue her dreams to travel.

He didn't want anyone stuck taking care of him this time. "I have to do this alone."

Mom's eyebrow arched, her face turning serious as she stood. "If you're dying, we'll be right there with you." She then turned and walked toward the kitchen, vanishing into the hallway. Perhaps his news was too much for her to bear.

"It's going to be all right, son." When Dad stood, he slapped Eric on the shoulder. "I'm leaving now. Call Joy."

Why was Dad so intent on having him talk to Joy? Didn't he realize it would only give her false hope? Eric considered Dad's suggestion when he ambled to the sunroom and retrieved his phone. Scrolling, he reread the first message Joy had sent him yesterday, two hours after she'd left.

Joy: I know you heard from the doctor. Please, don't push me away. I love you.

"I love you too," he mumbled the words to her paintings on the wall. Then he read another text.

Joy: I know you need space. You regret giving Josie space. I don't want to have any regrets. Please call me. I miss you.

Oh, Joy! So loving and tenderhearted. How he longed to see her. She was worried he'd do something foolish like Josie had done.

A sense of unease latched onto him as he read another text she'd sent early that morning.

Joy: Even if I knew you're five minutes from dying, I would choose you. I would rather love you for five minutes than have someone else to love for a lifetime. I love you so much.

His thumb hovered over the screen. His eyes were burning... itching with tears. *Why did she choose him?* He hadn't been in the best shape when she met him, yet she'd fallen in love with him. She'd seen him at his worst, rarely at his best, yet she loved him just as he was.

He needed to call her. A text couldn't express how genuinely sorry he was.

"Ahem."

He startled. The phone slid out of his hand and thudded on the rug when he spun toward Sabastian.

"Good grief, you scared me." Eric's hand flew to his racing heart.

"I'm sorry, sir." Sabastian put his hands on his chest and bowed apologetically. "I just, um..."

What was he doing in the guesthouse this late? Eric had to peer at the bright alarm clock on the bookshelf, the clock he used to use when he slept in the sunroom. It was ten thirty.

"Okay." Eric straightened, confusion flickering as he gave the man his full attention. "Can I help you?"

Sabastian clutched the back of his neck, his overly worn T-shirt and sweats indicating he was done with work for the day.

"I know it's none of my business, but I just... wanted to say something."

Eric must be radiating symptoms of death if Sabastian summoned him to talk. "Would you like to sit?"

Instead of taking the couch Eric ushered him to, Sabastian started talking, "I've seen you at your best, seen you at your worst." His lips twisted as if he was about to smile. "It was nice to see that you struggle with your faith like everyone else."

Where was he going with all this?

"It was also nice to see that Joy makes you happy."

Who was this man and what had he done with Sabastian? "Okay."

"Point is"—Sabastian's words flew out like rapid-fire this time—"you're the man who used to go to homeless shelters and speak about God's goodness. You gave me a reason to believe there's a God who cared for me. You helped many people. Do you ever go on the internet to read people's success stories after you help them?"

Before Eric could respond that he had no time to surf the internet, Sabastian continued speaking with his hands moving. "I've listened to you complain about how God abandoned you, how He doesn't care for you anymore. But you're not the only one who lost a family."

Ouch. He was right. The thousands of orphans were an answer in itself.

"At least you were adopted into this loving home with nice parents...." The man spoke as if he was relieving himself of the ten years he hadn't been able to talk to Eric. He must have spoken in Italian or Spanish somewhere in between his ranting, then back to English as he pointed out the things Eric could be thankful for.

"Whether you're dying or not, you have people to love you, to cry with you." Sabastian slammed his hand with a fist, his face agonized as his voice almost broke down when he reminded Eric to stop pushing people away.

"Joy loves you. And many people around the world like me, who pray for you every day." Sabastian blew out a breath, then clasped his shaky hands together, grimacing as if regretting pouring out his heart.

"You're done?" Eric asked, still shocked by Sabastian's boldness. He should be growling at him and sending him off to mind his own business, but he wanted the man to keep talking.

"Sorry." Sabastian then turned to leave, uttering a "God bless you" as he wandered back toward the kitchen.

Eric looked up to the ceiling, wondering how in the world Sabastian worked up the nerve to summon a mountain of words. He stood, replaying Sabastian's comments about God's blessings. Yes, Eric had been whining a lot lately.

In the past, whenever he got overwhelmed with life's circumstances, he'd help or pray for someone else in need so he didn't focus on himself.

It had been a while since he'd thanked God for the people who loved him. His parents, his siblings, and his friends. Of Joy's texts, one in particular resonated with him—*"I would rather love you for five minutes than have someone else to love for a lifetime."*

That alone constricted his chest. After Terrence picked him up tomorrow, Eric would stop by Joy's apartment on their way to the airport.

# CHAPTER 27

In a jumble of nerves, Joy twisted her grip on the steering wheel when she drove to The Peak on Saturday morning. After grinding her teeth, she tried to loosen her jaw and take in steady breaths. Still, her left leg kept jiggling, and she wiggled in her seat. She'd given Eric two days of silence. But he hadn't called her, and she didn't want to wait in suspense. She groaned. With her body jittery from all the Red Bulls she'd drank the last two days, she could barely sit still in the car.

Sleeping had been much harder than she'd expected.

Her phone chimed as she parked in the driveway, and she swiped to open a text from Ruby.

Ruby: Any news about Eric?

Joy would have to text as soon as she got an update, hopefully in the next ten minutes. Leaving her purse in the car, she raced for the house, and her whole body deflated when she didn't see Eric in the living room or sunroom.

It was only eighty thirty. Maybe he'd slept in. As she was walking back to wait in her car, the soft shuffle of feet through the main hallway caused her to backtrack and take a peek.

"I saw your car through the camera." Regina, dressed comfortably in black sweats and a blue T-shirt, ambled toward her in the kitchen. Since it wasn't a workday for Regina, her attire made sense.

"I came to see Eric."

"He left an hour ago," Regina said. "He was going to stop by your place."

Oh no! Joy's mouth hung open. She'd probably driven past him. "Let me go see if I can—"

"He's getting some tests done in Denver." Regina touched Joy's shoulder with a comforting hand. "If you don't catch up to him, he will be back tonight."

Maybe he was waiting for her at the apartment. A burst of adrenaline shot through Joy's system, and she squeezed her queasy stomach. Eager to know about his health, she asked, and Regina's face fell as she leaned against the counter.

"He has a brain tumor."

That was the worst disease he could have right now. The air left Joy's lungs, and she gripped her chest as if to pump oxygen into it.

"I know, sweetheart." Regina pulled Joy into a warm embrace and squeezed her while Joy's mind wandered into all the dark corners. "It's not cancerous though."

There was that hope. But anything dealing with the brain wasn't something to be taken lightly.

After a few moments of their hug, Joy eased out and sniffled, unable to contain the threatening tears. "I have to go."

Regina offered to have someone drive her, but Joy was already running toward the door and to her car with blurring vision.

When she reached for her phone, she noticed two missed calls from Eric and immediately called him back, but the call went to voicemail. She pounded her hands on the steering wheel a few times, then called again, but it went to his voicemail. He was still using the new phone, so he hadn't personalized his answering machine to his voice. There would have been comfort in hearing his voice.

Her usually thirty-minute drive turned into an hour when she encountered the Saturday tourist traffic. Then she got pulled over for running a red light. In her defense, it had been yellow when she drove through.

When she arrived at the complex's parking lot and didn't see the limousine, her heart sank. She threw her hands on her head and tugged at her hair, not caring if she pulled it out.

On days like today, she hated this town for the tourists, she hated it for the tickets they easily gave out, and she hated herself for not being home when Eric showed up. Burying her head against the steering wheel, she gritted her teeth and screamed, "Gaah!"

When she leaned back in her seat with slumped shoulders, everything looked blurry, even the cars pulling in and out of the parking lot. Thankfully, the early September air was brisk, and her car wouldn't heat up. It was a good place to hang out for the rest of the day.

"Is Eric going to be okay?" She attempted to pray, but her mind was busy spinning with endless ideas.

Joy had no idea how long she stayed in the car or how many times she checked and tried calling Eric, but the earlier sun had vanished behind clouds. Now her stomach growled. But she had no appetite.

When her phone rang, she grabbed it fast, hope flowing through her when she caught Eric's name.

"Eric!" she breathed his name through the phone.

"Oh, Joy." Emotion cracked his voice. "I'm so sorry for what I said."

"I'm glad you called." She wasn't concerned about what he said anymore. He'd been right after all, and maybe she'd needed to hear it. She'd dedicated herself to other patients because—yes, she remembered what it felt like to be helpless and afraid—but also a part of her unwittingly believed that, if she was there helping them, then she wasn't the one *needing* help. Since he'd laid her motives bare, she could work through them and put her trust fully in God, not any works of hers. Now, when she volunteered, she'd do it from a right place of her heart, not from fear of being the patient, of being helpless, of dying....

She shivered and tightened her grip on the phone, needing to hold onto him, be there with him, comfort him. "Are you okay?"

"I love you. It hurts that—"

"You're not going to die." Somehow, she spoke over the tight ball clutched in her throat. "What hospital are you at?"

"Olive Medical." A long, low breath rushed through the speakers. "I'm scared to leave you."

A cold shiver ran through her. She was terrified to go through life without him, but she hadn't given her mind the chance to wander into that dark moment. She was the one supposed to die before him, not the other way around.

Despite her doubts, she swallowed a breath. "You will not die." She could only pray, but deep down she wasn't sure what God's plan was for her life with Eric. She closed her eyes, sending a plea to God that He could give her Eric's pain instead. He'd been through so much.

"Joy?"

"Where does it hurt?"

"My heart." He was silent, and she stayed still, tightening the phone to her ear while listening to his escalated breathing. "For you."

He shouldn't be worrying about her when he had his health to deal with. The time on the dashboard showed three thirty. He should be on his way home by now. "When do they get your results back?"

"There were fibroids growing, and they might spread to other parts of my body...." That could be a disaster. "They're keeping me at the hospital."

Oh no. "Why?"

"They're preparing me for a procedure tomorrow. There's an operating room available."

All Joy could see was red and danger, but if he had a tumor, it needed to be removed. What if he didn't wake up from it? She'd almost died after her surgery.

"Can you please let my parents know?" Eric's words brought her back to the present.

"Okay." Not sure how else she could help, except for wanting to see him, she said, "I'll be there soon."

"I love you," he said.

She closed her eyes and relaxed her death grip on the phone, relieved he didn't argue about her going. "I love you too."

GETTING TO DENVER WASN'T as fast as Joy had thought. As soon as she called Eric's parents, she also texted her mom, asking for prayer and for her to update Ruby. After that, Joy packed her overnight bag, showered, and changed. She made it to Olive Medical in three and half hours, at almost nine p.m.

The petite nurse behind the counter helped point Joy in the right direction without asking too many questions.

As if expecting her arrival, Eric was wide-eyed, and his gaze pinned toward the entrance. When he sighted her, he grinned and shifted his head on the pillows propping it up. "Hi, sunshine."

"Hi, sweetheart."

An antiseptic smell permeated the room, and the heart monitor beeped as Joy sprinted toward him. She eased off her backpack and tossed it to the ground. With the IV hooked to his left arm, she threaded her arm around his neck and leaned in for an embrace.

"The sweet smell of Joy," he said, kissing her cheek.

Joy savored the warmth of his lips on her skin, then eased out of the embrace and knelt on the polished floor. "Are you feeling okay?"

He lowered the bed and patted the space next to him. "That floor is dirty."

"I don't care." She reached out her hand to his scruffy jaw. "I can see you better when I kneel here."

His smile tugged at her heart, and he pushed her curls back from her face, tilting his head to study her. "Your eyes are swollen."

She stared at the light blanket covering him, wanting to tell him
how impossible he was. For not responding to her calls and texts, for
pushing her away, and for all the events leading to today, she blew out
a frustrated breath. She was here now. No need to waste time on her
frustrations. "Thanks for the compliment."

"It's okay if you're mad at me." He held her chin in his palm so
she could look at him, and his eyes seeped with sorrow and pain. "I
thought I was protecting you."

"I don't like to be kept in the dark."

"I know." He swallowed. "Sunshine should never be in the dark.
You're supposed to be out there. Basking in your dreams, traveling—"

"I don't want to travel the world. I don't want to go anywhere
without you." How else was she going to make him understand what
he meant to her? "You're my dream."

A silence passed as they listened to the heart monitor beeping.

"You have a terrible dream."

Joy softly punched his elbow. "Shut up."

He let out a soft chuckle. "Have you eaten anything today?"

She had to think about it as she recalled her day from the time
she'd woken up and drove to The Peak. "A Red Bull."

His face turned serious. "Terrence got you a room at the Four
Seasons when I sent him to rest. You should eat and rest too."

"I didn't drive this far to stay in a hotel while you're in the hospital."

He shook his head. "I forgot how you have a hard time listening
to instructions." With his voice soft and playful, he reminded her of
those early days she'd worked at The Peak after he'd warmed up to
her. "I'm glad you stuck with me though."

"I'm glad you stuck with me too."

When a nurse walked in to check on his IV and take his vitals, Joy asked what steps they were going to take in preparation for surgery.

"We'll shampoo his hair with a surgical detergent."

Joy touched Eric's hair when the nurse said he'd be getting a haircut. They would need to cut out a section of the skull to reveal the brain and tumor underneath. She shivered at the details.

After the nurse left, Eric assured her that having the procedure was for the best. "Apparently, there's not enough room in the brain to accommodate a tumor. I wanted the surgery done right away. If I die, then you can move on faster than—"

"You're not dying." If she said it enough times, she might end up believing it herself. Her knees were hurting, giving her a good excuse to stand and lean in to plant a soft kiss on his mouth.

Wanting him to know she'd be waiting whenever he got out of surgery and needing a distraction from the unforeseen fate, she pulled her phone from her backpack and scrolled for the music app. "Here's the song I want to play at our wedding."

"Really?" A grin crinkled up his face.

Joy nodded and pressed play to "A Million Dreams."

When the song ended, Eric asked her to find "You Are My Sunshine" from her lullaby playlist. As she played the song, he entwined his hand with hers and closed his eyes. He squeezed their clasped hands at the chorus about her making him happy during gray skies.

Tears ran down her cheeks as she breathed in gasps. She must have been sobbing loudly since Eric unclasped their hands and reached out to swipe at her face. When the song ended and she pressed Stop, he said, "That's the song that comes to mind every time I think of you."

*He* was all those things, and she told him so.

As the night went on, he complained about his feet being cold, so she pulled her socks from her backpack and slid them on his feet.

"Please tell me that I'm not wearing butterfly socks."

She laughed. "Polka dots."

The rest of the night, the nurse came in from time to time to check on Eric's fluids. Joy read him different poetic psalms from her Bible app and browsed through her gallery to look at the photos they'd taken on their trip. She prayed for him, and at some point when he was struggling to keep his eyes open, she encouraged him to sleep. Tomorrow was going to be a long day.

SUNDAY MORNING STARTED with a briefing in the surgical waiting room. Eric's parents had arrived at four. They'd prayed and visited with him for an hour before the nurses took him to prepare for surgery. Then the surgeon summoned Kyle, Regina, and Joy.

Joy recognized Dr. Ryan Harper from his visit at The Peak, but in their brief meeting, she hadn't known his intelligence. Now, she detected his knowledge in the detailed way he explained a craniotomy and his steps during Eric's procedure. "I'll remove the tumor and fix the bone flap back into place with metal screws...."

Joy grimaced. Metal screws didn't seem right, but the doctor didn't grimace. He sounded like he'd done the procedure several times.

"We've given him Dexamethasone, a steroid to help keep the brain from swelling." Ryan continued explaining the medication Eric would have after the procedure.

"What causes brain swelling?" Regina asked, her brows drawn.

"Sometimes the tumor." Ryan shrugged. The thick hair she'd seen last time was now hidden beneath a surgical cap. "On rare occasions, the surgery gets complicated."

"How dangerous is this surgery?" Now second-guessing, Joy needed to hear the doctor's assurance, even if she couldn't convince Eric to back out.

Ryan crossed his arms over his navy scrubs, and his kind blue eyes peered into hers. "Like any surgery, it's always dangerous. I operate, but God determines the results."

There was comfort in Ryan's words and his trust in God's sovereignty over his patients.

When he pointed out the risks that could occur after the surgery, a wave of nausea hit Joy, and she could barely stand. But she didn't want the doctor to assume she needed to be admitted, so she crossed her legs to support her.

"Any more questions?" Ryan asked.

"Let's pray for you," Kyle suggested, and they surrounded Dr. Harper.

Kyle prayed for wisdom and God's guidance for Ryan as he navigated through Eric's head. He also prayed for all the doctors working with Ryan to be alert and have steady nerves and hands.

"Amen," they said collectively, and Regina wrapped her arms around Dr. Harper.

"May God be with you."

"You as well, Mrs. Stone." He gave a curt nod and promised to update them once he completed the surgery in three to five hours.

"You need to get some rest, Joy," Regina said after the doctor left. Her usually combed hair was rumpled.

Kyle was standing staring at the muted TV, frowning while he raked his hair. "We'll call you as soon as the doctor comes." He addressed Joy.

"I need to be here." Joy choked out the words as she held back threatening tears. The only place she'd go once she left the waiting room was the chapel. She'd spotted one on the way in. A stronger woman would pray, but she wasn't strong, not now. After all the illnesses Eric had tested positive for in the past, what were the odds God would let him have a successful procedure this time? She'd read Job's story, and Eric's trials weren't much different. If Eric was anything like Job, then there was hope God was still writing Eric's story.

She needed to do something, anything other than sitting and waiting for hours.

"Can I get you some coffee?" she asked instead, aware that the couple preferred coffee over tea.

"I'm good." Kyle lifted his hand.

"I'll have a coffee." Regina slumped into one of the vinyl-covered chairs. "Thank you."

Joy would go find herself some lemonade for her tea. As she stepped out of the room, she had no idea where to find the cafeteria or lounge. But when she peered down the hall, then to the opposite side, she caught a familiar face.

"Ms. Musana." Terrence smiled as he walked toward her with a disposable cup in his hand and a bag in the other.

"Good morning, Terrence."

"Here." He handed her the cup with a picture of a tree, and a hotel logo. "Mr. Stone had the nurse call me this morning."

Joy shook her head, amused how Eric had instructed Terrence to bring her lemonade tea and breakfast. Not having an appetite, she told Terrence so.

"He also said you need to eat." Terrence ushered her toward the hall. Perhaps it was the cafeteria.

"I need to take Regina her coffee."

As Terrence lifted the bag with the restaurant logo, the savory scent stirred her stomach to growl.

"I have omelets for the three of you. I'll go get Mr. and Mrs. Stone to join us."

Joy had no idea how Terrence convinced the couple to come out of the waiting room, but they joined her for breakfast in the cafeteria. The food didn't have its usual flavor, but she ate out of necessity. She needed to be strong for Eric when he woke up.

Kyle talked about their kids, and Regina said she'd called and informed them about Eric's procedure.

When they returned to the waiting area and slumped into chairs, silence settled over them, each person apparently lost in their thoughts. Sundays must be slow since they were the only ones in the room.

Kyle stared at the natural plant in the corner as if he was studying the vein and venules in the leaf. Next to him, Regina browsed through her phone, her fingers shaky as she carefully typed up something. Joy sat on one of the chairs across from the couple, and Terrence was slumped in a corner chair with his hand on his chin as he gazed through the window.

Joy checked her phone that she'd ignored since she'd used it with Eric.

Mom had texted to remind her she had her entire church praying for Eric. Ruby sent well wishes. Ruby's faith was neutral. She had nothing against God but cheered for anyone who pursued Him.

Joy should go to the chapel and pray, but she didn't feel like it.

Now that she had some time and nothing to distract her, she finally typed Eric's name in the Google search. It had been great to learn his personality through him opening up rather than her snooping, but it was high time she saw how the rest of the world saw him.

**Investment and Retirement perspective** was the first response from the search with ericstone.com. Joy clicked the link and read a brief bio of his early life as a Wall Street broker.

When she returned to the main search button, Eric was affiliated on the top billionaire list in America. His name was also linked to the *Forbes* website. The rest of the search results showed his name connected to charities, and as she clicked on each link, they led back to organizations Eric had helped start or sponsored. She read one testimony after another from adults who'd been kids in the orphanages he'd sponsored.

Several hospitals showed up with his name and his involvement. Small business stories from owners acknowledged him for the success of their businesses. Orphans, families, and stories in random newspapers... so many grateful people. Joy doubted Eric even knew about all of these testimonies.

Then came the internet stories about the loss of his wife and children, as well as the charity fundraisers he'd attended. Joy scrolled through pictures of him with his gorgeous wife. She was fashionable in all the event photos with her red hair draping over her shoulders.

One of the common themes on the charity websites was the announcement to pray for Eric Stone. Wow. Eric was so loved, and he didn't even know.

"Joy Musana?"

Startled, she dropped her phone on the thin carpet. She'd never met the middle-aged woman who'd walked in.

"I'm Martina Sanchez." With a light accent in her tone, Martina reached out and shook Joy's hand. "The case manager."

Martina then glanced at her clipboard. Then, with a paper in her hand, she surveyed the room. "Regina Stone?"

After Regina frowned and stood, she joined Joy and the woman in the middle of the room. Martina then read, "Kyle Stone?" and finally called Terrence's name. As Kyle and Terrence joined them, they all had drawn their brows in confusion just like Joy.

"Eric signed this yesterday, upon arrival." The woman lifted a paper with Eric's signature for them to see as she continued to explain what a medical proxy meant. "Joy has the power of medical attorney to make health decisions on his behalf."

Joy's mind was spinning while Martina spoke of what, Joy had no idea. "I wanted to make sure that you all know Joy."

While Regina nodded and Terrence responded with a yes, Kyle asked why they had to talk about Eric's health in his absence.

"This is something we do with every patient."

"Eric will be awake to make his own decisions," Joy added, not ready to process the worst-case scenario yet.

"I agree with Joy." Kyle ambled back to the chair, his hair disheveled. "But yes, I respect his decision for her to make any calls."

At Kyle's response, Martina handed Joy the paper to sign her name.

With her hands shaking as she wrote her name, she realized she'd never discussed death plans with Eric. Where would he be buried? Probably with his family in San Francisco since she was just his girlfriend. Besides that, she had no money to pay for a grave site for him.

It was surprising that he trusted her with his life decisions.

She hadn't known how deep and serious she was in his heart until now. The choice shouldn't be hard if it was between life or death. She would choose him to live in whatever condition God had him.

There were more things to pray about, and as soon as Martina left, Joy headed to the chapel. As she stepped into the dim atmosphere, something calming seemed to wash over her. The air seemed easier to breathe, as if cleansed from the antiseptic and medicinal scents—the taste of fear. A man kneeling at the altar raised his hands as he whispered. In one of the middle pews, a woman slouched on the bench, her face buried in her hands, probably praying.

Joy settled in the back pew and closed her eyes. Having no clue what prayer she hadn't prayed for Eric yet, she stayed silent, listening to God while she pictured Eric back on his feet and running his charities.

When she returned to the waiting room, Terrence offered to bring food to her and Eric's parents, but like everyone else, Joy wasn't hungry.

Just before one thirty, Dr. Harper walked through the waiting room's double doors. As Joy leaped up and Regina, Kyle, and Terrence did the same, Ryan's gaze encompassed all of them. "We got the whole tumor out."

Relief flooded Joy, and she drew out a breath.

Regina wrapped her arms around her husband. But Ryan's tired eyes were unreadable since he wasn't smiling when he delivered the good news.

"There's been a minor complication."

Regina tore out of her husband's embrace. "What?"

"Why?" Kyle asked.

"How minor?" Joy gripped her chest as blood thrummed through her veins.

Dr. Harper ran a hand over his exhausted face. "Bleeding and possible reaction to anesthesia."

Joy threw her hands on her head, feeling a dull ache. Eric's battle with illness was far from over.

She was always strong to pray for everyone else, but the last thing on her mind was to pray for herself.

# CHAPTER 28

Tolerating delay without getting upset is what Joy and Eric's family had done during the twelve hours after Eric's surgery. They'd had to keep him sedated to prevent restlessness and anxiety.

Thankfully, they'd made an exception for them to see him. Joy had been in his room briefly, but had come undone the moment she saw the tubes in his face and the wires attached around his head. All the memories of her time in the hospital became so real when it was Eric in that bed. She wished it was her lying there helpless, not him.

Terrence had taken his turn next, then Kyle and Regina went after. Joy was ready to go back in since she'd composed herself. She needed to see Eric and touch his face once more. What if he didn't wake up?

She paced in the hallway outside the ICU's heavy double doors. What was taking them so long?

The doctor said he was fine, so did Terrence. And that should be assuring, but as long as the love of her life's survival was uncertain, she was anything but assured.

Whenever someone opened and walked through the ICU doors, Joy's heart leaped with the hope it was Regina and Kyle. But, when they emerged, Kyle's creased forehead didn't put Joy at ease. Perhaps something had happened in the last hour or so. "Any change?"

While Regina shook her head, the garish light highlighted the dark circles under her eyes.

"I'll keep an eye on him if you want to freshen up," Joy suggested, now realizing they could do nothing but wait.

"I will drive you to your hotel."

At the sound of Terrence's voice, Kyle took his wife's hand. "I think it's a good idea."

So Joy promised to text them any updates. Then, desperate to get to Eric's room, she strode with urgency to his open door. There, she paused and sucked in a deep breath before entering. Her heart hammered at the sight of tubes and beeping machines still intact.

*Eric!* Her Eric still had his eyes closed, and a patch covered the shaven part of his head while the oxygen mask obscured half of his face.

An ache built in her throat at the sight of a strong man with a big heart, a hero to so many, physically weakened by illness. She took a shuddering breath as she moved forward, sank down on the polished floor, and reached for his hand. The warmth of his skin comforted her, promised life still throbbed through his veins.

She needed to remind him how much she needed him. "You have to wake up." Her voice was shaky.

As his chest rose and fell steadily, it was hard to tell how much of his breathing was aided by oxygen or done on his own.

She'd tried to be the strong one, lied to all the patients she visited that she was strong. But she hadn't had anyone this close to her have a brain tumor and, worse, end up with complications.

She fought back the tears since she'd promised herself she'd get it together. "Please come back to me."

There was the risk he may not recognize her or anyone when he woke up. While that would sting, Joy would rather have him back in any form. "I can't survive without you."

He'd become a part of her dreams, and yes, she could survive physically, but emotionally? She didn't even want to think about it.

"Okay, God..." She looked up to the ceiling, aware of God's presence in this very room even if she didn't see Him. "Please don't take Eric away from me. Please don't take him away from all those orphans." The ones she'd read about. He had people in place running the charities, but he wanted to add more businesses to support those kids in becoming strong adults.

She squeezed his hand and kept talking to him.

"Please don't forget about me." She pulled up to stand, remembering the backpack she'd left in the room when she came in earlier. She retrieved a pen and returned to Eric's side, then drew a butterfly and wrote below it—Remember Me. Joy.

She then pulled out her phone. It was three a.m. She scrolled for her Bible app and read different psalms to him while she played music, some of their favorites. She sang along to "You Are My Sunshine."

Nurses came in to fill his IVs and update his vitals on the computer. At some point, the doctor came in to check on him.

Joy had no idea how long she stayed, but daylight streamed through the window when another nurse introduced herself as Eric's nurse for the day.

Minutes later, Regina and Kyle arrived with Terrence. Regina rested a hand on Joy's shoulder. She'd changed into jeans and a T-shirt with Stone Enterprises emblazoned on it. Her eyes looked somewhat less tired. "Go to the hotel and get some rest, dear heart."

"I need to be here when he wakes up."

As Joy fought a yawn, Regina wrapped her arms around Joy. She smelled of fresh flowers and a sweet fragrance, making Joy remember the last time she'd showered. What was today anyway? She'd lost track. "Even if you don't sleep, at least go have a break."

She *did* need to smell decent when Eric woke up. "I'll keep my phone on."

Kyle gave a curt nod, and Terrence walked with her. "I can take you."

"My luggage is still in the car." She had a good parking spot, and if she left, it would be gone. "I'll go get a couple of my outfits and meet you—"

"At the main entrance."

At the luxurious hotel, Joy didn't have time to enjoy the inviting bed. She showered and changed and shoved her dirty clothes in her backpack. She didn't feel right about wasting money by not staying in the room they'd paid for, but she wouldn't sleep while Eric's fate was uncertain.

When she returned, the waiting area erupted with noise and commotion. Joy spotted Regina and Kyle amid the loud group.

"Joy!" Kyle beckoned, and the group of nine or ten new people stared at her.

"That's Joy?" A bubbly brunette ambled forward, and Joy swallowed. She must be one of Eric's sisters.

Joy surveyed the rest of the group. There was a daunting similarity to the family photo she'd seen.

"Hi." Joy lifted her hand to wave to everyone.

"I'm Iris." The brunette put out her hand and gushed on while Joy shook it. "Mom told me so much about you."

Heat tingled in Joy's cheeks as Regina introduced everyone. Joy had already forgotten their names by the end of the introductions, except for Logan and Iris.

"So nice to meet you guys."

"I finally get to meet you." Logan, slim and toned, spoke dramatically as he wiped mock sweat from his forehead. "Eric wouldn't let any of us near you."

"Wait till he finds out you met her without his permission," said another man with an accent similar to Sabastian's.

The siblings bantered until Kyle reminded them to take their turns in Eric's room. "Two at a time."

After another twelve hours of them going back and forth to Eric's room, the doctor said they'd be taking Eric off sedation. Since it was Joy's turn to return to his room, the doctor said she could come in.

PAIN EVERYWHERE... Thirst...

Eric heard her say his name. How he loved that voice, longed to reach out and touch her soft face!

He tried to move his hand, but everything felt heavy. He forced his eyelids to open as he listened to the machine beeping of his heart rate. His shoulder hurt, and his head slipped into a fog again. *I'm so sorry, Joy.* Sorrow crushed his chest until it burned. Gasping, he felt himself slip away into a trail on a sunny spring midmorning.

He was jogging on a familiar trail with different scenery. As he entered the lush forest, his feet crunched over old fallen leaves and rotten twigs. The air smelled fresh, mixed with another earthy aroma as the trees ended and the path snaked into a tunnel.

Light from the opposite entrance streamed into the tunnel, making the path clear as he kept a steady pace.

He winced into the bright light when he stepped out of the tunnel and stilled to catch his breath. With outstretched arms, he took in the picturesque scenery as the breeze seeped through his T-shirt.

The smell of freshly cut grass hung in the air. Beyond the expansive lawn was a field of colorful blooming wildflowers. Kids' cheerful voices rang out as an array of butterflies flew above the plants while others landed on random petals.

When he peered to the other end of the land, he saw a head whizzing through the field, then a face and a smile when the woman emerged from the field and to the grass. "Joy?"

She turned and lifted her hand, shielding her eyes. "Eric!"

She touched her baby bump before she started toward him. Eric's legs carried him forward to meet her in the vibrant grass. Those doe eyes seemed to widen with every step. Then his hands were cupping her face, the skin so soft, so perfect, his beautiful wife.

"I missed you this morning," she whispered.

"I didn't want to wake you." He'd left early for his run. His lips found hers, his heart pounding the way it did whenever he kissed her. Her fingers gently raked in his hair as he kissed her soundly.

"Mommy, Daddy..."

They tore apart at the sound of kids' voices.

"I hope the kids didn't see us." Joy touched her lips, and when Eric stared at several kids exposing their missing-teeth grins, he saw faces he knew and adored.

*Their kids.*

"I can't believe I'm a father," he said, pulling his wife to his side, "and a husband."

Joy smiled shyly. "With God all things are possible."

How was it possible when the doctors said he was infertile?

"Daddy..."

Their six-year-old, Dustin, bounded and threw his arms around Eric's legs. "We released the butterflies."

Eric lowered himself to the child's level and ruffled his soft curls. "You did that without me?"

His heart squeezed at the tenderness he felt for his family as Dustin jumped up and down. He had Joy's eyes and enthusiasm for nature. "Mommy said we're going to do it again when you get home."

Happiness flowed in his heart when he looked at Joy. Their three daughters were shoving each other on her lap, and she kissed the tops of their heads. "There's enough love for each and every one of you."

Eric could feel Joy's love as she spoke to the kids with tenderness.

Ariel had Eric's hazel eyes while the other two had emerald-green eyes. "Let's go fight for mom's lap too." He hoisted Dustin, and they ambled toward Joy.

"We made it!" Three more kids joined them as they raced toward them. "Group hug!" Xavier, their eight-year-old, shouted, and they fell over Eric, who fell on Joy and the girls.

"Tickle fight." Eric slid his arms under Joy's armpits, then the girls' one at a time.

Happy squeals sounded from his kids and his wife as he continued to tickle one of them at a time.

Contentment too strong to contemplate filled his heart, and he soaked in the happiness that had been sleeping far too long to stretch out inside. He wanted this feeling to last, but machines beeped and feet shuffled to interfere with his peace.

He could see moving shadows, not dark ones, thank goodness.

"He's awake," someone said, and there was a ruckus.

He winced at the bright light when his eyelids fluttered open. His head hurt, and his throat felt dry and thirsty. The shadows became more and more visible as his sight cleared. Lots of people dressed in blue.

"Eric, can you hear me?"

He opened his mouth to speak, but something was over his mouth. So he tried to lift his hand to move it. Ink swirled all over his palm. Notes and a drawing he realized when he squinted to get a better look.

Joy was here. He struggled to shift, but his hand was weak. He'd rather have it fall off as long as he read whatever she'd written in his palm.

A butterfly. His cheeks lifted as he read the words below the drawing. Remember Me. Joy.

He wanted Joy. He peered at the vacant chair to the far side against the wall and tried to shift his head to the side but couldn't. Didn't the nurse see that he needed help?

A commotion sounded, and a flood of people stormed into the room. "Eric, I was here first."

His siblings.

"We're going to let in one person at a time," the nurse said, and his siblings argued as to who should be the first.

"We should let Joy go first."

Joy! Just hearing the name flooded his heart with sunshine and warmth. The moment she walked through the door, he had no idea how he managed to lift his hand to his nose and yank off the mask.

"Eric!" Joy flew to him and threw her arms over the wires to wrap around his neck, weeping and laughing. She stepped back to look him over. "Do you remember me?"

"Yes." It was a scruffy whisper. His throat hurt for whatever reason. His eyes stung that he wasn't strong enough to carry her in his arms the way he wanted to. In his dream, she was his wife, but she didn't have a ring on her finger. He remembered clearly how he'd pushed her away before he went to the hospital.

"I'm so glad!" She kissed every part of his face she could reach. If it weren't for the wound on his head, she'd probably be kissing his head, as well.

Eric coughed when he tried to laugh, but when she kissed his lips, his body was instantly awake and his mouth alert. With the pillows propping his head and Joy leaning in close enough, he kissed her back, feeling the pieces inside himself come back together. He was still alive! Having Joy in his arms was a reason for him to believe he could start over.

When she pulled back breathless, she said, "Thank you for coming back to me." Her puffy eyes searched his, so warm and brown he knew she meant every word. "I love you so much."

"I love you too." His voice might be frail, but at least she could hear him.

The commotion outside the door escalated, and she must have heard it because she put the oxygen mask back on his nose. "I better let your siblings take a turn to see you." She then kissed his forehead and promised to be back as soon as possible.

Logan walked in first and took Eric's hand in his. "Man, you got a killer haircut."

"You're next." Eric put in an effort to speak louder, but he doubted Logan heard him through the mask. His brother was looking at the monitor.

"Your heart rate is in high gear." His brown eyes gazed at Eric's knowingly. "I told you I would meet your girlfriend soon."

He'd called at the house a few days after Bryce and Eric's other friends' visit. "You and Bryce..." Always causing trouble.

Logan talked about random topics—work, their family reunion and Christmas plans.

Now that he was awake, Eric could only hope he'd be healthy and strong to celebrate his first Christmas with Joy as his wife. He wanted to marry her soon.

If she'd stuck with him through those hard times, it didn't matter how long he lived. He would rather marry her for one day than not marry her at all.

The rest of his siblings took turns coming in to say hello before Mom and Dad walked in. He had the best parents in the world.

Mom was sobbing, and Dad was in terrible shape. So Eric managed to say, "Your hair looks worse than mine." He didn't have to look in the mirror to know he looked awful with one area of his head shaved. He'd get a haircut whenever Ryan thought it would be the right time to do so.

The next day, they moved Eric into a larger recovery room with a pullout couch, a full-size bathroom, and a fabulous mountain view.

Joy stayed with him during his remaining week at the hospital. She slept on the couch and was happy the bathroom had a shower. She was the first person he saw when he woke up and the last before he closed his eyes. She made him laugh, and her voice continued to soothe him as she read the Bible to him, prayed with him, and listened to music with him on her phone.

Maybe she was the reason he hadn't had nightmares that week. His siblings and parents checked in on him every day. Joy's mom and grandpa came by for the last two days. Sally was getting married to Alex on December 1.

Ryan stopped by with daily updates, and Eric was mending well. Thanks to Joy's presence, he didn't dread the hospital as much.

His siblings had flown back by the time Eric was sent home, but Joy's family stayed around. He encouraged her and her family to stay at The Peak the following week. He wanted them there when he proposed to her.

Having invested in some of the businesses on Main Street, Eric was friends with most of the owners—he also knew some from the years he'd led the annual small business conferences. When Eric approached the chairman with plans for his engagement, the man had spoken to the shop owners, and they'd been gracious to block the street for two hours in the evening with only foot traffic. The chairman said that it was a get-well-soon gift.

After being housebound for so long, Eric had forgotten the weather in Pleasant View was unpredictable. On the evening of his surprise visit into town—that's what he'd called it when he suggested to Joy they go to the art studio in mid-October—the weather started out pleasant.

Since Eric told her he'd bought it for her, she was always up for going to the studio. He could still hear the echo of her surprised squeals.

As they rode in the back of a horse-drawn carriage, he draped his arm over Joy's orange peacoat, enthralled by the wonder in her eyes. She peered at the squat redbrick buildings on one side, then the bank and boutiques on the other side.

"I love this town," she said as she stared up at the snowcapped roofs and then the sparkling lights interwoven across the street. Eric had paid to add the solar-powered lanterns now hanging on the vibrant yellow trees along Main Street.

"I'm glad you like this town," he said since he wanted to make it his home too. Not just his hometown, but his home as a resident.

"A Million Dreams" blasted from the coffee shop halfway toward the art studio, and her eyes sparkled brighter than the twinkling lights. "Do you hear our song?"

Eric feigned innocence as he pulled her closer. He'd paid the coffee shop and hired a DJ to play their favorites from Joy's playlist.

"I've never been here in the evening before." She spread the blanket on Eric's legs. "Is it usually this slow?"

Despite the random people enjoying the shops, there wasn't nearly half the crowd who usually perused Main.

"I think they're waiting for our carriage."

It wasn't true since the town only had carriage rides in November and December, but he'd requested the service.

When the carriage stopped in front of the art studio, the driver held out his hand for Eric to help him down. Eric took Joy's fingers into his, his nerves colliding into one another as fear bolted through him.

She tilted her head to the side, suspicious no doubt. One thing he was sure of whenever he looked into her brown eyes was love. She looked at him like he was the best thing that had ever happened to her, yet it was the other way around. He was so filled with emotion that he had no right definition for what was in his chest.

"I love you," she whispered.

His breath caught. He could write a story of his love for her, but a well of emotion was building up inside him. He'd better focus to see the night's mission through.

With his legs shaking, more nervous than he remembered ever being, he let go of Joy's hand and lowered himself to one knee. The cold asphalt seeped through his jeans as he pulled out a red box from his jacket and opened it. The diamond sparkled under the gallery's porch light.

"Eric?" A hundred emotions laced her voice, but he could only hope this is what she wanted too.

"Joy Musana..." His heart was in his throat as he continued. "Just like your name, you are my sunshine. You light up my world in a way that—"

"Oh, Eric." Her eyes were glossy.

"Will you do me the honor of becoming my best friend... my wife?"

A tear slid down her cheek as she nodded, her face a sunrise on a cloudy morning, warmth in the cold day.

He took her hand and kissed her fingers before sliding the ring on. The gallery door burst open with loud cheers and clapping.

"Everyone is here?" Joy asked, but before he was interrupted, Eric drew her in his arms and kissed her tenderly. His heart was so full he could hardly get the words out.

Cameras flashed around them. People shouted, but as Joy kissed him back, it felt like they were the only people in town.

# EPILOGUE

The night-light streamed dim light into the bedroom, revealing the glow on Joy's face. Her chest rose and fell, her breathing heavy. Evidence of her exhaustion from taking care of their eight children.

Eric wasn't creepy for admiring his wife while she slept, but his internal clock was set for their twins' feeding time. It was three a.m., and he hadn't heard a peep from the walk-in closet where they slept instead of their bedroom. Keeping their four-month-olds close was convenient with the night feeding.

There. That was Hannah's scream through the baby monitor. Eric tried to slide out of the bed quietly so he didn't wake Joy, but she shifted and fluttered her groggy eyes open. As usual, she could sleep through anything, but after a peep from their children, she instinctively woke.

"It's feeding time." She yawned and pulled the covers down from her shoulder.

Leaning up on his elbow, he pressed a tender kiss to her forehead, savoring her scent he'd never get tired of. "Go back to sleep." It was going to be a long day, and she could use all the rest she could get. "I'll feed them."

"Are you sure?" Her eyes were already fluttering closed. "You're the best, sweetheart."

"You trained me well."

Bottle-feeding both babies at once wasn't easy, but it always worked out somehow.

When their two-year-old triplets, Ariel, Dustin, and Gideon, had been born, Eric and Joy had shared the task of feeding. Thankfully, God had blessed Joy with enough milk to breastfeed the babies, and she pumped extra for whenever he fed them.

Aha. That was Violet's soft cry. Eric stepped out of bed and tucked the covers around his wife, pressing another kiss to her soft cheeks.

A contented smile lifted her face. "I love you," she said with her eyes closed.

"I love you too." He turned down the monitor volume on the dresser.

*Love.* Words couldn't describe the fountain of love he had for his wife, for his kids, and more importantly, for God and all He'd done for Eric. Now Eric understood why God had forced him to rest during the eighteen months of his illness. God was training him to parent infants and toddlers.

He had so many miracles and blessings he could tell for the rest of his life, their house being one of them. But the most shocking miracle was his ability to have biological kids.

They'd married in November, a month following their engagement. When Joy was sick and they'd gone to the doctor four months later, they learned she was pregnant. They both didn't believe it until Eric went back for his own fertility test.

Apparently, God had changed his infertility—something the doctors couldn't explain, just like they couldn't explain the negative results to his Lyme disease test and all the other diseases that used to dwell in his body.

Joy still went to her annual visits, and all was well by God's grace. They'd both agreed not to worry and panic about what could happen and what-ifs, but instead to embrace each day as God granted them.

Right before the birth of their twins, they learned Tao had Alzheimer's, and she'd made Joy the triplets' legal guardian. He and Joy loved them and treated them no differently from their own kids. On Sunday afternoons, they took them to see their grandma in memory care, an event that was often gut-wrenching when Tao didn't recognize them.

With so much to do, Eric had transferred the CEO role to his brother, Logan.

He spent more time with his family as they invested in expanding the charities in countries that needed one or more. He also encouraged Joy to pursue her art. In fact, she'd been hired by the hospital to draw a mural in the children's ward. The studio was still her getaway to relax, but she wanted to host an open gallery once a year to showcase work by other local artists.

Looking back over his life and the family he'd lost, Eric knew God had comforted him when He brought Joy into his life.

Joy was good at initiating the trips to the cemetery twice a year so they could put flowers on the graves. But the past seemed like fog, and the future was full of possibilities. His heart could burst with God's praises, and Eric wanted the world to know there was a God who still performed miracles every day. For that reason alone, he and Joy had agreed to tomorrow's party and press conference in their home.

THE SUN ROLLED OUT of the horizon, casting touches of golden rays on the steaming mountains as Bryce Solace crossed the freshly cut lawn. He waved at a couple setting up the cameras for the day's event.

For whatever reason, he'd felt compelled to take over this operation. It was the least he could do after everything Eric Stone had done for him and for a lot of people. Even though Bryce had been knowledgeable in the field, Eric had taught him the ins and outs of investment.

Despite Bryce's skepticism about God, deep down he was starting to believe there might be a God, but he wouldn't tell Eric or anyone else, for that matter.

Eric was fully restored to health, and after everything he'd been through, he still clung to God. That was a statement in itself.

People lingered throughout the yard as servers passed drinks and decadent appetizers. A line of cars with names on the license plates still headed up the long driveway to Eric's mansion. Decorative lanterns hung over the drive, and Bryce nodded, content with the outcome of his doing.

He'd started a GoFundMe page for Eric about the time he had a tumor. The fund only proved what Bryce already knew about Eric and the people who appreciated him. The page went viral, and in less than a month, the funds had surpassed ten million dollars. Money kept rolling in, and knowing Eric, he would use the money to build more charities.

Bryce utilized some of that money and had a Realtor approach the ranch owner of Eric's dream house in Pleasant View. He'd given such a generous offer the owner couldn't turn it down. Bryce didn't have to walk to the other end of the endless acreage to know there was a waterfall. It was hard to hear the creek with the DJ testing the microphone, but it was a peaceful sound—a sound he intended to listen to whenever he felt the need for solitude.

As he neared the tent where some of the family members sat, Bryce snatched a tart from one of the passing waiters.

"I bet you're floating on air," Logan said, glancing at the six tents arranged on the property. Even if they were best friends, they rarely saw each other due to the distance in their jobs. Logan was the reason Bryce had come to be a part of the Stone family. "Heard there's a couple of presidents here."

"Of companies, of course."

Logan pushed his wavy hair from his face. "No. Some countries in Africa or was it South America?"

Bryce hadn't expected the presidents to show up. "I spoke to the secretary of Zimbabwe but..." Come to think of it, maybe he'd invited them, after all.

"So this was your idea of a reunion, huh?"

Bryce shrugged as he stared at the media truck taking up the space by the entrance. "As long as all your family is here." He then asked, "Where are your siblings?"

Logan cast a glance toward the tent where kids were squealing as they ran around the white chairs. "Playing with the kids, I hope."

"And Eric?"

"Iris and I are on baby duty." Logan gestured behind them. "I'm headed to the house to get the twins."

"Where's the nanny?" They had to have someone to help them with that many kids.

"We gave her a break."

No doubt all the siblings wanted to play a part in their nieces and nephews' lives.

"Good luck, man." Knowing he may not see Logan for a while after the event, Bryce asked, "Coming home for Christmas this year?"

"Oh yeah, we should get those snowmobiles out. I doubt Eric will use his cabin this winter."

He had reservations about the cabin, but it was also hard to make personal plans when he visited his mom. "I'll check with my mom—"

"Dude." Logan chuckled and shook his head. "When will you ever stop your mom from making your schedule?"

Having someone remind him about Mom defining his routine stung. "I live in New York." But Mom called every day to inquire about each step of his business plans.

Logan snorted. "No wonder you and Liberty will never get back together."

Ouch. Bryce rolled the ring on his finger. Pathetic that he still wore it, even if they'd been separated for ages. "Have you seen her lately?"

Logan shook his head, his accusing expression crumpling into sorrow. He then pointed his chin behind Bryce. "But Iris does."

The last thing Bryce needed was Iris's sarcasm.

"What are you two talking about?" She joined them, her pumps lifting her to almost the same height as Bryce.

"Logan and I are thinking of taking the snowmobiles out this winter."

"That's if your mom lets you." She tossed an olive in her mouth.

"What do you mean?" Bryce glanced at Logan for backup, but his friend lifted his hands, shrugging like "I told you so."

There was no sense in trying to defend himself. Defending himself against the very reason their one-year marriage failed wouldn't bring Liberty into his life.

"I'm gonna get Eric and Joy." Bryce walked away. Time to move the festivities along.

The camera crew seemed ready since they were standing guard by the main tent. Striding toward the house, he yelled at the two siblings, "You'd better come tend to the kids."

The main room was quiet when he let himself in. The kids were probably sleeping. He walked around the stairs to another room where paintings took up wall space—drawings that had inspired Eric through his dark days. He was opening the room for people to come and pursue that evening.

As Bryce walked out through the back entrance and into a hallway, he followed the voices toward the open door, then stopped short the moment he saw Eric kneeling before Joy. Dressed in a yellow one-shoulder dress, she gazed into Eric's eyes with a tenderness that tugged at Bryce's heart.

It was hard to hear what they were talking about, but the way Joy clung to Eric's words and the adoration in Eric's eyes—Man! Bryce froze at the door. What he wouldn't give to have what Eric and Joy had, to have Liberty back in his life, and to hold her once more.

He swallowed. The pain of loneliness felt more real than he cared to admit.

"Are they ready for us?"

Bryce blinked at Eric's voice. Embarrassment flushed through him, and he squeezed the back of his neck. "Yes."

Later that evening as Bryce listened to Eric's responses to the media, the man's love for God and his family rang through his genuine words. The compassion he had for the orphans, the homeless, and all who needed help left Bryce wondering if he'd ever made a difference in anyone's life.

Of course, the check he would be presenting to Eric tonight—the rest of the money from the fundraiser—would no doubt go toward building another hospital, a homeless shelter, or an orphanage.

When the event ended, ten thousand emotions coursed through Bryce. For the first time in his life, he had no idea if he could still refuse to believe what he'd worked so hard not to believe.

-THE END-

Check out all the other books in the Series on my Amazon Page.

Stay tuned for Eric's siblings in the spin off series-The Billionaires' Reunion.

Also Stone Enterprises Will be featured in The Office Heartthrobs.

If you would like to connect with me, join Rose's Facebook group[1] and connect with other readers as well. **Rose Fresquez's Reader Group.**

---

1.    https://www.facebook.com/groups/243932449976110/?ref=pages_profile_groups_tab&source_id=435344610252020

# Next in the Caregiver Series!

# *The Investor's Wife*

**They need a Christmas miracle to save their marriage. What they get is a perfect storm.**

Confident investment broker Bryce Solace has few regrets in life, but never fighting for his marriage is one of them. Although he still loves his wife, it's too late for a second chance—until a friend invites him on a guys' trip to a mountain cabin for some sledding and snowboarding.

Single Mom, Liberty Solace is swamped by the demands of running a homecare business and parenting. She never wanted to end things with Bryce or keep his baby a secret from him—just from his toxic mother. When a friend convinces her to take a week away without the baby, Liberty isn't sure what to expect. Definitely not her ex waiting at the cabin in the mountains!

With a fallen tree blocking the road, these two former spouses are stuck together with only their regrets and secrets to keep them company. Will old flames be rekindled, or will their friends' matchmaking plan only reopen old wounds?

Order your copy on Amazon.

# A NOTE FROM THE AUTHOR

Thank you for reading *The CEO's Companion*. If you haven't already figured out after reading, this story is inspired by the book of Job from the bible. I struggled to get through this book, since I had eight people die within a month. Mostly friends and acquaintances, and it became a challenge to put reality into fiction. By God's grace and my editor's support, the story came together the way God intended.

It's always a blessing to meet new readers. And to those who have read all my stories, thanks for giving me another chance and for your reviews and notes of encouragement.

I can never forget to thank God who enables me to create these stories. Thank you Lord!

You can connect with Rose on Facebook or email her at rjfresquez@gmail.com

# ABOUT THE AUTHOR

Rose Fresquez is the author of the Buchanan -Firefighter series, Romance in the Rockies, The caregiver series, two short stories and two family devotionals.

She's married and is the proud mother of four amazing kids. She loves to sing praises to God. When she's not busy taking care of her family, she's writing.

Printed in Great Britain
by Amazon

39848785R00179